Verse of the Vampyre

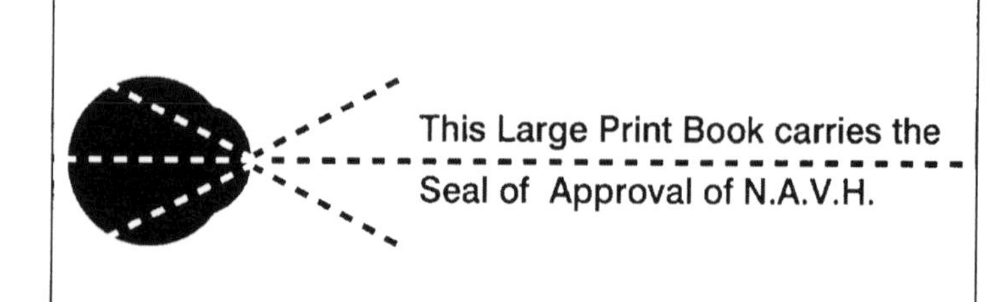
This Large Print Book carries the
Seal of Approval of N.A.V.H.

Verse of the Vampyre

Diana Killian

Thorndike Press • Waterville, Maine

This book is a work of fiction. Names, characters, places and incidents are products of the author's imagination or are used fictitiously. Any resemblance to actual events or locales or persons, living or dead, is entirely coincidental.

Published in 2005 by arrangement with Pocket Books, an imprint of Simon & Schuster, Inc.

Thorndike Press® Large Print Mystery.

The tree indicium is a trademark of Thorndike Press.

The text of this Large Print edition is unabridged.
Other aspects of the book may vary from the original edition.

Set in 16 pt. Plantin by Al Chase.

Printed in the United States on permanent paper.

Library of Congress Cataloging-in-Publication Data

Killian, Diana.
Verse of the vampyre / Diana Killian.
p. cm.
ISBN 0-7862-7248-1(lg. print : hc : alk. paper)
1. Socialites — Crimes against — Fiction. 2. Lake District (England) — Fiction. 3. Americans — England — Fiction. 4. Literary historians — Fiction. 5. Stalking victims — Fiction. 6. Amateur theater — Fiction. 7. Women teachers — Fiction. 8. Large type books. I. Title.
PS3611.I4515V47 2005
813′.6—dc22 2004061713

To Kevin,
my very own Prince of Darkness,
with love.

National Association for Visually Handicapped
serving the partially seeing

As the Founder/CEO of NAVH, the only national health agency solely devoted to those who, although not totally blind, have an eye disease which could lead to serious visual impairment, I am pleased to recognize Thorndike Press* as one of the leading publishers in the large print field.

Founded in 1954 in San Francisco to prepare large print textbooks for partially seeing children, NAVH became the pioneer and standard setting agency in the preparation of large type.

Today, those publishers who meet our standards carry the prestigious "Seal of Approval" indicating high quality large print. We are delighted that Thorndike Press is one of the publishers whose titles meet these standards. We are also pleased to recognize the significant contribution Thorndike Press is making in this important and growing field.

Lorraine H. Marchi, L.H.D.
Founder/CEO
NAVH

* Thorndike Press encompasses the following imprints: Thorndike, Wheeler, Walker and Large Print Press.

Acknowledgments

I wish to thank my agent, Jacky Sach, for all her hard work, but even more for her enthusiasm and faith. I also wish to thank my eagle-eyed editor, Christina Boys — my traveling companion on these journeys to the imaginary village of Innisdale.

Thanks also to my family (the funniest and most brutal of my critiquers) and to my partners in crime at Wicked Company.

And last but not least, a very big acknowledgment to the booksellers who gave Grace, Peter, and me a place to tell our story. To all the Jeans, Johns, Juans, Juannas, Reginas, Deannas — to you Mystery Mavens everywhere, thank you.

Prologue

> I have a personal dislike to Vampires, and the little acquaintance I have with them would by no means induce me to reveal their secrets.
>
> – Lord Byron

The figure in the shadows watched with gray dead eyes as the young man in the bed ran his hand through black, already disheveled curls. The tears on his cheeks had dried; his dark, red-rimmed eyes stared into the yellow glow of the still-burning gas lamps. Though the heavy draperies held daylight at bay, morning prowled outside the windows. A coach rumbled down elegant Great Pulteney Street. The house creaked, rising from sleep.

The whispers began.

Blinking sticky lashes, the young man saw again the Turkish cemetery. Cypress cast fingers of shadow across the turbaned tombstones. The smell of red pine, the murmur of a hidden spring replaced the scents and sounds of the English dawn. With a whir of black-tipped wings, a stork took flight, serpent writhing in its long beak.

Fantasy or memory? He was no longer sure. And if fantasy . . . his own or that other's? That *hated* other . . .

The creature in the gloom stirred. The seal ring on a bone white finger caught the candlelight that illuminated the Arabic characters carved within the red stone.

The young man's lower lip quivered. He bit it hard. Head turning on the pillows, he gazed at the crooked stack of leather books on the shelf over the fireplace mantel. His journals. His proof. His vindication. His eyes traveled the room once more, but already it seemed strange and foreign to him.

So we'll go no more a-roving.

He sat up and with a steady hand poured from the decanter on the bedstand. Blood red splashed, dissolving the white powder in the bowl of the goblet.

The young man smiled a bitter smile. The watcher in the shadows returned the smile, but the pale eyes were unchanged and cold.

" 'Tis well," said the young man.

He lifted the goblet and drank.

1

In Grace Hollister's opinion only a character in a book — or a real idiot — would agree to a midnight rendezvous in a graveyard. So it was truly aggravating to find herself crouched behind a thicket in the Innisdale cemetery waiting for Peter Fox.

Not that this was exactly a "rendezvous," and not that she was exactly "waiting" for Peter. No, this fell more under the heading of "spying on," and that was truly the most aggravating thing of all. To be reduced to — but here Grace's thoughts were cut short as the rusted gate to the graveyard screeched in warning.

Ducking back into the branches, she listened to footsteps crunching down the leaf-strewn path near where she hid. She waited, holding her breath, till the newcomer passed, his shadow falling across her face and gliding away. Grace swallowed hard.

The October night was cold and smelled of damp earth and something cloying. A few feet to her left, a tangle of wild roses half concealed the entrance to a crypt, and

Grace blamed the night's funereal perfume on the colorless flowers twisting up and over the cornices.

Cautiously, she peered through the thicket. She knew that confident, loose-limbed stride — that long, lean silhouette — even without the telltale glint of moonlight on pale hair. And with recognition came bewilderment. *What in the world was going on?*

What was Peter up to?

For that matter, what was Grace up to? After all, if Peter wanted to arrange midnight assignations with women . . . it wasn't like he and Grace really had an "understanding." Well, not an understanding that most people would . . . understand. Grace's parents certainly couldn't comprehend it. Her ex-boyfriend Chaz didn't get it. Even Grace sometimes wondered if she had failed to read the fine print when it came to her relationship with Peter Fox.

Peter started down the hillside, taking himself from Grace's view. She weighed the risk and left her hiding spot, scuttling across the grass to crouch behind a tree.

The tree offered poor concealment; so after a moment's hesitation, she scooted over to a headstone. Peering over the top she spotted Peter a few yards down the slope. He stood very still, apparently scanning the nightscape; then he continued along the path that jogged down the hillside. In a moment he would be out of sight.

What next? wondered Grace. The more she moved around, the greater her chances of being discovered, but there was no point in following him if she couldn't figure out what he was doing.

She looked around, but her next move would take her into the open.

Peter gave a low whistle that could have passed for some nocturnal birdcall. Instinctively, Grace leaned forward, watching him pass through the crowd of stone lambs, sleeping marble cherubim and tilting crosses that stretched across the clearing to the dark woods beyond.

Was someone out there, hiding and watching from the dense shelter of the forest? It was a creepy thought.

Tree branches stirred in the night breeze, but no one appeared. Grace looked toward Peter, but he stepped to the right, out of her line of vision. Once again she was tempted to leave her hiding place, but the ornate headstone provided good cover. And she knew from past experience how sharp Peter's hearing was.

Beyond the graveyard, pine trees stood in black attitude, their jagged tops resembling fangs. Grace tried to make out a shape that shouldn't be there. If anyone was out there, she stuck to the shadows. It would be a woman. The voice on the phone call that Grace had inadvertently overheard had definitely been female. And a woman would indicate romance, a tryst perhaps; although the caller's husky, mocking voice, while seductive in tone, had held a hint of threat. Had there been something familiar about that voice? All afternoon Grace had tried and failed to pin down the caller's identity.

High above, the moon was veiled in mist, its diffused light shimmering on the headstones. The inscriptions wavered like incantations.

Another bird trill issued from the direction Peter had gone. At least, Grace assumed it was Peter. Maybe it really was a bird this time.

But again the signal, if it was a signal, met silence.

Grace smothered a yawn. Surveillance work was tiring. She peered at her watch. Difficult to read the tiny Roman numerals in the gloom, but it had to be late. Very late. Decent folk would be in bed. Bed. Longingly, Grace thought of her flannel sheets and goose-down comforter. It was chilly, and she had put in a full day at Rogue's Gallery, where she worked to supplement her sabbatical income. The knees of her jeans were soaked from kneeling on the damp ground, and her legs prickled pins and needles.

She shifted her cramped position. Peter was still lost to view behind a flat box tomb. Uneasily, she glanced back to the overgrown crypt. Trails of mist were rising off the ground like ghosts taking form. She shivered.

This is crazy, she told herself. What if he catches me? How am I going to explain? The truth was, there was no explanation. Her decision to come here tonight had been on impulse, triggered by Peter's odd behavior the last few weeks. Now that she thought about it, he had seemed to change right around the time the jewel thefts had started.

That's right, a little voice in her head jeered. This is about saving him from a life of crime. It has nothing to do with moonlight tête-à-têtes with sultry-voiced females.

Quick footsteps returning up the path had Grace flattening herself against the sheltering headstone. Peter was coming back.

There wasn't time to move, to find better concealment. Grace shrank down and held her breath. He didn't pause, didn't glance her way. He was a shade moving through the silver shadows.

Diana's foresters, gentlemen of the shade, minions of the moon.

The quote from Shakespeare came unbidden; Grace bit back a rueful grin. She couldn't believe that Peter Fox, ex–jewel thief extraordinaire, had returned to his former profession, but something was going on. If he wasn't involved in the recent rash of jewel robberies, she bet he knew something about them.

In a few moments Peter's footsteps died away. The gate groaned and clanged shut. Grace was left with the sleeping dead and her own less-than-comfortable thoughts.

The tree above her creaked in the wind. Grace gave it a quick look. Just her luck if she was knocked out by a falling limb.

In the distance she heard the engine of Peter's Land Rover revving up; the hum of the engine died away, leaving only night sounds. Lonesome sounds.

Feeling very much alone, she stared up at the sky, at the milkweed dust of stars. How long did she have to wait? Absently, she massaged her thigh muscles.

Listening to the soft tick of her wristwatch, she pictured Peter driving down the country lane back to Craddock House. The cemetery was out in the middle of nowhere; so the chances of running into anyone else were infinitesimal — unless his quarry was still lurking about, and that seemed unlikely.

At last Grace moved to rise, reaching for the headstone to pull herself up. Abruptly, she realized that this was not a park; she was kneeling on someone's grave. The thought jolted her. In the shifting moonlight she could read the words carved there.

And all is dark and dreary now, where once was joy.

It sort of put things into perspective. With a silent apology, Grace gathered herself to stand.

Midrise, a scrape of sound froze her. She listened.

Nothing.

Cautiously, she raised her head over the smiling cherubs atop the tombstone.

There was movement to her left. Something inside the portico of the crypt stirred. Grace's eyes widened.

There it was again. Motion. And then, as her brain tried to assimilate this, a figure in a cape stepped out of the doorway and into the moonshine.

Grace's hand covered her gasp.

Even across the distance of grass and

graves she recognized the tall, gaunt figure of Lord Ruthven, Innisdale's newest resident. His hair was black and lank; his obsidian eyes shone with fierce intelligence in his bony face.

Not that Grace could tell in this light what his eyes were shining with — or if they were even open — but she'd had plenty of opportunity to study the man during the past weeks.

Am I dreaming? Grace wondered. Did I fall asleep waiting? That would make sense. What didn't make sense was Lord Ruthven, the London producer who had volunteered to help with the local theater group's production of *The Vampyre*, hanging out at the village cemetery. Granted, Grace, who had been roped into acting as technical advisor to the production, had pegged Ruthven as an eccentric, but this was turning into an episode of *Tales from the Crypt*.

Could Lord Ruthven have been the person Peter intended to meet?

Then who was the woman who had called Peter? Lord Ruthven's secretary? That would be some job. Grace smothered a jittery giggle. But if Ruthven had arranged to meet Peter, why would he remain hidden?

No, hard to believe as it was, it did appear

as though Lord Ruthven had also been observing Peter.

As she stared at the caped figure, the moon slipped behind the tattered clouds; its lanternlight flickered and went out.

Even a year ago Grace would not have dreamed of doing what she did now, but acquaintance with Peter Fox had been . . . empowering. (Although that was probably not the word Ms. Winters, principal of St. Anne's Academy, would have used.)

Grace slid down and began to crawl very slowly and cautiously across the wet grass for a better view. Her knees and elbows dug into the soggy ground as she moved ahead foot by foot.

But the treacherous moon glided out of its cloud cover, and the glade was bathed in radiance once more. A radiant emptiness.

Grace sat and stared.

Lord Ruthven had vanished.

"You're late," Peter said, when Grace arrived at Rogue's Gallery the next morning. He was wielding a crowbar on a wooden crate with the nonchalance of a man who had more than a casual acquaintance with proper crowbar usage.

Rogue's Gallery, the antique shop where Peter now earned an honest living, took up the lower level of Craddock House. Peter lived upstairs.

The gallery was a magical place. Everything in it was beautiful, rare or amazing, from the carved mahogany mermaid suspended from the vaulted ceiling to the man-sized Tsubo jar that took up an entire corner of the floor.

And the framed antique maps with their delicate tints and exotic place names seemed to promise all who entered the door that adventure lurked just around the next corner. This had certainly proved true for Grace.

She said, "I know. Sorry, boss." Avoiding his keen blue gaze, Grace headed for the stockroom. She shrugged out of her mac and hung it behind the door. Peter must have received a shipment. There were several pieces of Staffordshire creamware sitting on the floor. She placed the pieces on the desk. Not that Peter ever dropped or broke anything. She had never met anyone more surefooted (or light-fingered) than the owner of Rogue's Gallery Antiques and Books.

Grace made herself a cup of tea using the hot plate in the back room. She refilled Peter's mug, joining him on the shop floor. He took the mug with absent thanks, busy examining the contents of the wooden crate.

Books. More books. The entire landing of the shop's second story was devoted to books. Old books, rare books, beautiful books. What had started out as a private passion had developed into a lucrative side-line. This lot looked to be mystery books. Vintage paperbacks with lurid and inviting covers. Peter smiled faintly as he read the back of *Silken Menace*, its cover decorated by a reclining blonde in naughty purple undies.

Grace stared out the bow windows over-looking the front garden and the road. It was raining, one of those misty autumn rains that did wonders for the garden and very little for hairstyles. Especially Grace's, as a quick glimpse in a foggy antique mirror confirmed. Her French knot was slipping, and her cheeks looked hot and pink.

She tucked a damp chestnut strand behind her ear, and said briskly, "I guess I'll finish cataloging the Stark collection."

Peter caught her wrist as she moved past him. "What's up?"

She stilled. "Nothing. What do you mean?"

"I've never known you to be late. And you seem rather . . ." He considered her for a moment. "Edgy this morning."

And she thought he wasn't paying attention? She steeled herself to meet his gaze. Grace was no good at lying, and Peter was a difficult man to fool. He studied her, his eyes curious, his thin mouth quirking in that unreadable half smile. His long fingers circled her wrist lightly, but she could feel his touch in her bones.

It was hard to believe that she had once thought he wasn't handsome — but perhaps "handsome" was too weak a word. Elegant bones, the contrast of dark brows and pale hair, startling blue eyes beneath eyelids as hooded and mysterious as an Egyptian pharaoh's. Maybe "striking" was a better word.

"You look guilty," he murmured. "What have you been up to?"

"Oh, the usual. Murder and mayhem."

"When did you take up the mayhem?" Peter queried, and Grace laughed, slipping her hand free.

She glanced through her notes on the Stark library. She was about three-quarters through cataloging the two-hundred-book collection, a tedious process of noting each book's title, author, subject, publisher, date of publication and ISBN number — although most of the books in the estate's library were too old to have ISBN numbers.

While Grace worked, she unobtrusively

kept an eye on Peter. She thought if anyone seemed edgy, he did. She caught him staring out the window a couple of times, as though watching the road, and each time the phone rang, she was sure he tensed.

What's wrong? she wanted to ask. But she had already asked during the past weeks, and each time Peter had acted as though he didn't know what she was talking about. It was as though they had reverted to the initial days of their acquaintanceship, when neither quite trusted the other. If she forced the issue, she might make matters worse; but Grace feared that day by day they were slowly growing apart.

Perhaps because of the rain, or maybe because October was the off-season, they had few customers that day. Generally Grace loved such mornings: she and Peter bantering with each other or working side by side in comfortable silence. Peter usually fixed lunch, or they went down to the pub together. It was friendly and relaxed. Companionable. She had begun to believe that this was the way she was supposed to spend the rest of her life.

Most evenings were spent with each other. And Peter made no secret that he found her attractive. He wined and dined her, kissed her and flirted with her, but he had yet to attempt — in the vernacular of the young ladies of St. Anne's — to put the move on her. That had been fine with Grace. She wasn't a woman to rush into anything. Knowing Peter's reputation with the feminine populace, she had found his restraint flattering. Until recently.

At noontime they retreated upstairs to Peter's living quarters and shared a ploughman's lunch of hot crusty bread, a thick slab of farmhouse cheddar, pickled onions and a pint of ale from one of the small local brewers.

Grace loved this kitchen, with its gleaming kettles hanging from convenient hooks and old oak-leaf china sparkling from inside glass-fronted cupboards. The hardwood floors shone like glass. The scrubbed pine table and chairs nestled in a cozy nook overlooking the garden, where roses and peonies made bright splashes of color.

The autumn rain pricking against the kitchen windowpanes had a forlorn sound. Grace looked up from her plate to find Peter studying her.

"What?" she inquired.

He said at last, "How's the play coming?"

Her thoughts a million miles away, Grace had to rack her brain for a response. "Oh," she said finally. "Well, there's been another program change. Now we're doing Polidori's *The Vampyre.*" Or rather, a play based on J. R. Planche's play based on the short story by Polidori.

"Dr. John William Polidori? I thought you were doing Byron."

"It turns out Byron doesn't have a version of the play. There's a fragment of a story, but it's not enough to base a play on."

Peter seemed more amused than sympathetic. "Bad luck. Still, I can't imagine most of the others care whether the play is based on Polidori, Byron or Wes Craven. Are the Iveses still committed to the project?"

"Theresa is. I think Sir Gerald is beginning to resent the time she's spending away from the home fires. He's stopped coming to rehearsals. Not that any rehearsing is going on at this point."

"Foxhunting season officially opens a week Monday," Peter commented, and it was not an inconsequential remark given that Sir Gerald Ives was Master of Hounds of the Innisdale Pack. In these parts, foxhunting was more religion than sport. The hills and fells of the Lake District were home to the legendary Six Fell Packs and birthplace of Sir John Peel, the eighteenth-century farmer and MFH who had gained immortality when his friend John Woodcock Graves honored his hunting exploits in the song "D'ye Ken John Peel."

"I don't think he's going to convince her ladyship to abandon the boards. She definitely seems to have the bug." Privately, Grace suspected that the bug Lady Ives (fifteen years younger than her hunt-obsessed husband) had was less for the stage and more for Derek Derrick, one of the other actors. It wasn't hard to see why. Not only was Derek capable of talking about something besides whelping, foaling and cubbing, he was as gorgeous as a Saturday matinee idol. Tall, blond, blue-eyed . . .

"Your eyes are glazing over," Peter remarked.

"Hmm? Oh. Well, the truth is," Grace admitted, "it's not the greatest play in the world."

"No!" Peter leaned back, quoting in mock dramatic tones, " 'But when they arrived, it was too late. Lord Ruthven had disappeared, and Aubrey's sister had glutted the thirst of a VAMPYRE!' "

Grace chuckled. Although the Romantic period in literature was her field, Grace had been unaware of Dr. John William Polidori's contribution to the genre. In fact, her impression of Lord Byron's doctor was solely based on unflattering cinematic portraits in films like Ken Russell's *Gothic*. Greater familiarity with Polidori's creative efforts reinforced her sympathy if not her critical respect for the tragic figure of whom Byron had written, "A young man more likely to contract diseases than cure them."

"I know, I know. I guess it's sort of a classic, but it's melodramatic and overwrought and . . . goofy." She thought it over. "And it *is* kind of a weird coincidence that our producer/director has the same name as the title character. It would be one thing if his name were Lord Smith."

"I don't believe in coincidence," said Peter.

What was it in his tone? Something . . .

"But what else could it be? Maybe Ruthven is a stage name, and he was attracted to the material because of the PR opportunity."

Peter raised a skeptical brow. "Photo ops from a provincial production?"

"Don't ask me. He's supposed to be very well known in London theater circles. Derek Derrick has done some television at least. He thought the project was worth his time."

"Ah yes. Who can forget his stirring portrayal of the devoted spouse of an allergy sufferer?"

Peter didn't own a television, so it was unlikely he had seen Derrick's work with his own eyes. Someone besides Grace was keeping him updated on the cast and crew of *The Vampyre.* The entire village of Innisdale was probably snickering into its collective pint.

She would have liked to tell Peter about Lord Ruthven's peculiar behavior in the cemetery, but she would have had to confess her own peculiar behavior.

"Well, why else would they — ?" But the downstairs buzzer proclaimed that a customer had finally discovered them on their quiet country lane, and the conversation ended. Peter went downstairs, and Grace cleaned up the remains of lunch.

"So how is it that you don't ride to hounds but you're still invited to the Hunt Ball?" Grace inquired later that afternoon as she was finishing up the Stark catalog.

"Eligible bachelors are welcome at any social event," Peter informed her.

"Eligible?" she mused.

He corrected, "Willing to dance with anyone." He studied her. "Your first Hunt Ball. My, my. You are moving up in the world."

She laid aside her pad. "I know it's old hat

for you, but I'm very excited."

"I know you are. It's rather sweet. Did you buy a new frock?"

Frock. He really was something of a throwback.

I met a traveler from an antique land . . .

"I can't afford to. The riding habit was expensive, even getting the jacket secondhand."

Peter shook his head.

"I don't expect you to understand," Grace said.

"I understand. You're suffering an acute case of Anglomania. If I find you buying champagne glasses with the queen's portrait, I'll have to take steps."

"I probably watched too many episodes of *Masterpiece Theatre* at an impressionable age," Grace agreed. "I used to dream about going to balls and foxhunts and village fetes."

"My dear girl, you can't really tell me that your life's ambition is to rub elbows with overfed, undereducated boobs whose aim in life is to kill small animals with as much pomp and circumstance as they can afford." He had gone back to scanning a bill of lading, so perhaps the grimness in his voice had to do with freight charges.

"Since you put it that way, no. But if I'm

here, it seems a pity not to experience everything offered."

" 'Everything' covers a lot of ground. Your sabbatical is nearly over, isn't it?"

She didn't know how to take that. She knew her sabbatical was nearly over as well as he did. And she remembered, if he did not, why she had taken this sabbatical.

Anything she might have said was cut off as the shop door opened with a jingle of bells. Mrs. Mac, Peter's "char lady," backed in, shaking out her dripping umbrella.

"Afternoon, dearies!" she chirped.

An apple-cheeked dumpling of a woman with a mop of gray curls, Mrs. Mac could have passed for the grandmotherly type except for the sharp cold of her faded blue eyes.

"Wet through, I am." Mrs. Mac dropped her umbrella and heavy carpetbag on the counter. "Such a to-do in the village!" Her eyes twinkled with wicked pleasure. "I could do with a cuppa." She started for the stockroom, shedding her black raincoat as she went.

"Neither rain nor wind nor sleet nor snow," said Grace.

Peter said, "I was thinking more along the lines of 'In thunder, lightning or in rain.' "

Grace chuckled at the reference to *Macbeth.* Mrs. Mac did look a bit like a witch.

"What's happened in the village?" she asked, when Mrs. Mac returned, mug in hand.

Mrs. Mac made an unlovely sucking sound at her tea before pronouncing, "Vandalism. Someone spray painted the side of the chapel."

"Obscenities?" Grace inquired. Peter had already lost interest. Vandalism was not his idea of crime.

"No, no." Mrs. Mac chortled. "It said, 'The vampire walks'!"

2

The gallery windows flashed white, and with the kind of timing for which amateur theater productions are famous, Mrs. Mac's startling announcement was nearly lost in a deafening crack. Thunder boomed so loud it sounded artificial. The lamps flickered, then brightened. Above them, the suspended mermaid swayed gently, cresting invisible seas.

"It was a dark and stormy night," Peter drawled, as the rumble faded away, and Mrs. Mac laughed uneasily.

Grace barely heard them, blinking at the recollection of the caped figure of Lord Ruthven flitting around the graveyard the night before. "Could the graffiti be publicity for the play?" she suggested doubtfully.

Mrs. Mac cackled, though whether in agreement or derision was impossible to know. She hied off to begin her afternoon's chores. Mrs. Mac might look prone to shortcuts and sweeping under the carpet, but when it came to cleaning, whether by mop or magic wand, she got results.

“Publicity?” Peter inquired, raising one black eyebrow in a characteristic gesture.

“Lord Ruthven’s a tad eccentric.”

“Vandalizing a church is a lot eccentric.” Peter had surprising streaks of conservatism — surprising considering his criminal background.

“It’s probably just some kids acting up. Halloween is only a couple of weeks away.”

Before moving to Innisdale, Grace had been under the impression that the British did not celebrate Halloween. It turned out that while trick-or-treating did not seem to be a local tradition, there was an annual village fete to celebrate All Hallows’ Eve. Perhaps that explained Lord Ruthven’s costume, but somehow she didn’t think so.

“Very likely. Did you want to redo the pottery display?”

Grace spent the rest of the afternoon rearranging the newly acquired Staffordshire pottery amongst the other pieces artfully displayed on the furniture throughout the shop.

It was hard not to become attached to some of these treasures. She had been sorry when the merry-go-round horse that had sat in the bow window the day she first found Rogue’s Gallery was sold. Perhaps in some secret corner of her mind she had pictured that merry-go-round horse in a particular nursery. Now the window shelf was filled with a collection of Victorian children's toys, including a tall penny-farthing cycle and porcelain dolls.

It was getting dark when Mrs. Mac, the day's hurly-burly done, came downstairs. She gathered her things.

"G'night, dearie!" she called to Grace. The rain was thundering down. It poured off the eaves and splashed on the stone walk as Mrs. Mac opened the front door.

Grace called good night. It was closing time and, with rehearsal tonight, she, too, should be leaving. She wondered if Peter would ask her to stay to dinner. Up until a few weeks ago, she had taken these invitations for granted. What did he do on the evenings he no longer spent with her?

Her attention was on positioning a creamware pierced basket and undertray to best vantage; so she almost failed to overhear Mrs. Mac whisper to Peter, "I hear there was another jewel robbery last night." Grace's ears pricked up, but she didn't turn her head.

"Where?" Peter, too, spoke undervoice.

Mrs. Mac's laugh was as dry as a stick breaking. "As if you didn't know, my lad!"

The shop door bells jangled behind her.

* * *

Grace drove cautiously through Innisdale Wood, headlights illuminating the throng of dripping trees and darkness. Oily black rain pooled in the narrow road beyond her glistening windshield. She decelerated, splashing through a puddle that was deeper than expected. The road would be flooded soon.

Grace had not done much driving in bad weather before her stay in the Lake District, but she was learning fast. Other lessons took longer.

A year ago she had visited the Lake District to research her doctoral dissertation on the Romantic poets. It had been a trip designed to combine business with pleasure: Grace was on vacation with her friend and fellow instructor at St. Anne's Academy for Girls, Monica Gabbana. Every mile, every minute of that long-awaited holiday had been carefully planned, then . . . Fate had intervened.

So Grace was officially on sabbatical, and the doctoral dissertation had expanded to a proposed book that promised new insight into the nineteenth-century Romantic poet and rake, Lord Byron. But, as much as she loved the Lakes, and as much as a successful academic career required publishing *some-*

thing, that was not really why she had stayed.

Caught in the beam of the Aston Martin's headlights, eyes gleamed out of the undergrowth, and Grace swerved on the slick road. Better not to think of affairs of the heart when she needed to concentrate on her driving. She could think about the play instead. Or she could think about Lord Ruthven's mysterious behavior. Or she could think about Lady Ruthven.

Grace was a people watcher, and she found Catriona Ruthven fascinating. She reminded Grace of a line by Shelley, "A pard-like spirit, beautiful and swift." It wasn't all attitude. Her hair was a magnificent shade of red, and instead of the freckles that should have been hers, her skin was the pale gold of honey. Old whisky was the color of her eyes.

The only mystery about Lady Ruthven was how she ended up with Lord Ruthven. She was vibrantly alive, almost . . . elemental. And he was pretty much your standard-issue dried stick. Or so Grace had thought before she found him pulling his Count Dracula routine the night before.

Rounding a bend, she braked sharply at the sight of flares in the road. Her tires skidded, and she had to fight to correct. A giant moving van had gone off the pavement and was partially blocking her way; for one frightened moment, before she regained control of the car, Grace feared she might career into it. Two figures in hooded rain slickers slid in and out of her headlights before she straightened out.

Grace pulled to the side, turned the engine off and took a couple of deep breaths. Her hands were shaking. Ahead, she could see the men in slickers gesturing and shouting. She had probably scared them even more than herself.

She got out of her car, walking toward them. She could see that two of the moving truck's big tires were mired in the roadside mud. Rain pelted down. It was a horrible night to be stranded.

"I'm so sorry! I nearly lost control," she called to the nearest man, a short burly figure in olive green. "Is there anything I can do? Do you have a radio? Have you called for help?"

His face was a white wet blur as he waved her away. "Dinna fash yerself!" he said in a broad Scots accent. "We've got it under control." He made another push-away motion.

The other man had returned to wedging wood beneath the truck's tire. His back was to Grace, and he did not acknowledge her presence. The first man went to join him.

Grace hesitated, but it was not a moment for small talk, and there was apparently nothing she could do to help them. She called good night, which went unanswered, and hurried back to the warmth and safety of her car.

With a ghastly shriek of hinges — suitable to the material to be rehearsed that night — the door to the Innisdale Playhouse opened.

Unlike Keswick's Theatre by the Lake ("Home to Cumbria's Leading Professional Theatre Company!") or Ulverston's stately Coronation Hall, where the South Cumbria Music Festival was held annually, the Innisdale Playhouse was small and dilapidated. While some Lake District theaters could boast romantic histories, the Playhouse was merely old. Jazz festivals and touring ballet companies generally declined the opportunity to grace the Playhouse's weathered boards, and so far no benevolent grand dame of the London stage had bestowed any favors upon its sparsely shingled roof.

Which, in Grace's opinion, and despite her earlier comments to Peter, made Lord Ruthven's interest in a local production of

Polidori's *The Vampyre* all the odder.

But then, Grace reflected, letting the heavy side entrance door slam shut behind her, everything about the production was odd. It wasn't only that Ruthven had voluntarily involved himself in an amateur theater production that seemed unlikely to further his — or anyone else's career — but Derek Derrick had signed on. Granted, Derrick was a struggling TV actor who believed working with Ruthven would be good for his career.

As for Grace, she had agreed to help out because she was a firm believer in getting involved. If she was going to live for any length of time in Innisdale (assuming there was any point in staying beyond the run of her sabbatical), she would have to cultivate more friends, discover independent interests, make her own way. And, well, she had thought the play sounded like fun. That had been back in the good old days when she was still under the impression that Byron had written *The Vampyre*.

The stage was lit, and the cast and crew of *The Vampyre* assembled in front of a painted backdrop of Transylvanian-looking landscape complete with cliffs, bats and gloomy castle.

Tall and strikingly beautiful, Catriona

Ruthven sat on a packing crate with her legs boyishly crossed, managing to make jeans and a leather jacket look like haute couture. As Grace made her way through the aisle between velvet-covered tip-up chairs, she heard the other woman drawl, "The time for discussion is past."

A rhythmic thudding followed Catriona's words. Grace was familiar with the sound of Lady Venetia Brougham's ebony walking stick hitting the stage boards. From a distance, the local Byronic scholar looked like a child; the synthetic gloss of her black bob and the bright blue of her silk dress disguised the fact that she was about eighty years old. The pounding was followed by her imperious, "If I am to finance this spectacle, I believe I should have a say!"

"You had a say. And then some." Catriona met the reptilian glint of Lady Vee's gaze and raised one supercilious eyebrow. It was a very irritating expression, as Grace well knew, because Peter had the same trick.

"Ladies, please." Lord Ruthven looked up from his clipboard. He sounded wearier than ever — and no wonder, thought Grace. She was feeling the lack of sleep herself. "We have covered this ground." The play's producer and director wore black jeans and a black turtleneck; he generally wore black, reflected Grace. He also wore eyeliner. Perhaps he was a fan of Goth. That might explain his appalling taste in dramatic material.

"Not to my satisfaction!" snapped Lady Vee. Then her tone changed. "Ah, my *deah!*" she purred, greeting Grace like an old friend, as Grace joined the enclave on stage. "I know *you* will see my point."

Grace nearly glanced behind, seeking the person Lady Vee addressed, but caught herself. It appeared that she and Lady Vee were enjoying one of their periodic truces.

"Sorry I'm late," she apologized to the group, most of whom she already knew. "The road through the woods is starting to flood." She shrugged out of her raincoat, draping it with the others over a stage prop coffin.

"You're not the problem," Lord Ruthven muttered, glancing at his watch again. "Derrick is the problem. Where the devil is he?"

Someone volunteered having seen Derrick at the pub, and the director's face grew grimmer.

A rummage sale's worth of chairs in a variety of shapes and styles was spread around the brightly lit stage. Grace pulled a peeling captain's chair next to Roy Blade, who said out of the side of his mouth, "You haven't missed much," in his disconcertingly cultured voice.

With his long dark hair, eye patch and collection of ornate tattoos, Roy Blade looked like a biker, which he was. He did not look like a librarian, but he was that, too, as well as another expert on poets of the Romantic age. Given the presence of two equally opinionated scholars, Grace wondered if she hadn't been brought in as tiebreaker.

Lady Vee, perched on a claw-footed monstrosity that looked vaguely like a throne, articulated around her foot-long ivory cigarette holder. "Grace, I have suggested to the group that Byron's *Manfred* would be a more suitable project than Polidori's *The Vampyre*."

The sighs, mutters and rustlings from the rest of the group spoke volumes, though no one said anything. Roy's big hands, the backs embellished in the black scrollwork of tattoos, kneaded his thigh muscles as though he were restraining himself from strangling somebody.

No wonder there was tension in the air, Grace thought. "Uh . . ." she began. Uh-oh was more like it.

"It's too bloody late," Catriona exclaimed, rising to her feet. With a dark look at Grace, she whirled and strode down the stage.

"Catriona!" Lord Ruthven's tone cut across the startled silence.

What's that look for? Grace wondered. How is this my fault? Lady Vee was a law unto herself. Grace wasn't encouraging her.

"Well, we did vote on this," she tried to point out reasonably.

"Thank you, Susan B. Anthony," Catriona commented from downstage.

"What's *her* problem?" Lady Ives murmured.

Wife of the local baronet and MFH, Theresa Ives was the county equivalent of the traditional CEO trophy wife: blond, blue-eyed and — years Sir Gerald's junior — built to last. As befitted the queen of the horsey set, her laugh was high and whinnying like a pony's.

"Vote?" Lady Vee repeated as though the word were foreign to her. "How many here are qualified to vote on this subject?"

More rumblings. Grace had a feeling the Innisdale Players were a hairsbreadth from turning into the Innisdale Lynch Mob.

The side door to the theater banged open again, and Derek Derrick struggled to shut it against the rain. A blast of storm-scented air wafted up the aisle. Grace shivered.

"Christ! It's a hurricane out there!" Derrick made his way through the rows of chairs and vaulted onto the stage. "Were you waiting for me? You didn't have to do that!" He offered his white and practiced grin, unfazed by Lord Ruthven's glower.

"We're not rehearsing," Theresa informed him. "Lady Venetia has found another problem. This time it's the entire play." Derrick dropped beside her and squeezed her shoulder sympathetically. Grace tried not to notice that familiar gesture.

"It is not as though rehearsals had really progressed," the devil in the blue dress said defensively.

"How can they progress when you're raising an objection every step of the way?" Catriona stalked back across the stage in their direction.

For the first time, and probably because of her chance encounter with the moving-van man, Grace noticed that Catriona's voice had the faintest trace of a Scottish burr.

Grace replayed the voice of Peter's mysterious caller in her head. Could it have been Catriona?

"Anyway, who's to say *Manfred* is the stronger piece?" growled Roy Blade. "Within two years of its publication, *The Vampyre* was translated into French, German, Spanish and Swedish. Even before Polidori's death it had been adapted for the stage."

Everyone began to speak at once.

Lady Vee bristled. "*Any* work by Byron would be a *fahhhr* more suitable choice than Polidori, who . . ."

"But there are no roles for women in it!" Theresa protested.

The idea that Lady Ives might have actually read Byron's masterpiece momentarily dumbfounded the others.

Into the silence, Grace placated, "After all, Polidori's work was strong enough to be mistaken originally for Byron's own. Goethe even called it Byron's best work."

"It's influenced a hell of a lot of writers," Roy Blade declared. "Sheridan Le Fanu, Edgar Allan Poe and Bram Stoker to name a few." He warmed to his theme, oblivious to the signs of restlessness in his audience. "True, it may not be the seminal vampire text, that credit would go to Burger or perhaps Goethe for *Die Braut von Korinth* —"

"Brilliant bloke," Derrick commented to

Theresa, who put her hands to her head as though she felt a headache coming on — or wanted to cover her ears.

Lady Vee ignored all this, speaking solely to Grace. "Goethe was being *ironic.* Vampires!" She made a noise of disgust. "I agreed to invest in a work of cultural significance. Polidori was a sycophant. He plagiarized the idea of a vampire from Byron, who had the good sense and exquisite taste to abandon the project as unworthy."

Roy Blade rose, towering over the elderly woman — who puffed up like an adder. "Perhaps if Byron and his snotty crowd of effetes hadn't deliberately set out to humiliate and punish Polidori for having committed the unforgivable sin of working for a living instead of being born to aristocrats or intellectuals —"

"*Work?* He was a leech by profession and nature. He was hired to *spy* upon B. by his publisher."

"Would that be Polidori's publisher or Byron's?" Derrick queried with great interest.

"I think we're getting off the track," Grace said.

Catriona curled her lip. "You have the gift of understatement."

"And you have the gift of unproductive

commentary." Years of dealing with smart-ass adolescents had sharpened her tongue, but Grace regretted her hasty words when Theresa uttered a pleased, "Ooh!"

"Please continue, Grace," Lord Ruthven said. She assumed he was not encouraging her to attack his wife, but to address Lady Vee's issues.

"In fairness," she went on, "while Polidori admitted he was inspired by Byron, his work was written and published before Byron ever penned his fragment."

Roy Blade burst out, "Who knows what he might have achieved if he hadn't been driven by Byron's ridicule and ostracization to take his own life. He was only twenty-six. A boy! He had a brilliant mind. The youngest man ever to receive his medical degree from the University of Edinburgh. Had he found an ounce of kindness or encouragement, he might have —"

"Now, I don't think you can blame what happened to Polidori in England on Byron," Grace objected. "As far as I know, Byron never said anything disparaging about *The Vampyre* other than to make it clear it wasn't his own."

"You're not helping," Catriona informed her. "Look, we've had this out. As *Ms.* Hollister points out, we voted." She turned to Lady Vee. "*You* were outvoted, if you will recall." As she moved, she trod on the stage trapdoor.

With a cracking sound, it gave way beneath her.

3

As Catriona dropped through the black square, Theresa screamed. There were outcries of shock and horror from the others.

Catriona's hands shot out and grabbed the edge of the stage. She hung there for a moment. Strangely, she never screamed, never made a sound. Her hands flattened out, then flexed as she tried for better purchase on the wooden floor. Her elbow worked its way over the edge, then the top of her head appeared.

It was only a matter of seconds; then the paralysis of disbelief that had held the group, shattered.

"Oh, my gosh!" cried Grace, springing forward to help. She had the notion that Roy Blade moved with her, but it was Derek Derrick beside her as her hands closed over Catriona's wrists. Though distantly aware of people running, of footsteps pounding across the stage, of doors banging, of commotion and chaos, all her focus was on hanging on to Catriona.

Catriona's hands felt callused and unexpectedly strong as they locked on Grace's wrists. For a beat Grace felt her own balance go; then Derek's hand clenched a fistful of the dangling woman's leather collar, taking her weight.

"Catriona, my God!" Lord Ruthven helped them draw her up. His face was bloodless. "My God!"

The others circled round, babbling shock and relief.

Catriona shook her fiery hair out of her face and laughed breathlessly. "Quick reflexes, Grace. I owe you."

"Not as quick as yours." Anyone else would surely have crashed through to the basement.

Catriona's eyes flicked to Derek Derrick's. "Ta," she said coolly.

"Close call, eh!" He looked like Grace felt: badly shaken. Staring down into the trap, he called, "All clear. We pulled her up."

Roy Blade called back, his words muffled. A light went on from below.

He had broken records in his charge down to the basement, but he would not have been in time, Grace realized. It was a chilling thought.

"But how could it have happened?" Theresa was protesting, as the group milled, offering suggestions, comments and general opinions. A couple of men offered to put boards across the opening.

"It's an old theater." Lady Vee's voice trembled.

Grace knelt, peering cautiously through the opening. "Good heavens, what a drop. It looks like it goes straight down to the basement." She called, "Can you tell what happened?"

Roy Blade's negative response floated up.

"They say the theater is haunted," Theresa whispered. Derek Derrick chuckled and slipped an arm around her slim shoulders.

"Balderdash!" Lady Vee said. "Grace, I can't imagine what you hope to accomplish in that *most* unflattering position."

"Shouldn't there be a lift or something?" When no one answered, Grace rose and dusted off her hands and knees.

If someone wanted to stage an accident, a theater was an ideal setting. Even in a new, well-maintained theater, trapdoors, pits, balconies, catwalks and stairs offered a variety of deadly possibilities for falls and electrocution. And Grace had seen plenty of TV shows where victims had been conked by falling battens or counterweights. For that matter, real-life actors and crew alike fell off stages with distressing frequency.

The Innisdale Playhouse was poorly lit, the wiring was old, and most of the stairs and scaffolds did not have rails. Why am I thinking like this? Grace wondered. Perhaps because from the moment she had walked in that night she had sensed a certain peculiar energy in the air, something she recognized from years of teaching. Mischief. That's what it was. She had felt mischief in the room.

"It could have been an accident," she reflected aloud.

"What do you mean!" exclaimed Lady Vee. She clutched Grace's arm as though she needed the support. "Of *course* it was an accident!" The others chimed in, staring at Grace as though she had committed some social solecism.

It was Catriona who said, after staring at Grace for a long moment, "I don't believe in accidents."

She sounds like Peter, Grace reflected. *I don't believe in coincidence,* he had said in much the same tone of voice.

Catriona pushed through them, making her way backstage. The black curtains with their scarlet-stenciled masks of tragedy and comedy rippled in her wake. The others followed in uneasy silence.

Navigating the backstage obstacle course of props, leads and electrical cords, Catriona found a light switch and continued to the theater basement.

"For God's sake, watch your step, everyone," Lord Ruthven ordered, as they clattered down the stairs. "This place is a death trap. We'll get the inspectors in tomorrow."

In the narrow stairwell they met Roy Blade. Catriona brushed past him. Blade backed against the wall so that the others could file past. Slowly he followed them.

The basement was dank and poorly lit. It smelled of old plumbing and something acrid. An electrical short? White light streamed in from the open trapdoor about twelve feet above them. There was an old-fashioned lift, but it had been shoved to the far wall. The broken trapdoor lay on the floor.

Grace picked it up. It looked all right to her inexpert eye. No saw marks, no obvious signs of tampering. The wood showed splintering around the hinges, but that seemed in keeping with the nature of the accident.

"Drag that table over here and give me a leg up," Catriona ordered.

Derek and Roy moved to obey. A heavy, battered table scraped its way across the cement floor and was positioned beneath the trapdoor.

Lord Ruthven took the broken trapdoor and examined it himself. "Don't break your neck falling off that damn table," he dictated, as Catriona joined Derek on the table. Derek cupped his hands, and nimbly she stepped up, reaching for the open trap. With one hand outstretched, she steadied herself on the frame, craning her neck to examine the latch that had given way.

Grace watched Lord Ruthven watching his wife, and wondered again if Lady Ruthven had been the woman Peter had gone to meet. It did give Lord Ruthven a reason for being in the cemetery that time of night. Perhaps he had been spying on the missus?

But if Catriona had been the woman who called Peter, why had she not shown herself?

"I remember sitting in this theater during an air raid," Lady Vee said suddenly, her voice echoing against the cement walls. "We had decoy sites just outside of Penrith, you know. To lure the Germans away from the ironworks in Cleator Moor and elsewhere. We were watching a production of *Night Must Fall* when the siren went. It's the last time I recall sitting in this theater."

"T-That's World War II," Theresa accused, teeth chattering. Her tone implied the topic was past its expiration date. "How long must we all stay down here? It's like a morgue!"

"What do you see?" Lord Ruthven called up to his wife.

She dropped lightly down to the tabletop. "Nothing. Not a damn thing." She smiled, but it was not a pleasant smile. "Perhaps the latch did simply give."

"What else?" Theresa asked blankly. She stared at the others. No one had an answer.

"It's not a very sure way of — of —" Grace stopped, uncomfortable with where her thoughts were leading her.

"Of killing someone?" Catriona finished for her. "It's not, is it?"

"All right, ladies. Gentlemen," — Lord Ruthven was brisk, shepherding the others out of the basement before they had time to react to Catriona's extraordinary comment — "I think we've all had enough for one night. We'll meet back here tomorrow evening."

They began to file back up the stairs.

"We haven't resolved which play," Lady Vee began, stopping in her tracks.

With less than his usual patience Lord Ruthven said, "Lady Venetia, your concerns are commendable; that's one reason I wanted your input on this production, but the group has selected the material, and it is a strong piece, ideally suited to the season. If you can't reconcile yourself to it, we shall have to arrange financial backing elsewhere, I suppose."

There was a long silence, filled in by the drum of distant rain somewhere far above them.

"We shall see what we shall see," Lady Vee said ominously.

There was a dwarf in Grace's garden the next morning. He wore green leggings and a red cap and had a long gray beard. A ballerina in a pink tutu accompanied him.

"Wow!" Grace said, opening the door.

She was renting a small cottage on the grounds of Renfrew Hall. The Gardener's Cottage was a cozy bed-sitter painted a fanciful pink. The door was bright red, as was the trim on the windows. An iron stove kept the cottage toasty in the winter, and in the summer Grace woke to the sound of doves cooing beneath the eaves and the scent of apple blossoms. A far cry from the convenient but characterless apartment she rented in Los Angeles.

"You two look terrific. Is this a dress rehearsal for the Halloween fete?" She glanced up at the somber blue sky. It was going to be a gorgeous day. The cottage's silvery shingles steamed in the sunlight. Raindrops glittered on the grass and flowers.

The dwarf advanced, hopping a large puddle. The ballerina skirted the sides.

"I'm a princess," the ballerina informed Grace. She was a bit stubby for the ballet, and her love of peppermint bull's-eyes was bound to prove detrimental. Her name was Patricia Smithwick, and she was the four-year-old granddaughter of Grace's landlady.

"She's a ballerina," the dwarf corrected in an unexpectedly deep voice. His beard was coming unstuck. He licked at the gray fringe, attempting to retrieve it with his tongue. Jeremiah Smithwick was the ballerina's brother. He was six and had inherited the same tilted hazel eyes, freckles and sandy curls. They stood together in the shade of a velvety green Chinese astilboides, obscurely reminding Grace of "The Elf and the Dormouse," a poem she had been required to memorize in grade school.

"A princess ballerina!" she admired.

"Just a princess," the ballerina assured her. She studied Grace's cinnamon-colored turtleneck dress and matching cardigan, her snub nose wrinkled in thought. "Are you going foxhunting?"

"Not this morning. I'm going to work." She held up her purse in illustration.

"Granny used to go foxhunting."

"I didn't know that." It was difficult to picture her landlady sailing over hedges and fences, but of course Sally Smithwick had not always been a comfortably sized grandmother.

"Granddad was afraid of horses. He's in heaven now. I'm going to have a pony for my birthday. I know his name."

"No you *don't!*" the dwarf objected.

Patricia stuck her tongue out at him, which was not something princesses or even ballerinas did much in England.

"I was only a year or two older than you when I learned to ride," Grace said, hoping to defuse the looming hostilities.

"I'm going to hunt foxes," Patricia confided.

"No, you're *not!*" the dwarf informed her. "A fox would eat you up!" To Grace, he said politely, "Granny wants to see you."

Oh dear, thought Grace. Late for work two days in a row; she had always prided herself on her punctuality. "I'll stop by on my way out," she promised the pint-sized posse.

Accompanied by Jeremiah and Patricia, Grace got her battered Aston Martin DB4 out of the carriage house that served as garage. The car's engine disturbed the swallows nesting in the rafters, and to the children's delight they circled in Disney-like formation before swooping out of the double doors.

The car had belonged to Sally's late husband, and she had sold it to Grace for a pittance despite the fact that it would have fetched a terrific price from a collector. Grace loved the baby blue sports car, for all its dents and dings. Every time she turned the key in the ignition she felt like Mrs. Peel in *The Avengers*.

She drove around to the front of the red-brick house and parked. A former vicarage on the edge of the village, Renfrew Hall was run as a bed-and-breakfast during tourist season.

Sally met Grace at the door, her freckled face troubled, although she went through the motions of offering tea and polite conversation.

The interior of Renfrew Hall was a homely hodgepodge of styles and personalities. Flea market finds and gorgeous antique pieces roosted side by side. Slipcovers in checks and flowers competed gaily for attention. It was a home designed to accommodate children, dogs and cats. The clock tick-tocked comfortably on the fireplace mantel. Scents of vanilla and cinnamon hung in the air.

Grace declined tea. Sally sent the children to change out of their Halloween costumes, then at last came to the point. "Grace, I caught Miss Coke snooping around your cottage last night."

"Who?"

"Miss Coke." Sally looked over her shoulder in the direction the children had gone, and said undervoiced, "The local witch."

"Are you serious?" Grace was smiling.

Sally was about sixty, friendly and sensible. During the past year Grace had come to consider Sally a friend. She reminded Grace of many of the women she had taught with at St. Anne's, the kind of woman Grace understood. Or usually understood. This was something new.

Sally shook her head at Grace's tone. "I know what you're thinking, Grace, but she's the real thing."

Coke is the real thing? Grace had to bite back a laugh. She said curiously, "Do you mean she puts spells on people?"

"Sometimes. She's a queer old duck.

Anyway, I found her trying to hang this on your front door." Sally reached into her cardigan pocket and handed Grace what at first glance appeared to be a wooden toy.

Grace stared down at the shriveled figure. It was amorphously female. Brown threads were glued to the walnut-sized head. A snip of flowered material that appeared to be from a skirt Grace had thrown out a few months earlier was stuck to the body. A hatpin was jabbed through the doll's throat. Fashion statement? Unlikely.

"I guess this is the season for it. But, Sally, surely you don't believe in — well, whatever this is supposed to be. What *is* it supposed to be, by the way?" Grace asked, studying the doll again.

"It's a . . . a poppet." Sally's hazel eyes were grave. "I think it's a warning. Miss Coke is mad on the subject of animals. She probably has fifty cats in that ramshackle place of hers, and of course she's working night and day to save Squirrel Nutkin."

"Of course," Grace said blankly. Squirrel Nutkin? She had heard something about a campaign to preserve the area's native red squirrel from the encroaching grays. Perhaps that's what Sally meant?

"Naturally she's staunchly antihunting, and every year she gets worse. Well, they all do. The sabs, that is."

"The sabs?"

"Saboteurs. Of the hunt."

"Oh."

"I suppose Miss Coke learned that you're going to be taking part in the hunt this season."

" 'Taking part' is probably an exaggeration. I just want to see what it's like, really."

Sally didn't say anything.

If the grandchildren were correct, and Sally had formerly hunted, Grace supposed that she must not be antifoxhunting, but it was a heated debate in Britain. The use of hounds for hunting had even been banned in Scotland.

Grace had yet to make her own mind up on the subject. She liked animals, but she was not above eating meat or wearing leather. She had heard both sides of the foxhunting argument, and agreed that both sides made good points. She knew that opponents of the sport were highly organized and as fanatical as proponents. She said slowly, "Did you — ?"

"We had words," Sally said tersely.

"Oh dear. Sally, I'm sorry. Do you think it would help if I spoke to her?"

"I do not. I'd stay clear of her, Grace. She's more than a tad odd. I only . . . wanted to show you this and tell you to be careful. You won't be the only one she's harassing. She had poor Theresa Ives in tears last week."

"Harassing?"

"Stalking."

"Stalking? Can't the police do something?"

Sally shook her head, a gesture that seemed to indicate that Grace just didn't get it.

And, in fact, Grace didn't get it, unless Sally was sorry for the old woman, or there was some village social hierarchy at work.

"All right," she said. "Thank you for telling me, and I promise to be careful." She was still smiling although Sally's manner was troubling. Sally seemed too grounded to be taking this kind of thing so much to heart. And of course it was unpleasant to think that a stranger actively wished one harm.

Sally said again, "Please do be careful, Grace. Bad things have happened to people Miss Coke has ill-wished. Very bad things."

Though the circumstances had not been conducive to falling in love, Grace had been in love with Craddock House from the moment she laid eyes on it, a winding, climbing affair of white stone and silver slate framed in tumultuous rose and wisteria. Despite the exhaustion, fear and confusion of that long-ago day, she still had a vivid memory of her first impression of the old house: the stately chimneys, diamond-paned windows, and graceful crooks and angles of seventeenth-century architecture. That day she would have welcomed the sight of a police car parked out front, but today Chief Constable Heron's black Bentley filled her with unease.

Not that Grace didn't like the chief constable; she did. He was a shrewd but kind man, and had been most sympathetic to her during her first visit to Innisdale. The problem was, his main ambition in life seemed to be to see Peter behind bars. It put a crimp in an otherwise beautiful friendship.

Heron, accompanied by one of his rosy-cheeked constables, was crossing the trim lawn as Grace started up the cobblestone walk. She sped up and reached the front door to Rogue's Gallery as the representatives of the law did.

"Morning, Miss Hollister," Heron said in his gruff way, as she opened the door for them. She sensed he was not thrilled to see her, and her anxiety grew. Something was up.

Behind the counter, Peter was reading the *London Times*. He glanced up casually. Though the lower level of Craddock House was half-concealed from the road by trim hedges and banks of flowers, she could tell by his cool expression that he had already observed their approach and was braced for whatever was coming.

"Ah, Chief Constable," he greeted in that insufferable tone he got when he was talking to the police, like the Scarlet Pimpernel facing down Chauvelin. He folded the paper in crisp quarters. "Always a delight. Is there anything in particular you're looking for this time? Some bauble for Mrs. Chief Constable, perhaps?"

"May we speak privately, Mr. Fox?"

"Certainly." Peter's eyes found Grace's. "Mind the store, love?"

Grace assented and watched Peter lead the constabulary to his back office. As soon as the door closed behind them she darted around to an alcove and lifted down a heavy gilt-framed painting of a foxhunt. Soundlessly, she inched open the panel concealed beneath.

She had learned the hard way last year that Craddock House was riddled with secret passages and "hidey-holes." Peter had once said he wasn't sure that even he knew all the old house's secrets, but this was one secret he had shared. Though she couldn't see into the back office, Grace could now hear the men's conversation, and it was not encouraging. Heron was not wasting any time on pleasantries.

"May I ask where you were the night of the fifteenth, Mr. Fox?"

"Thursday night?" Peter sounded indifferent. "What time?"

"Between the hours of midnight and two."

"Here. At home."

"Can anyone corroborate your whereabouts?"

Peter was silent for a moment; then he said, "No."

"Did you receive any phone calls or visitors during that time?"

"Not that I recall."

Why meet in the cramped office? Grace wondered. It was more of a stockroom than an office, really. Why not his flat upstairs? Her mind worried at it for a few moments; then she knew. The entrance to at least one of the old house's numerous secret passages was in that office. He must be considering making a run for it.

But that didn't make sense. Surely the situation was not that desperate? Unless . . .

unless Peter *was* involved.

She listened tensely. There was silence in the office. Then Heron said bluntly, "You don't ask us what this is about, Mr. Fox."

Peter's voice was suddenly edged. "We both know what this is about, Chief Constable. You're hoping to nick me for the Thwaite job."

"Not just the Thwaite job," Heron said, sounding almost jovial. "The jobs you pulled at the Potter-Grahaems' and the Crosbys' as well."

"I hate to disappoint you, but I might have an alibi for one of those evenings."

"We're all ears, sir."

"Then again, I might not," Peter admitted.

"You enjoy games, Mr. Fox."

"Backgammon is a game, Chief Constable. I find the idea of prison less amusing."

"You'll find it less amusing still with a charge of homicide against you."

"Homicide?" Peter sounded stiff. After a moment he said, "I wasn't aware anyone had been killed."

"You need to keep up on these things, Mr. Fox. The security guard at the Crosbys'? The man injured in the robbery? He died this morning."

Peter seemed to have nothing to say to that.

Grace was having a bit of trouble herself. Someone had died as a result of the local robberies. She was ashamed to realize that until this moment she had not taken the crimes seriously. They had seemed the stuff of drawing room comedies: daring cat burglars scaling the roofs of wealthy nobs, scooping up jewels from well-insured people who could easily afford to buy more, and vanishing into the night. But a man who had simply been doing his job had been killed. Someone's husband or father or son — it was too terrible to think about.

"Constable," Heron barked, startling Grace out of her reflections.

They were going to *arrest* Peter? Just like that?

She didn't wait to hear more. Abandoning her listening post, she flew up the aisle and around the corner as the door of the office opened. She narrowly missed crashing into Heron's solid bulk. "Wait!" she got out.

Peter stood behind him. His blue eyes met hers, any emotion veiled.

He didn't run, Grace thought in amazed relief. She had been so afraid he would that she had to rethink what she planned to say.

"Wait!" she repeated more calmly.

As though he had expected this, Heron shook his head regretfully. "I do wish you wouldn't, Miss Hollister."

"But I — I must." The constable smiled sympathetically. He had a nice face. Encouraged, Grace went on. "You're making a mistake!"

Avoiding Peter's gaze, she forged ahead. "I have an idea what this is about, but Mr. Fox was with me on the night in question."

"The night in question?" Like she had stumbled out of the pages of an Agatha Christie novel. "Thursday night, I mean," she clarified. "We were together. Me and Peter. Peter and I, I mean."

"I think they've got that part," Peter told her.

If he had an alibi for Thursday night, then he was probably in the clear for the night the Crosby house was burgled. She knew it, and so did Heron. He sighed a long and weary sigh, then nodded to his constable, who stepped past Peter. Apparently they had not actually slapped the handcuffs on him. Perhaps Grace had been premature.

"If you had an alibi, you should have spoken up, Mr. Fox," the chief constable said sternly.

Peter studied the older man sardonically.

"Life is simple for you, Chief Constable."

"It is for most honest folk."

"Honest folk or folk lacking in imagination?"

Heron disregarded this, turning his attention back on Grace. It was not easy to hold his shrewd gaze. "You'd be willing to testify to Mr. Fox's whereabouts between the hours of twelve and two on Thursday evening, Miss Hollister?"

Grace nodded. "If it comes to that."

"It may very well come to that." Heron seemed to brood over this. Then, reaching a decision, he said, "We'll have a look around then, Mr. Fox, unless you've an objection."

"I'm sure my objections won't delay your search long."

"Not long."

Peter made a gesture that managed to be both graceful and rude. "Have at it."

It was more than a look around. Accompanied by Grace they made a thorough search, opening every single crate and box in the stockroom, checking article after article of furniture in the shop against a long list. When they had finished inside they went out in the back garden to inspect the potting shed and garage.

At a nod from Peter, Grace grabbed her coat and followed them out.

The back garden had evolved from the original vegetable patch to beds of herbs and flowers. In the spring the fragrant pastel of sweet peas entangled with climbing vines and rambling roses. Blue delphiniums, red poppies and yellow daffodils bloomed in joyous abandon. Thyme and rosemary burst from their beds in scented bouquets. But at this time of year the yard was muted in brown and rust red. The rabbits and squirrels and birds had departed, leaving a sort of desolate quiet.

Grace stood to the side where cabbages and potatoes grew behind the potting shed. She could smell the damp earth and the odd myrrh scent of the antique roses overgrowing the shed's roof and doorway.

Beyond the hedgerows she spotted sheep grazing peacefully near the remnants of the old Roman wall. No place could have seemed further removed from crime or the underworld.

The police finished diligently poking through the clay pots and watering cans and at last marched round the front and reentered the gallery, followed by Grace.

"Everything in order?"

Heron did not respond to the raillery in Peter's voice. "We would like you to come down to the station this afternoon, Mr. Fox.

It would be helpful to . . . have your perspective on these crimes. It's only a request, you understand."

"I understand," said Peter. Grace saw the look the two men exchanged before the older man turned away. All these dark and meaningful looks. It was like watching a foreign movie without subtitles.

The shop bells rang cheerfully behind the police officers.

Peter went to the front window, observing them cross the lawn and get into their car.

Grace watched Peter watching the cops. His profile gave nothing away.

"Don't think I'm not grateful for the alibi," he said, turning from the window, "but what the hell were you thinking?"

"That you'd do the same for me?"

The corner of his mouth twitched in amusement. "I don't suffer from an overly tender conscience," Peter pointed out. "You, on the other hand, agonize over every little white lie."

"Well, you were free to speak up. You could have told them the truth."

His blue eyes mocked her. "I hope I'm not so ungallant as to naysay a beautiful woman intent on ruining her good name in my honor."

"I don't know how good my name is

around here anyway," Grace muttered. "I'm sure everyone in the village thinks we're sleeping together."

"That's the spirit." But his mind was not on her; his eyes narrowed at some inward vision. "Didn't it occur to you that they'll check your story? When they verify we weren't together —"

"We were together," Grace said. "In a manner of speaking."

"What manner of speaking would that be? The forked tongue variety?"

From the first she had known her deception would have to come out, but she had hoped to delay the moment until their relationship was again on solid ground. Assuming that day ever arrived. "I wasn't lying. I was —" Grace swallowed on the word.

"You 'was'?"

"Spying."

"Spying?" His expression was blank. Gradually understanding dawned. "On me?"

Grace nodded.

"You were spying on me Thursday night?" Peter seemed to be struggling to absorb it.

"Yes."

Very rarely had she seen him at a loss for

words, but she saw it now. "Why?" he asked at last. Face and voice were expressionless.

"It was by accident."

"This should be interesting."

"Not the spying, the phone call I overheard."

He started to speak, then stopped himself. Grace hurried on, "What I mean is, I accidentally picked up the phone when you did. I didn't mean to listen in."

"Perhaps you should have hung up." The suggestion was put in a silky tone. She did not like the look in his eyes. This was going to be worse than she had imagined, and she had gone into it knowing that he would see her actions as betrayal.

Grace plowed on. "I heard her . . ." She hazarded a guess, "Catriona —" His eyes flickered, and she knew her guess had been correct. "Telling you to meet her at the graveyard. She sounded — it sounded — I thought —"

"You put it so well," Peter murmured. "So you decided to follow me?"

"Actually," Grace said with a hint of spirit, "I was there ahead of you. Which is how I know you weren't robbing the Thwaites."

He watched her warily. "I was only there for a few minutes. I could have joined my confederates at the scene of the crime."

"You waited for thirty minutes," Grace said. "When I drove by here about twenty minutes later your car was parked outside. I waited on the road maybe another thirty minutes until your lights went out; so unless you took a taxi to join the robbers for the last half hour, I think you're clear."

"You do, do you?"

She didn't like the derision in that. She retorted, "Unfortunately, I can't alibi Lady Ruthven, since she never showed."

His expression altered. "Be very careful, Grace," Peter said. His tone caused the small hairs at the back of her neck to prickle.

The gallery door jingled behind them, and Grace nearly leapt out of her skin.

"Cheerio, you two!" fluted Theresa Ives.

Grace watched Peter's features rearrange themselves into a smile. Her knees felt weak with the release of tension.

"To be continued," he warned, and brushed past her.

4

"Nothing I say could persuade you to join us on the field next weekend?" Lady Ives held up the opal glass perfume atomizer for closer examination. "Lalique?"

"Schneider. Circa 1895," Peter replied.

"Schneider. Of course." She bit her lip. "But you do ride. I've seen you riding with Allegra Clairmont-Brougham. You ride *beautifully*." This last was said with a certain appraising glint in her narrow-set eyes.

"I'm afraid I don't care much for hunting," Peter apologized. "Too much sympathy for the fox."

Grace gritted her teeth as Theresa Ives gave her neighing laugh. "How much?" Lady Theresa inquired.

"For you? Three hundred quid." Since the regular price was two-fifty, Lady Ives was indeed getting a special deal. Grace inwardly shook her head as Lady Ives gave that annoying laugh again.

Grace had been observing them bat the conversational ball back and forth for about forty-five minutes. Her ladyship, a collector of antique perfume bottles, was one of Peter's regular customers. Since she did spend a fair amount of money at Rogue's Gallery, Grace knew it was cynical to suspect that part of Theresa's interest was in the shop's owner. But then a disproportionate ratio of Peter's clientele was feminine.

"Grace will be joining us on Saturday," Theresa murmured.

"Grace does so many things I would not."

Theresa gave that laugh, and said to Grace, "He's awful, isn't he?"

"Yes."

She confided to Peter, "Gerald says that Grace has an *admirable* seat."

"Oh for a seat in some poetic nook," quoted Peter. "Just hid with trees and a sparkling brook."

Theresa squealed with pleasure. "Poetic nook. That's brilliant. Did you hear that, Grace?"

"Wasn't I meant to?" She was tired of being the butt — or rather *seat* — of Peter's wit, and tried to change the subject. "Is there really a lot of antihunting sentiment locally?"

Theresa shrugged. "Not a lot. A few malcontents who care more about the rights of animals than other people."

"In the States many of the hunt clubs use a drag scent."

Theresa widened her baby blues. "In the States some clubs hunt *coyotes,*" she pointed out, as though such barbarians were capable of anything.

"I thought it was all about the Thrill of the Chase. What does it matter what you chase?"

"It doesn't. A hare, a stag, a fox. But it has to be *real.*"

"Otherwise, the local game get so apathetic," Peter put in.

Theresa laughed, making a snorting noise. "You're *wicked!*"

Grace bit her tongue. The best thing was to keep out of hearing range, and there was certainly plenty to keep her occupied and out of Peter and Theresa's vicinity, but somehow she kept tuning back in. Theresa's voice carried. More annoying was the fact that Peter's didn't.

She could hear Theresa complaining now about what a nuisance Lady Vee was over the play and how they couldn't get any rehearsing done.

". . . And you should have heard them going on and on about who was responsible for whose death, when the truth is they'd *all* be dead by now!"

"Assuming one could tell the difference." He was egging her on, but Theresa didn't seem to notice. Apparently *not* the keenest hunter in the pack.

"We had poetry in school, of course. Poets. Ugh! Utter wet weeds. Someone dying because someone wrote a bad review, then someone else writing a poem about *that!* Of course I don't pretend to be an intellectual like Grace."

"Does Grace pretend to be an intellectual?"

Lady Ives gurgled her delight. Grace was less delighted. She slapped the dust rag down hard and came around the corner (in a cloud of dust) to find them at the front counter. Peter was wrapping the fragile swirled glass in tissue. He looked up with a bland expression.

"I think I'll leave early," Grace announced a little loudly.

"Oooh. Not feeling well?" Theresa was all sympathy.

"Not awfully."

Grace retrieved her things from the back. Peter met her at the door, holding it in place when she started to open it. In a voice for her ears alone he said, "Need I tell you to keep your mouth shut about what we discussed this morning?"

"Since you put it so nicely, how can I refuse?" She shoved hard against the door, and he let go, which caused her to stagger out onto the cobblestones.

The gallery door closed firmly behind her.

He was angry, Grace thought, as she sat in the library basement later that day studying past editions of *The Clarion*. Angrier than she'd ever seen him. Well, so was she. The thing that made her angriest was the knowledge that she was handling this all wrong. Skulking around graveyards, lying to the police, running away and now snooping.

But was trying to learn more about the robberies technically snooping or was this simply doing the required homework? After all, she had more than a little at stake, too. She pushed her glasses back into place and resumed reading.

The first robbery had occurred early in August, one week before Lord and Lady Ruthven had set up house in Innisdale.

Coincidence? thought Grace. I think not. But it probably was.

Mr. and Mrs. Benjamin Potter-Grahaem had been on holiday when their home was burgled. The house's somewhat antiquated security system had been easily disarmed, and the thief or thieves had made off with several hundred thousand dollars' worth of silver and art.

As robberies went it was rather a no-brainer. The house had been uninhabited by other than an elderly and hard-of-hearing butler who slept through the excitement; and the security system had presented no challenge at all. The police assumed that at least two persons had been involved in the crime, mostly owing to the amount of loot removed from the premises.

To Grace this did not sound like Peter's "MO," but since her knowledge of Peter's past was based mostly on imagination, that didn't mean much.

The truth was, she knew very little about Peter's background, criminal or otherwise. He had admitted once that jewels were his specialty, and that he had been known in "the business" as the Ice Fox, following a spectacular diamond heist early in his career.

But she had no idea how he had operated and whether he had occasionally branched out to old masters or small appliances.

The second burglary had required more effort on the part of the thieves. The security system was up-to-the-minute, and both servants and the Crosby family had been in residence. In fact, Mrs. Crosby's jewels had been stolen from a small safe in her bedchamber. Along with the jewels had vanished a number of valuable *objets d'art,* including a Faberge egg and a priceless Isfahan rug.

The rug struck Grace as sheer cheek.

Unfortunately, the estate's security guard had been hit by the escaping thieves' vehicle. This was the incident to which Heron had referred. The guard had been in a coma at the time the newspaper article had been written.

That's not murder, Grace thought. Manslaughter at the most, surely?

The police went on record declaring the two robberies to be the work of the same cunning and expert gang.

Gang? That fact must eliminate Peter. Peter had always worked alone, although, come to think of it, Grace wasn't sure whether she had formed that opinion on her own or whether Peter had said something to give her that impression.

What were Peter's finances like? She had no idea. He lived very very well, and the shop seemed to turn a brisk dollar. Then again, business was slow during the tourist off-season. He had told her once that he had made a number of fortunate investments. It could be the truth, but considering it objectively, she could see why the police might find his bank accounts worth checking into.

The third and most recent robbery had taken place at the estate of Reginald and Evadne Thwaite. This had been by far the most daring job. In addition to a complicated security system, the Thwaites owned two dogs, which the thieves had neutralized with doped butcher's bones. They had managed to clear off with a half million dollars' worth of jewels, paintings and antiques in just over two hours.

Where are they stashing the stuff? wondered Grace. The idea that occurred to her left her lunch lying like a lump of lead in her stomach.

What better place to hide antiques than in an antiques gallery? No wonder Heron had wanted to search the shop after the Thwaite robbery. And how convenient: Peter was frequently on buying trips; he would be expected to return with a van of merchandise. While he was traveling he could fence the jewels and unload the items that would be too hot to move through Rogue's Gallery.

For a few moments Grace sat, unhappily chewing the end of her reading glasses. Her task was to prove that Peter couldn't be involved, but the more she learned, the easier it was to understand why the chief constable thought Peter might, as the mystery novels said, "look good for it."

Returning upstairs, she handed over the basement key to Roy Blade at the inquiry desk.

After exchanging a few pleasantries, she asked, "Are you taking part in the hunt next weekend?"

Blade laughed his buccaneer's laugh. "Do I look like the foxhunting type to you?" His good eye glinted. "Anyway, I'm always on the side of the fox."

"That's what Peter said." She remembered something else Peter had once said about having been in love with a woman who had hair the color of a fox and a temper to match. Maybe she should have paid closer attention.

"What do you think of Catriona Ruthven?" she heard herself asking.

Blade shrugged his broad leather-jacketed shoulders. "Good stage presence. Good speaking voice."

"I mean as a woman."

Blade raised his eyebrows. "A handful, I'd say." His black eye gleamed with curiosity. Grace dropped the subject. Excusing herself after a moment or two, she went to reexamine the much-thumbed current issue of *The Clarion*.

As she read over the account of the security guard's death it seemed to her that there was something noncommittal in the official police comments. Had the guard been in on the burglary? Was his death not an accident?

Grace was frowning over this when a young woman reading *British Vogue* suddenly leaned across to her, and said softly, "What they're afraid to tell you is his body was drained of blood."

The hair on the nape of Grace's neck stood on end. "I beg your pardon?"

The young woman swept her heavily frosted hair off her face, glanced over her shoulder as though the king's spies were everywhere, and whispered again, "His body was drained of blood! They're afraid to put it in the paper, but it's true."

"What do you mean, 'drained of blood'? How do you know that?"

"Everyone knows it."

Across the way an elderly gentleman glared at them and made a shushing sound.

The woman gave her a meaningful look, then returned to her keen perusal of armor-plated cocktail dresses.

Grace hesitated, glanced at the elderly gentleman who had resumed scowling over *The Economist*, then leaned toward the *British Vogue* reader. "But *how* do you know it's true?"

"My boyfriend works for *The Clarion*. The police won't let them print it. They don't want to start a panic."

Rehearsal that evening broke up early, with both Derek and Theresa excusing themselves for urgent appointments. They departed in much-emphasized opposite directions, which only served to focus suspicion on them.

Catriona laughed off her husband's dark expression, teasing, "Oh, to be young and in love with someone you're not married to."

"Are you speaking from experience?" Ruthven retorted.

This served only to entertain Catriona further.

As the Innisdale Players cast and crew packed it in for another night, there was a general invitation to head over to the pub for a pint. To Grace's disappointment, Catriona declined. Having had her suspicion that Catriona was the woman Peter had expected to meet in the graveyard confirmed, Grace was increasingly curious about her.

Of course Catriona was married, but who knew what that might mean in this day and age. It meant something to Grace, and she hoped it meant something to Peter.

She had managed to convince herself that the change in Peter coincided with the first robbery. But Grace couldn't help wondering if she was trying to deflect the blame for her troubled relationship by coming up with some wild theory of a connection between Peter and Catriona — the connection being these burglaries? How much easier on her pride to blame Peter's waning interest on his criminal past rather than on her own inadequacies.

It was almost certainly coincidence that the arrival of the Ruthvens had shortly followed the first robbery.

I don't believe in coincidence. Wasn't that what Peter had said? And not so long ago.

Grace had to be satisfied with the knowledge that the equally inscrutable Lord Ruthven had said he would stop by later for a pint, and she joined the others at the Cock's Crow.

The pub had a low open-beamed ceiling and sixteenth-century dark paneling. The old-fashioned fixtures gleamed in the mellow light. There were candle sconces on the wall and vintage signs from the 1940s.

"Where is everybody?" Grace asked, glancing around. Almost none of the cast or crew was present. One of the stagehands glanced over his shoulder.

"It's this talk of vampires."

Grace laughed, then realized the man was serious.

"You've heard about Bill Jones?" The stagehand was an ordinary-looking man, middle-aged and clean-cut. His expression was perfectly sincere.

Grace shook her head. "Who?"

"The Crosbys' security man. His body was drained of every drop of blood. And there were strange marks on his neck. Marks —" The other man nudged him, and the stagehand broke off.

"That can't be true," Grace protested.

The stagehand shrugged, not looking at her. He turned back to the bar. Grace found herself sharing a table with Roy Blade. They ordered a round and some cheese and apple tartlets.

"I'm afraid the old bat was right. *Manfred* would have been the stronger work," Blade said, pushing a pint of beer toward Grace. "Somehow this version simply isn't living up to the promise of Polidori's vision."

"It is challenging," she said tactfully, re-directing her attention to the play.

Though Grace secretly agreed with Lady Vee, she focused on the bright side. According to Roy, who possessed all kinds of strange and arcane knowledge, there was a

German opera based on Polidori's tragedy called *Der Vampyr*, which had been updated by the BBC in the early 1990s and retitled *The Vampyr: A Soap Opera*. So Grace counted her blessings. Maybe they weren't doing *Manfred*, but at least there weren't any singing vampires in her immediate future.

"The old witch pushes my buttons with that *Upstairs, Downstairs* stuff," he grumbled.

No question of which old witch he was referring to, although Grace suddenly remembered the poppet that she was still carrying in her purse. She had intended to show it to Peter but had never had the chance.

She noticed that the stagehands excused themselves after one round and departed. "I guess like all of us she's a product of her generation," she offered vaguely, her thoughts circling back to Bill Jones's mysterious end.

Blade snorted, blowing foam from his brew. "What generation is that? Crustacean? She's the reason people have revolutions."

Absently, Grace sipped from the mug.

The beer was locally brewed, one of those golden bitters with a hint of citrus. Before her stay in Innisdale, Grace hadn't known a lager from a malt liquor, but Cumbria was home to many famous breweries, like Jennings, which had been around since the 1800s, or Barngates, which named its beers for the dogs that had lived at the Drunken Duck Inn.

Microbrewing was a thriving cottage industry in the Lakes. In fact, every June there was an enormous beer festival in Keswick, attracting nearly four thousand partiers.

She said, a little tentatively, "You haven't heard anything about there being something strange about the security guard's death, have you?"

"What security guard?" Blade looked blank.

"Bill Jones. The man who worked for the Crosbys. The one who was injured during the robbery."

"No. Well, just that they may have tried to run him down deliberately. Why?"

"I don't know. I've heard a couple of rumors."

"That what you were researching downstairs this afternoon?"

"Oh *that.* No." She changed the subject quickly. "Anyway, Lady Vee seems to have bailed." Lady Vee had not been in the theater that evening, so it appeared she was making good on her threat to abandon the project if she couldn't control it.

"Don't get your hopes up. Lady Be Damned isn't happy unless she's got everyone chasing their tails. Look at the summer before last."

Grace knew to what Blade referred, but thought it tactful to ignore this. "At least Allegra hasn't deserted us," she said.

The Honorable Allegra Clairmont-Brougham, Lady Vee's niece, had played a large and somewhat unpleasant role in Grace's adventures the previous year. But her relations with the Hon. Al, who was the art director for the play, had improved fractionally since Grace had joined the production. Grace put this down to the social principle of Misery Loves Company.

Blade wiped the foam from his beard with the back of a tattooed hand. "I've known the Honorable Al since we were kids. My dad used to work in her ladyship's stables."

"Oh. Right." The biker and the aristo? She couldn't really picture Blade and the Hon. Al together, but there were people who probably couldn't see the schoolteacher and the ex–jewel thief as a couple.

"What the hell," Blade said. "I know I don't have a chance with her. It's a miracle she never married some git like Gerald Ives."

She would have liked to reassure Blade that the feudal system was a thing of the past, but he knew as well as she did that for old families like the Broughams, the ruling class was alive and well. And Allegra was very much a creature of her upbringing. Besides which, Grace suspected she still had a thing for Peter. But then Grace was beginning to suspect every woman had a thing for Peter.

She had another ale to be polite. The conversation returned inevitably to the play and literature.

"You're quite a fan of Dr. Polidori," Grace remarked.

Blade's lips twisted. "I admit he's not in the same class as Byron or Shelley — let alone Keats — but I think he deserves kudos for providing us with our modern conception of the vampire."

"I beheld the wretch, the miserable monster whom I had created."

"*Frankenstein*, Chapter Five," Blade said automatically. "Born the same night as Polidori's vampire."

Blade was referring to the ghost story "competition" between Byron and the Shelleys at their Lake Geneva villa one rainy summer night in 1816. Mary Shelley had concocted Frankenstein's monster, Byron a vampire, Polidori a skull-faced woman. Percy Shelley, demonstrating artistic restraint, had abstained.

"Yes, that was some slumber party at the Villa Diodati."

Blade seemed to find this funny, or perhaps it was the effects of the third round of ale. "Yeah, they sure don't write them like they used to. Murder, monsters, revenge, lust —"

"I don't know. Sex and violence are staples of contemporary drama," Grace objected.

"Right, but it's not the same. Modern drama lacks the blood and guts of the true Gothic melodrama. Byron, Shelley — even Polidori — their fiction reflected their lives. They were larger than life. Byron's death in the Greek War for Independence, Shelley's drowning, Polidori's suicide. Even their ends embodied the dark romance of their lives."

Grace swallowed ale thoughtfully. It was true that the biographies of the great Romantics read like fiction, mirroring the dark elements of Gothic literature.

"Passion," Blade said. "They lived and died with passion. Nobody feels that kind of passion nowadays. It's inconvenient, embarrassing, politically incorrect."

"And dangerous," Grace added.

They left the pub together. A giant low-hanging moon made a silhouette of the chimney pots and rooftops of Innisdale.

As the theater was just a short distance, Grace declined Blade's offer of a lift back to her car.

His bike roared off into the night as she crossed the street, walking briskly past the park. The preparations for the coming fete were under way. Gaily striped tents puffed and sank in the night breeze as though they were breathing. A merry-go-round with beribboned lions, camels and other exotic animals, mouths open in soundless roars, stood in the moonlight. Playbills tugged against hastily hammered nails promising fortune-telling, fireworks and all manner of earthly and unearthly delights.

It was strange, Grace reflected, to think that these lighthearted celebrations were based primarily on the ancient pagan festival of *Samhain,* honoring Amhain, Celtic Lord of the Dead. The ancient Druid bonfires and animal sacrifices heralded the season of cold, darkness and decay. Celtic tradition held that on this single eve the Lord of the Dead allowed departed souls to return to their earthly homes. On *Samhain,* the border between the dead and living faded, and creatures of the night were at their most powerful.

A little knowledge, Grace thought ruefully.

The streets were quiet; cheerful lights shone behind curtains and blinds, and the scent of wood fires spiced the autumn night.

Grace was just reflecting how she would never have dreamed of walking alone at night in Los Angeles, when she caught the sound of footsteps behind her.

She glanced back. There was no one there.

Mindful of her numerous self-defense classes, Grace cut across the road, keeping her pace quick and her posture confident. Her ears were attuned to any sounds. All she could hear was the echo of her own footsteps down the empty streets.

But then there was a faint furtive noise a yard or two behind her. Without bothering to check, she crossed the street again. As she reached the opposite pavement she threw a look over her shoulder. This time she caught a glimpse of something and felt her scalp prickle.

It had to be a trick of the light, but she could have sworn that her follower wore a cape.

Lord Ruthven on his way to the pub? No. He would say something, call out to her. And, although it was hard to tell, she didn't think the figure was tall enough. If she could get a better look . . . but actually this was as much of a look as she wanted.

Suddenly the familiar streets seemed dull with shadows, and menacing. There were no homes along this stretch of road, and the shops were closed and dark. The police kiosk was on the other side of the village. She hated to think what she would say to one of her girls who let herself get into a situation like this.

And had she really believed it was worth the savings not to carry a cell phone here? For a smart woman, Grace, she told herself, you really can be an idiot.

Still walking, she felt around in her purse, pulled out her compact and held it up, half-turning. "Look, if you don't clear off, I'm calling the cops!" She hoped her voice sounded more confident than she felt. She hoped that from this distance and concealed by her hand her compact might be mistaken for a cell phone. She hoped she didn't fall over something while walking backward.

Eyes probing the gloom, Grace weighed her options. She didn't have many.

There. Something moved by the corner of

a building. She glimpsed white. A face? No, too white, too stiff. A mask? She faced forward again.

She could see the theater marquee in the distance, featuring nothing and starring no one. The theater lights were dark, the parking lot empty. She began to jog. She heard footsteps behind her break into a run.

This time she didn't stop to look. Grace ran, too, purse clutched against her side and feet pounding the pavement. Puddles shimmered in moonlight. She saw the blur of her reflection as she raced past. And the reflection of something right on her heels. She ran faster. She ran for her life; adrenaline gave her wings.

The Aston Martin sat by itself in the empty parking lot.

Her keys were already clenched between her knuckles, blades out, as a last-resort weapon. Now she fumbled with them, jamming the car key into the lock.

It didn't fit. Was it upside down? The wrong key? She turned it this way, that way, for agonizing seconds before the car door opened. Jumping in, she slammed the door shut behind her and banged down the lock.

She scrabbled to fit the key into the ignition. Again it seemed too big for the lock. She poked blindly. Her eyes raked the car park for her pursuer.

Nothing. The shadows shifted with the moonlight, but there was no one there.

The Aston Martin roared into life, and Grace peeled out of the lot.

She was as angry as she was scared. Her heart banged against her ribs in that fight-or-flight reaction, or perhaps from her mad dash. Her hands gripped the steering wheel too tightly. Slowly, she drove down the narrow street, the car's headlights spotlighting the corners and alleys of the road. There was no sign of her pursuer.

5

Grace woke to a morning as dark as night. Needles of rain glittered in the gloom outside the front window. For the first time she realized that all this rain could get on her nerves. From the chesterfield, which made into a bed, she spotted Miss Coke's poppet lying on her dresser and was filled with uncharacteristic depression. She was homesick. She missed teaching. She missed her family. Witches were casting spells on her.

She sat up, her feet touching cold floor, and shivered. Winter was coming. She caught a glimpse of herself in the dresser mirror. She needed a haircut.

"Anything else wrong?" Grace asked her reflection.

Well, there was the fact that someone had deliberately tried to scare the heck out of her the night before. Grace debated whether she had made the right choice in not going immediately to the police station. But what would have been the end result? She had been followed but not assaulted. She did not have a description; she was not positive that her follower had been in costume. And if she did reveal her suspicion to the police, they would surely dismiss it as a Halloween prank. For all Grace knew, it *was* a Halloween prank. She hadn't been harmed; she hadn't even really been threatened.

She should still file a complaint; that was common sense, but she didn't want to bring any more police attention to herself than she could help, because of Peter.

Peter.

There was another problem. She really did not feel up to facing Peter this morning.

After several minutes of pacing she decided to call him.

For a split second she believed she was going to get away with talking to the answering machine, but Peter picked up on the second ring. She could picture him, hair damp from the shower, bare skin smelling of soap and shaving lather. He would be barefoot, bare-chested, a white towel draped around his shoulders. The kitchen would smell of coffee and bacon as he moved through his comfortable morning routine.

His voice, a bit huskier in the mornings, answered.

"Hi, it's me," she started in. "I've been thinking about yesterday, and um . . . I think it would be a good idea to . . . um, give each other some space."

She could imagine what he thought of that euphemism. There was a pause during which the line seemed to crackle with things unsaid; then Peter was crisp and to the point. "I'm leaving on a buying trip this morning, so you'll have all the space you require."

She was both relieved and disappointed. "How long will you be gone?" she asked after a moment.

"I'm not sure. A few days perhaps." Before the previous day it would have been natural to question him; now it was like talking to a stranger.

"All right," Grace said, equally crisp and to the point. "In that case I'll cover for you. At the shop I mean." Of course she meant at the shop; she hardly needed to clarify that she wasn't covering for his involvement in a crime — she knew he wasn't involved in any crime!

"Thanks." His tone was dry. There was another pause. Grace waited. Her heart was pounding hard. Love or an anxiety attack? It was beginning to feel like the same thing.

Peter severed the connection.

He was gone for a week, and there were

no robberies. That was the good news. It might also be the bad news. She didn't know how the police might interpret it. She only knew that she missed him. Peter had gone on buying trips before, but then his absence had been eased by phone calls and even a postcard or two. This time there was nothing. He might have dropped off the face of the earth.

Grace tried not to miss him or even think about him. There was plenty to do between rehearsals, her book and minding the store. Of the three, working at Rogue's Gallery was the least demanding. Peter had everything organized so that the shop practically ran itself. But Peter's absence was most noticeable at Rogue's Gallery. The littlest things reminded Grace of him: his coffee mug sitting on his desk, his olive waxed jacket hanging on the coatrack, the silver fountain pen he always used. Reminders of his presence were everywhere.

Everything in the shop had been handpicked by him, from the vintage movie poster for the 1925 *Raffles* to the red lacquer Japanese screen embellished with a terrifying dragon — and a terrifying price tag. Peter catered to clients of imagination and exquisite taste — and fat pocketbooks.

"Have you heard anything more about

the robberies, Mrs. Mac?" Grace asked the charwoman one morning early into Peter's absence.

"Like?" Mrs. Mac wasn't nearly as chatty without Peter around, Grace had noticed.

"I don't know. I heard a couple of weird stories about the security guard. Did you go to his funeral yesterday?"

"And why should I? Did I know the man?"

Grace shrugged. "A lot of people went, I understand."

No response. Grace studied the formidable broadside of Mrs. Mac.

"Have you lived in Innisdale long, Mrs. Mac?" She was suddenly curious.

"Two years this spring."

"I don't know why I thought you had known Peter longer." Grace scrambled to shift chairs and rugs out of the path of Mrs. Mac's mop.

Mrs. Mac grunted and jabbed the mop into an alcove as though something dangerous lurked there. "That's right. Knew him before."

"Knew him before what?"

Mrs. Mac's colorless eyes flicked to Grace's face. "Before he moved to Cumbria."

Here was a wealth of information on

Peter, Grace recognized, but it would not be easy to crack the safe of Mrs. Mac's reticence.

"Was it hard getting used to the country life?" she asked casually, returning to the counter.

"Makes a change, it does," Mrs. Mac said indifferently. "You should know, dearie."

"I guess you have to go where there's work."

"That's right. When I got — er — when I was looking for work, Mr. Fox offered me a job, and I took it. He was always looking out for the re —" She cut herself off.

Looking out for the re . . . st? Rest . . . of us? And what would the rest of them be? What was Peter Fox? An ex–jewel thief. A former criminal. Was this what he held in common with Mrs. Mac? Yes, Grace could believe that Mrs. Mac might have a criminal record. There was an edge to her that was more than hardness. *When I got — er — When I got . . . out?*

Grace made a stab in the dark. "But he never went to prison. He was never caught — in this country."

Mrs. Mac shoved the mop so hard it nearly flew out of her grasp. She straightened up. "He told you about that? About the Turkish job? He's never talked to anyone, not so's —" She caught herself. Her mouth compressed.

"I don't think he told me everything," Grace admitted, which was the understatement of the year.

Mrs. Mac's laugh was as harsh as a crow's. "No, I imagine not, ducks."

She turned away, jabbing at corners with her mop in a way that probably indicated as much irritation with herself as with Grace. Grace considered her plump and unrelenting back.

What did it mean? Had she really learned anything new? Apparently Peter's internment in Turkey had been the result of a botched caper. She had pretty well worked that much out for herself, but the caper had been big enough that his former confederates (if they *were* former!) knew of it — although not the details.

To Grace, Turkey meant Lord Byron. The notorious rake and poet had died fighting the Turks in the Greek War for Independence, and many of his Eastern-influenced works showed familiarity with and interest in Islam.

In fact, Byron's own fragment of a vampire novel had been set in Turkey.

. . . the sudden and rapid illness of

> my companion obliged us to halt at a Turkish cemetery, the turbaned tombstones of which were the sole indication that human life had ever been a sojourner in this wilderness. The only caravansera we had seen was left some hours behind us, not a vestige of a town or even cottage was within sight or hope, and this "city of the dead" appeared to be the sole refuge of my unfortunate friend, who seemed on the verge of becoming the last of its inhabitants.

But it was unlikely that a notorious jewel thief had been hunting antiquities in that "wild and tenant-less tract." From the little he let slip, Grace gathered Peter had approached his former profession with a pragmatic and cynical attitude. Jewels had equaled cold cash; he found nothing magical or romantic about them. They were easy to grab and easy to liquidate. Antiquities, on the other hand, were a much riskier proposition.

Had Mrs. Mac revealed anything else? Was Peter fostering his own thieves' den in Innisdale? Or perhaps by hiring Mrs. Mac he had simply been giving an old colleague a break. Loyalty wasn't a bad trait in a man. Nor compassion.

When Mrs. Mac glanced her way, Grace quickly looked down at her book. After a few moments she began to read in earnest.

She had recently started Tom Holland's *Lord of the Dead*, a diverting blend of fact and fantasy that worked from the premise that Lord Byron, going by the name of Lord Ruthven, was in fact a vampire.

The Ruthven name had certainly gotten a workout in connection with Lord Byron. In her melodramatic novel *Glenarvon*, Lady Caroline Lamb had named the villain (a thinly disguised caricature of Byron) Lord Ruthven. Then Dr. Polidori had continued the nasty in-joke by naming his vampire villain (also a thinly disguised caricature of Byron) Lord Ruthven. Now Holland had taken it to the next logical step: a vampire named Lord Ruthven was, in fact, Lord Byron.

It made Grace wonder again about the uncanny coincidence of Innisdale's own Lord Ruthven. True, Lord Ruthven had appeared before the season's play had been selected; but, thinking back, Grace couldn't recall who had actually suggested doing Polidori's story. Had Ruthven himself suggested it or had someone else, perhaps unconsciously influenced by Ruthven's name, proposed the idea?

If Ruthven had manipulated the Innisdale Players to perform *The Vampyre*, what could be his purpose?

For that matter, was Ruthven even the producer's real name?

Am I becoming completely paranoid? Grace wondered.

But, since she was indulging her paranoia, why *had* Grace been brought in? Granted, when she had been invited to take part, the theater committee was still discussing doing a work by Byron; but even so, with Roy Blade and Lady Venetia present, there were more than enough experts on the plays and poetry of the Romantic Age — jokes about being the "tiebreaker" aside.

It was all very odd. Now they had some nut running around in a Halloween cape and spooky mask. It could be a coincidence. It was the kind of prank an adolescent might think up.

It could be someone's idea of a publicity stunt.

Or someone could be seriously disturbed.

On Tuesday the Innisdale Players arrived at the theater to find the front of the building spray painted. THE BLOOD IS THE LIFE, proclaimed three-foot red letters.

A small crowd gathered outside.

"I know that quote. Why do I know that quote?" Grace caught Blade's out-loud thought over the others' exclamations and expressions of dismay.

"It's from the Bible," she answered.

His black brows shot up as he recognized the source.

"It's also from *Dracula*," Grace added.

"*Dracula*?" Lady Theresa laughed uneasily. "Tell him to get his own show."

"Look on the bright side," Derek said cheerfully. "Free publicity never hurt anyone."

Catriona said to Grace, "You seem awfully well versed on your vampire lore."

"I've been reading up. That's my job, right?"

"Right." With one skeptical word Catriona managed to suggest that Grace was not above vandalizing public property. Grace told herself it was beneath her to respond to Catriona's baiting.

Not for the first time she wondered at Catriona's antagonism. Surely this undercurrent as much as anything confirmed there was something between Catriona and Peter — something that made the other woman resent Grace. And if Catriona resented Grace, that was a good sign, right?

That meant she wasn't having it all her own way.

Lord Ruthven turned from the defaced building. Grace didn't know what to make of his expression. Anger? Fear? Low blood sugar?

"Perhaps we should get the police," Catriona said to him. There was a challenge in her tone.

Ruthven stared at her with his dark hollow eyes and said nothing.

If the police were called in, Grace saw no sign of them. After a day or two the front of the theater was scrubbed down and repainted.

Rehearsals continued remorselessly, for all the good they did.

It wasn't until Wednesday that Grace noticed she was being followed.

The woman was standing by the gate when Grace pulled out of the drive of Renfrew Hall. She noticed her in the rear-view: a tall thin figure in black standing motionless among the trees.

It shook Grace, but there were a dozen explanations, and she was happy to seize on the first one, which was that the woman had just been passing by.

That explanation didn't work so well

when Grace spotted her the next afternoon, across the road from Craddock House.

Grace had been indulging in some Cinderella-like daydreaming as she dusted cups of a Czech lusterware tea set. Her thoughts were preoccupied with what to wear to the Hunt Ball. Her budget was limited, and she had previously planned to wear her good black dress.

It was against her principles to "compete" for a man's attention, but common sense told her Catriona Ruthven would use every weapon in her arsenal if she was after Peter. Grace intended to stick to her principles, but the less-disciplined portion of her brain kept picturing herself sweeping into the Hunt Ball in a drop-dead glamour dress.

She was smiling at this vision when she noticed movement in the trees across the way. She went to the window.

Yes, the woman in black was standing outside the shop. Just standing there, staring.

Grace headed for the door, hesitated, then went outside, crossing the lawn.

"Can I help you?" she called.

The woman stared. She was wearing a black dress, black walking boots and a black scarf. Nothing too sinister about her, unless you were the fashion police, but creepy all the same.

"What do you want?" Grace called.

The woman continued to gaze unspeaking.

It was too bizarre. Grace went back inside and considered calling the police, but again she didn't want to bring attention to Peter or his shop.

Was she the local witch, Miss Coke? Or merely some deranged homeless person? Was she practicing witchcraft or intimidation?

Grace watched the woman for a few minutes more and decided that her uneasy attention was what Miss Coke (if it was Miss Coke) wanted.

However, after this unpleasant experience Grace concluded that she did deserve a treat of some kind. Since she couldn't afford a ball gown, she resorted to the time-honored tradition of having her hair done. She'd been wearing her long chestnut locks in the same simple style since she'd started teaching, and she felt it was time to make a change; maybe go for something more contemporary — even a bit sexier.

Halfway through the perm process she realized it might look like she was copying Catriona's signature style. She stared at her wired-for-sound reflection, thinking that if this kept up she would end up like the narrator of *Rebecca*, trying to compete with a ghost.

But in the end, she needn't have worried. Her soft curls looked nothing like Catriona's coppery mane, and the new sophisticated cut flattered her fine features. Grace felt so thrilled with the result she splurged and bought her favorite brand of lipstick and eye shadow in the new "Fall Palette."

Her efforts must have been successful, because Derek Derrick flirted with her quite outrageously at rehearsal that night — much to the chagrin of Theresa Ives.

They formed a truce later when she caught Theresa on her way out after rehearsal. Derrick waited, holding Theresa's white raincoat, as Grace said, "This may sound strange, but I wanted to ask you . . . do you know anything about a woman named Miss Coke?"

"That woman!"

"What does she look like? Tall, thin, dressed in black?"

"That's her." Theresa's face changed. "Don't tell me she's after you!"

"I'm not sure what she's after, but she's been following me around. Has she ever said anything to you? Threatened you?"

"She doesn't say anything," Theresa told

her. "That's why the police won't do anything. She simply stares in that ghastly way like — like Isis."

"Isis?"

"Or whatever her name was. The goddess of revenge."

"Nemesis, you mean?" The Honorable Allegra Clairmont-Brougham, a model-thin rather handsome woman in her forties, tied the belt on her camel hair coat. Grace realized that their conversation was more public than she had planned. "I suppose you're speaking of Miss Coke. Just ignore her," Allegra instructed Grace.

"That's easy for you to say," Theresa said, pouting. Derek put a hand on her shoulder in a gesture both comforting and proprietary. Grace's gaze caught that of the Hon. Al. It wasn't often they saw eye to eye, but apparently on this point, they were agreed.

"It's easy enough to do," Allegra retorted.

Grace said, "But if she's harassing people —"

Allegra tossed her black hair. "Oh, harassing! She's a harmless old crackpot."

"But I heard that" — it sounded silly but Grace pressed on — "bad things have happened to people who . . . got on Miss Coke's bad side."

Allegra made another impatient sound. If she wasn't careful, in a few years she would be saying "bah!" or "pshaw!" like Lady Vee. "*Anyone* can break his neck foxhunting," she said, and swept out through the theater doors.

6

The dawn cast an eerie bloodred tint over the dale.

A covey of quail started from the underbrush as Grace swung up into the saddle. The mare sidled, hooves powdering the frost on the ground. Grace quickly righted herself, putting a hand to her black velvet cap. Safely mounted, she looked around, past the horse trailers and Land Rovers and milling people in the "north forty" of Ives Manor, to the vista beyond.

In the distance she could see mountains, towering and dark, and she reflected on the irony that it was really those mountains that made Lakeland unforgettable.

O! for the crags that are wild and majestic, the steep, frowning glories of dark Lochnagar, Lord Byron had written of Scotland, but his words held true for Helvellyn or Scafell Pike, England's highest mountain. The crags and fells of the Lake District gave the country its distinctive character, a character reflected in the "kept-stone" spirit of its natives.

Grace had yet to hike any mountains, and she resolved that before she left this island — assuming she did not break her neck that morning — she was going to treat herself to scaling one of those slate-and-granite ridges right up to the point where earth met sky.

That said, she was just as glad that today's meet was on relatively flat land, although she knew that beyond the immediate fields and woods were heather-topped hills studded with stony outcrops, and it was as easy to take a header down a little hill as a big one.

The mare snorted and tossed her head. She was on loan from the Ives stable, and Grace was not too sure of her. She was not too sure of any of this, but she loved the smell of horse and leather and crisp morning air . . . she wasn't quite as crazy about the whiff from the flask Sir Gerald Ives waved under her nose.

"Have a nip," he invited.

Sir Gerald was about fifty, big and raw-boned with a face like a slab of good English beef.

"Good morning!" Grace said.

"She suits you." He again proffered Grace a swig from the silver flask, which she declined. "Takes the chill off."

"Oh gosh, no thanks. I don't eat break-fast."

She was joking but the baronet replied seriously, "You should have had your breakfast. Takes a hell of a lot out of you, hunting." His breath smoked in the chill air. It was about five-thirty in the morning, cold but reasonably dry — though in the Lake District a cloudless sky could be a temporary phenomenon.

Shrugging, Sir Gerald recapped the flask, his attention wandering. He rode a big, bad-tempered black, who chewed his bit with neurotic fervor. Grace resolved to stay well out of their way.

Already the red sky was paling to pink, and as the sun rose the fields shimmered gold; the surrounding trees seemed to blaze into life, foliage brilliant in scarlet, orange and yellows. The clearing was crowded with cars and horse trailers, but nobody seemed to be interested in the splendid scenery.

As Grace watched, horses were saddled and mounted swiftly. Riders greeted each other jovially. Thermos cups of coffee or something stronger were handed round. A young woman was slathering her face with sunscreen.

Do ye ken John Peel at the break of day, do ye ken John Peel in his coat so gay . . .

Several of the men, including Sir Gerald, wore scarlet coats. Everyone else was dressed in black hunt coat, white shirt, white stock tie, and black riding boots.

She smiled a little at the memory of a quote, though she couldn't remember where she had heard it: *"It isn't mere convention. Everyone can see that the people who hunt are the right people, and the people who don't are the wrong ones."* She knew what Peter would make of such nonsense, but probably many of the people here believed it.

She wondered if she really looked the part in her secondhand black jacket and brand-new breeches, or if something about her gave her away as an American. She put a hand up to check her cap again, but the eighty-seven bobby pins she had used seemed to be holding her hair in place.

She thought it interesting that although every child present wore a sturdy helmet, not one adult had deigned to safeguard his head — herself included.

A pack of lightly built fell hounds snuffled the covert, tails wagging, noses sniffing the air, sneezing violently as they worked the area for the scent of the fox. The Huntsman, a weathered-looking man by the name of Milliken, was in conversation with Theresa Ives, looking very smart indeed in her riding kit.

As Grace watched, Derek Derrick

brought his horse beside Theresa's, and the woman turned, smiling. Derek made a fine figure in his black coat. He could have ridden straight off the set of *The List of Adrian Messenger*.

"Your first ever hunt, is it?" Sir Gerald asked, clearly doing his duty as MFH and local gentry. "You should have joined us for cubbing season."

Grace might be yet undecided about foxhunting in principle, but she was squarely against the idea of hunting baby foxes. However, she was the guest. She murmured something about scheduling conflicts, and Sir Gerald said, "The hunt requires discipline and commitment. It builds character. That's why we encourage the children to participate."

"Do you have children?" Grace was surprised.

"No."

"Hoick together!" called the Whipper-in to straying hounds. The Whipper-in was the Huntsman's right-hand man. "Hoick, hoick."

There were a number of familiar faces present in the field, which consisted of about seventy. Grace spotted Chief Constable Heron on an enormous gray hunter.

If she got the chance, she wanted to ask

the chief constable about the rumors surrounding Bill Jones's death. But at the moment he was in conversation with the Hon. Al. Tall and boyishly slim, Al had the perfect figure for riding clothes. The chief constable sat as straight as a cavalry officer. He wore a scarlet jacket with a navy collar, which Grace understood to mean he had been awarded colors.

Al's collar, too, was navy. She was the official Field Master, which Grace found interesting. She would have expected Theresa, a devoted sportswoman and Sir Gerald's lady, to have been awarded that honor.

As though on cue, Theresa's laugh rang out, earning disapproving looks. Sir Gerald's hunter backed up as though his hands on the reins had suddenly tightened. Grace glanced his way.

"Good hunting, then!" he told her curtly. He trotted off to join his wife and her companion.

A heavyset man on a motorbike gunned the engine, catching Grace's attention. A pair of bright-eyed terriers sat in a cage on the back of the bike.

This, she realized, must be the Terrier Man, the person whose job it was to dig out and bolt (or shoot as the case might be) the fox when it went to ground.

Grace wondered how she would feel if she saw a fox shot. Her mount tossed its head restively and worked the bit. She stroked its neck with the butt of her crop.

Feeling a tiny bit on the outside, she spoke to the mare, whose ears twitched in response. Grace was a little anxious, although not about her riding skills. While other small girls her age had been shuttled to dance and music lessons, Grace had been learning dressage. She frequently substituted for St. Anne's riding instructor when he was ill or on vacation. No, her uncertainty revolved around hunt protocol, which she knew was rigorous. She prayed she wasn't going to inadvertently commit a faux pas like passing the Field Master or getting in the way of a hound.

Smiling at faces she recognized, she guided her horse through the crowd, declining offers of the stirrup cup. She couldn't help hearing bits and pieces of the conversations flowing around her as the Innisdale Pack greeted each other, talking and laughing. She knew that for most of these people, the hunt was a social event, and the killing of a fox was incidental.

"The police are always on the verge of making an arrest, aren't they? I don't suppose it really means anything."

"At last estimate the ban would leave over fourteen thousand hounds jobless. That doesn't include terriers, harriers, beagles, bassets . . ."

"Scottish, my dear. One of these obscure titles. *He's* very well known in theater circles."

It was at that moment that Grace spied Catriona Ruthven, sleek and stylish in black livery. She was mounted on a leggy sorrel whose burnished coat seemed color-coordinated with Catriona's coppery hair. The horse danced nervously but was easily checked by its rider. They made a lovely picture.

Grace glanced around, seeking Lord Ruthven, but couldn't see him. Perhaps he didn't ride to hounds. He didn't seem like the sporty type. In fact, she couldn't remember if she had ever seen him out in the fresh air and sunshine.

She wondered if Catriona's hunter was also on loan or if the Ruthvens kept their own stable. She began to consider the size and nature of the Ruthven household.

She knew they had taken one of the large Georgian houses at the edge of the village. The Monkton estate. An old house with a mysterious past. And how appropriate, although it was a big place for two. *Was* it just the two of them? Grace couldn't imagine the Ruthvens with children, but then she knew so little about them.

If Catriona was up to no good, surely her husband would have to know about it? Was that why he had followed her to the cemetery that night? Did he suspect her of something? Or was he in on it, too — assuming there was anything to be in on.

Servants would probably be aware of any irregularities in the household. Did they have a large staff? She seemed to recall the village gossips reporting that the newcomers had a German man working for them.

A thought occurred: Did Mrs. Mac "do" for the Ruthvens? If so, did that have any special significance?

Grace continued to study Catriona. As background to her thoughts, one of those snooty voices was droning, "They need about a three-hour head start to effectively disrupt a hunt. Changing the meet location at the last minute helps prevent the sort of fiasco we had last week when one of the hooligans called the pub and informed them the hunt had been canceled owing to rain . . ."

Saboteurs, Grace realized. The speaker was talking about organized efforts to disrupt the hunt by antihunt protestors. Sabs were inventive. Their tactics included everything from "prebeating" the planned covert, spraying foliage with scent dullers like citronella, opening up blocked earths so that cornered foxes might escape, and setting "rook scarers," various noise devices to scare the animals away.

Allegra guided her horse up to Grace. Her cheeks were flushed with cold and excitement. "Watch yourself," she said curtly. "The terrain's bloody past the ash grove. We're one of the few Lake District packs to hunt on horseback. Most hunt on foot."

Grace was still trying to reconcile the picture of a foxhunt on foot when a white-muzzled bitch lifted her head and let out a baying sound.

"Fiver's hit a line," Allegra exclaimed, and reined her mount away.

This Grace knew was the opening. The other hounds circled Fiver, the strike hound, barking and whining, "honoring" her voice, and the Huntsman's horn rang out, startling against the babble of hounds.

A frisson glided down Grace's spine. Were these crisp silvery notes from "The Peeler," the hunting horn that local legend claimed once belonged to John Peel — now the property of Sir Gerald Ives?

And then there was no time to think about anything because the chase was on.

The hounds tore off in full cry, presumably in chase of a fox invisible to Grace, who was busy guiding the mare through the heaving crowd of horses and riders.

"Tally ho!" shouted Derek Derrick, passing Grace at a gallop.

"Ass," grunted someone near Grace. She glanced back, then out of the corner of her eye caught movement.

Catriona veered her way. The sorrel kicked out at Grace's bay. The bay shied, eyes rolling, her muzzle wrinkling to bite. Grace tightened her knees, guiding the mare clear of Catriona's horse.

"Hey!" she protested.

"Ride 'em cowboy," Catriona quipped, urging her horse past. She was lost in the lunge of riders heading for the woods beyond.

Grace dug her heels into the bay.

Choose your line, she warned herself. Pace yourself. Don't crowd. Don't thrust.

The thud of hooves was like thunder as they crossed a mile or so of meadow. The trees neared, towering.

Grace ducked a low branch and slowed her horse, as it fought the bit. The woods were alive with the babble of hounds, the pounding of hooves on damp ground, the crackle of dead leaves and breaking branches.

What happened to the rule about going slow in woodland? Grace asked herself as riders charged ahead. Despite the mare's displeasure she took it more cautiously, while the hounds tore through the woods, followed by riders weaving in and out of trees, red and black coats flashing. She was still in the rear as dogs and horses burst out of the forest covert in arrow formation, chasing across the acres of green-and-gold checkerboard.

To horse and away, to the heart of the fray!
Fling care to the Devil for one merry day!

It's just like the books! Grace thought delightedly, as the field fanned out before her.

Her heart was in her mouth as they approached the first jump, one of the endless snaking stone walls left by Roman armies. It had been nearly two years since she'd jumped, and never in a crowd. She felt the mare's muscles bunch and instinctively leaned forward. And then they were soaring. The mare landed cleanly and sprang forward. Grace laughed with sheer exhilaration.

The pack sped on through wet fields, over rickety stiles, past silver meres glinting like glass in the now bright sunlight, chasing past fences behind which sheep grazed in apparent disinterest at the passing tumult.

Hounds racing tirelessly ahead, they took the first of several small hills. Purple heather dusted the gold in patches, hooves echoed against stone. They galloped on, horses and riders swarming the next rocky hill and spilling down over the side.

Grace caught her breath in surprise and pulled back. Below, a wide stream tumbled its blue way over rocks and boulders.

She spotted Catriona well out in front, starting across the streambed. As she watched, Catriona's saddle slipped, and she fell sideways. She put her arms out to save herself, falling headfirst into the stream.

The sorrel, saddle slipped well to the side, trotted to a stop while horses parted around Catriona, hooves narrowly missing the ball she had rolled herself into. One or two riders slowed and stopped to ascertain she was unhurt. Catriona climbed soddenly to her feet, waving them on.

Grace's horse waded in. Bending down, Grace caught the reins of Catriona's mount, leading him back. She tossed the reins to Catriona as Derek Derrick, even farther back in the field than she, pulled up beside them where they stood on the pulverized bank.

"What happened?" he asked, looking from Grace to Catriona.

"My girth billets broke," Catriona said, examining the hanging saddle. Her wet and mud-streaked face was grim. Kneeling, she ran her hands down her horse's forelegs.

"That brute's fine," Derek said. "You're soaked through."

It was cold down by the water. Catriona's teeth were beginning to chatter, as she said, "I'll live." Her look implied that someone would not.

"I'll go back with you, will I?" He offered a clean hanky, and Catriona took it, wiping her face and taking a better look at her saddle girth.

"How could both billets give at the same time?" Grace questioned, watching Catriona scrutinize what looked to Grace like cut leather.

After a moment Catriona said, "Perhaps it's defective." But she didn't sound convinced.

"You seem to be having a lot of accidents," Grace commented.

"And you always seem to be around when I'm having them."

This was such an unreasonable retort that Grace was momentarily at a loss for an answer. She noticed that Derek seemed to be trying to catch her eye.

"I've got this under control," he assured her. "Why don't you rejoin the field? No point all of us missing out on the kill." Maybe he thought Grace was aggravating the situation, or was every woman on Derek's menu? Grace gave him an "E" for Effort. Catriona was liable to eat him alive.

"Go ahead," he urged, as she hesitated. "I'm not that keen on —"

He broke off as a large brown fox came splashing across the shallows of the stream, passing within a few feet of them. The three humans exchanged looks.

It occurred to Grace that she was supposed to shout "Tally ho" or wave her cap to indicate having spotted the quarry, but the sight of the fox, trotting as fast as his legs would carry him, pink tongue hanging . . .

"Tally ho baaaaack!" Shouts echoed across the water. Horses and riders wheeled, hooves kicking up clots of grass and mud as the pack came thundering back, dogs baying outrage as they cut through riders. The notes of a hunting horn drifted over the churning surface.

Catriona hastily led her mount downstream as a tidal wave of water, horses and dogs crashed past.

Since Catriona was unhurt and more than

a match for Derek, and since Grace wasn't wanted by either Catriona or Derek, she decided she might as well rejoin the hunt. Saluting the other two, she kicked the mare forward into the plunging mass of bodies lumbering back up the hillside. A final glance over her shoulder showed Derek dismounting to join Catriona on the stream bank.

By now Grace felt the effects of her strenuous ride, especially in her legs and tailbone. Her arms ached. Her — recalling Peter's smart-assed comment — "poetic nook" ached. They had been riding hard for more than ninety minutes; she estimated they had covered well over ten miles. This was probably the hardest riding that Grace had ever done. She was tired and chilled and, having had a good look at the fox, wasn't keen to see it slaughtered.

In full cry the pack retraced their course across meadow and field, over the stone wall and down the rocky hills. When they reached the woods, the hounds lost the scent. The sound and fury of the hunt seemed to dissolve into green silence. Horses and hounds moved through the trees. Twigs snapped. A horse whickered.

"Yo hote, Yo hote, Yo hote," singsonged the Whipper-in, urging the hounds on.

Heads down, snuffling loudly, the hounds cast for scent in the humus.

As they reached the edge of the trees, Grace found herself riding beside Theresa Ives.

"Has he gone to ground?" Grace asked undervoice.

"I don't think so. He's a wily one, is Charlie," Theresa answered. There was a red welt across her cheek where she must have collided with a tree branch.

"Charlie?" Images from numerous war movies flashed through Grace's mind.

"Charles James Fox? The fox."

Still casting for a scent dissipating as the day grew warmer, they continued slowly back the way they had come. The meadow hummed with bees. The smell of wild-flowers mingled with horse and sweat. With relief Grace saw the meet point up ahead.

And then there came a most unofficial sound, a sound that seemed equal parts an-guish and a train letting off steam. Riders yanked reins, horses shied, birds took flight. Only the hounds seemed unfazed. Yards ahead, they raced in full cry up the hillock jammed with cars and horse vans.

The pack swept through the cars and horse trailers and ran great circles around the vacant flattened turf where Sir Gerald's silver Jaguar had been parked. Frustrated yips cut the sharp air.

Sir Gerald had dismounted and was cursing colorfully, calling God and the entire hunt membership as his witnesses.

It took Grace a moment to register the cause for alarm. The missing Jaguar was bouncing across the meadow heading for the main road, wildflowers strewn in its wake as the driver accelerated with shocking lack of regard for the car's undercarriage.

"Bloody hell!" Sir Gerald was shouting. "Hooligans! The bloody bastards! Is there nothing they won't stoop to!"

No head was visible over the backseat rest.

Like a silver bullet the car shot up the main road and disappeared around a curve.

Even the hounds seemed to be looking at each other for explanation.

At last someone remarked, "I say. Now that *is* a clever fox!"

7

A week to the day after his departure, a parcel arrived addressed in Peter's bold black scrawl.

Grace opened it with trepidation, but there was no message. Apparently it was just what it seemed: items for resale. She lifted out an alligator hatbox and matching makeup case. The kinds of things glamorous film stars from the forties used to lug around. The kinds of things Peter knew Grace loved.

The hatbox was empty, but the makeup case contained fascinating odds and ends: Limoges lipstick cases, an enamel pillbox (with tiny pink pills that Grace promptly tossed in the trash), delicate jeweled hair combs and a fragile silk scarf that still whispered scent. Precious junk, she thought. The sum of an unknown woman's life. A pair of rhinestone cat's-eye glasses in a velvet case made her smile.

For laughs she slipped them out of the case and tried them on.

"The better to see you with?" Peter inquired dryly.

"Peter!" It came out in a yelp of surprise. "You startled me!" How had she not heard him come in? But he always moved quietly and with an economy of movement. Lost in her pleasantly melancholy thoughts, she hadn't noticed a thing, and now he was standing right over her.

She blinked up at the magnified vision of him. She had forgotten how brilliant his eyes were. She was reminded of a line by Keats: *laughs the cerulean sky*.

He wore Levi's and a lambs' wool pullover in a muted plum color. The neck of his undershirt was crisp white against his tanned skin. He'd had time to take his jacket off.

"I didn't hear you come in."

The corner of Peter's mouth quirked with private amusement. He removed her specs, tossing them on the desktop.

Grace tried to keep her voice measured and hoped her cheeks weren't as pink as they felt. "How was your trip?"

"Interesting." He bent and kissed her, a swift, sure, make no mistake about it kiss. Grace's mouth seemed to tingle from the warm pressure of his.

"Oh."

"What have you been up to?" he asked, smiling faintly.

An exasperating man and far too sure of himself, but it was no use pretending she wasn't happy to see him. The relief of having him back, of the kiss that answered one thing at least, seemed to open the floodgate; and Grace poured it all out, the weird happenings at the theater, Miss Coke's nebulous threat, Lord Ruthven's peculiar behavior, the caped man who had followed her from the pub. She barely paused for breath.

Peter had the knack of listening with total attention, making a woman feel she was the only thing of interest in his world. He didn't interrupt, he didn't ask questions, he simply listened. At last Grace rolled to a full stop. He waited a moment to make sure she had truly run out of gas, then questioned, "Why the hell didn't you tell me any of this before I left?"

"I wanted to, but there wasn't time. Besides, most of it happened after you'd gone."

"It's nice to know you've been spending your time productively." He raked a hand through his pale hair. "Grace, this may sound funny coming from me, but one of the chief things I like about you is your honesty. Your directness. You speak your mind. You don't play games." His gaze found hers, and he added simply, "I need that."

Were they still talking about mysterious happenings, or had they moved on to their own relationship? She wasn't sure. Catriona would be direct, although Grace had no idea how honest she was; but for most of the women Peter knew, for most of the women he had romanced, love was a game, and Peter was first prize.

The tone of his voice, the expression in his eyes gave her the courage to ask, "What is Catriona Ruthven to you?"

From beside Grace the phone rang.

"You've *got* to be kidding!" said Grace.

Peter's smile was wry. He picked up the phone and replaced it on the cradle. Then he removed it, listened, and set the receiver on the desk.

"I don't like to lie to you, so we'll leave it at this. Nothing between Cat and myself has anything to do with what happens between you and me."

Cat. The casual intimacy of the diminutive smarted.

She had hoped for a denial; so this admission that there *was* something between them hurt. She was surprised that the sound that came out was a laugh. Well, sort of a laugh. "That's not an answer."

"It's the only answer I can give you."

Do you love her? she wanted to ask, but

she was afraid to hear the answer. She looked down at her hands, her slim bare fingers, then up into his face. "Okay, well then, what *is* between you and me?"

His smile was twisted, and there was a darkness in his eyes that was almost sadness. His expression said more than his words, and the message frightened Grace in some indefinable way.

He said huskily, "Everything and nothing. How's that for an answer?"

It felt like time stopped. Or maybe it was her heart. But Grace being Grace was analyzing his words before he'd finished speaking them, and after the initial emotional recoil, common sense reasserted itself.

"Uh, well, actually . . . am I grading by points or on a curve? Come on, Peter, how am I supposed to respond to that? As you pointed out yourself, my sabbatical is nearly over."

Peter, who had been half-sitting on the desk, straightened. He wasn't looking at her, as he said unemotionally, "I'm not in a position to make promises."

She knew he wasn't married, but there were other kinds of commitment. Grace sighed. "Swell. Okay, has it occurred to you that you're being set up by Cat Woman?"

That got his attention although he didn't say anything.

"I'm not stupid, Peter. Well, not most of the time. Obviously you know her from the bad old days. She's the girl with hair like a fox and the temper to match."

His mouth opened, but nothing came out. Which made a nice change. Usually Grace was the one left speechless. "You told me about her ages ago," she said with a blasé air that took a fair amount of work. "At Penwith Hall, remember?"

"No."

"Well, you did. And, unless I miss my guess, besides being your paramour, she was your partner in crime."

"My what?"

"Partner in —"

"No, the other." He was laughing at her now.

"Your lover."

He was still laughing, but she knew him well enough to know that, behind the teasing, his brain was calculating how much she knew and how much was guesswork.

"You can laugh all you like, but I've watched her. Granted, it's not hard evidence, but Catriona has some of your mannerisms and expressions. The same turn of phrase. And she does that thing with her eyebrow."

On cue his own eyebrow raised.

"You must have known each other a long time." Sister? Cousin? Wicked Stepmother? Grace wished she could convince herself of any of those.

Peter was no longer laughing; his expression was guarded.

"She's the only person I've ever seen with reflexes like yours. When that trapdoor gave way, any normal person would have fallen through. She has terrific upper body strength and amazing balance."

"Perhaps she escaped from a circus," Peter quipped.

Grace thought, but did not say, *And like you she's living by her own rules, her own code. She's larger than life and probably believes herself outside the law.*

"And things started to change between us from almost the moment she arrived here. That's also when the robberies began — or just about then."

"Grace, this is unwise." He was moving away from her, heading toward the door, ending the conversation.

"You can say that again. Do you think it's a coincidence that she arranged a rendezvous on the night of a robbery, leaving you without any alibi?"

His laugh was without humor.

"She tried to set you up. It almost worked."

"Let it go."

"Fine. I'll let it go. But there's something else you should probably be aware of. I think someone's trying to kill her."

If she was expecting some dramatic reaction, she didn't get it. True, he went still and thoughtful for a moment before saying, as he disappeared through the door, "It wouldn't be the first time."

After Peter went upstairs, Grace could hear him moving about, hear the restless beat of music. The Waterboys. Peter's first choice when he was, as the poets put it, "unquiet of soul."

She felt unquiet of soul herself; you couldn't force someone's trust — and for the first time it hit her squarely that Peter did not entirely trust her. She was so used to questioning whether she really did — or should — trust him that it came as a little bit of a shock to realize that he might feel the same.

Lost in her thoughts, only gradually she became aware that the seductive scent of cooking was wafting down the staircase and that Peter was calling her to close the shop and come up.

Grace found him in the kitchen braising pieces of chicken in butter and shallots. Hot water boiled on the stove top.

"Chicken with Riesling over noodles," Peter informed her.

"Smells delicious." She went to the glass-fronted cupboard and took down plates.

As she set the table, Peter asked her about the play. He seemed to zero in on how they had selected their material. "Why not *Dracula*?" he pressed. "Who originally came up with the idea of doing Polidori?"

"That's something I've tried to pin down, too," Grace said. "Do you think it's important?"

He did not answer this directly. "You wouldn't be involved in this production if it hadn't started out as a work by Byron. If early on the material had been switched — for example — to *Dracula*, you probably would have withdrawn."

"Maybe. That's true of Lady Vee, too."

"Yes." She thought she detected a "but" in there though Grace couldn't guess what it was.

He seemed to change the subject. "Polidori killed himself, didn't he?"

"Yes. He drank prussic acid. To spare the

feelings of his family the coroner pronounced death by 'visitation of God.' "

"Any reason for suicide?"

"Mental instability?" Grace hazarded. "He wasn't the most wholesome character. He had tried to kill himself at least once before during his stay with Byron at the Villa Diodati."

"What a delightful houseguest."

"Byron had fired him. They had fallen out by then, and although Byron saved his life, apparently that was the last straw." She fell silent as Peter ignited the cognac with a long match. When the flames subsided he poured in the white wine and covered the pan. Grace enjoyed watching him cook. The contradiction of a virile man capably performing tasks traditionally regarded as feminine was just plain . . . sexy.

"I take it they were more than friends?" he asked, disrupting her reflections.

"Friendship seems to have had little to do with it. Polidori envied and emulated Byron, who was never the most patient of men, let alone lovers. He, Polidori I mean, fancied himself one of the unrecognized literary giants of his era. I guess Byron thought he needed cutting down to size. He was pretty savage."

"The Chinese have a saying, 'Better make

a weak man your enemy than your friend.' "

"Byron would have agreed with that. He hadn't much tolerance for human frailty. Including his own. And poor Polidori did seem to bring out the worst in people."

The kitchen was redolent with the luscious scent of chicken simmering in wine and butter. Her mouth was starting to water.

"Did Polidori write anything besides *The Vampyre*?"

"Yes. The problem was that when *The Vampyre* was published it was attributed to Byron. Byron disassociated himself from it, but for some reason people were slow to accept his word. And when Polidori laid claim to the work, saying that only the original concept was Byron's, he was accused of plagiarism. The charge stuck, and nothing else that he wrote was taken seriously."

"Should it have been?"

"It's hard to say. Byron and Shelley dismissed his efforts, but it is possible their criticism wasn't objective."

"Do me a favor and open the wine."

Grace took wineglasses out of the Italian cabinet painted with ivy and tiny purple flowers. She found the corkscrew and uncorked the bottle of Riesling.

While she poured the wine, Peter drained

the boiling noodles in the sink. They finished preparing the meal in a companionable silence and sat down to eat.

"How's the book coming?"

She smiled across the table at him. Peter smiled, too, and she knew he was also remembering the adventures they had shared not so very long ago: the mad race to find the stolen "gewgaws" that Grace had believed would lead them to a lost work by Lord Byron. For a moment it was as though the doubt and misunderstandings of the past month had never happened.

"You may close your eyes to the truth, my dearest Aubrey, but there are things in this world that no mere mortal can comprehend until his fate is upon him. Swear upon the love we bear each other that you will return this night before the power of these fiends walks abroad."

To say that rehearsals were progressing would be an exaggeration, but they did continue — thus giving new meaning to "horror genre." Grace wasn't sure why her presence was still required, but when she suggested to Lord Ruthven that her role was complete, he seemed so distressed, she continued to attend.

Grace didn't mind the opportunity to observe Catriona. She still hoped to find some clue as to what was between the woman and Peter. Evening after evening she sat watching the Innisdale Players run through their lines, trying to decipher the riddle that was Catriona.

Rehearsal recommenced, with Blade as Aubrey reassuring Ianthe that he would return from vampire hunting before nightfall. Grace's mind wandered while Ruthven blocked out the next scene with his cast.

There were a number of set changes once the play's action moved to Greece, and Grace had to admit that Allegra, who was in charge of art direction (which meant she designed and painted most of the backdrops herself), had done a super job. The painted wasteland could have been Byron's own Turkish cemetery. Perhaps her great-aunt had influenced Allegra's artistic vision.

Speaking of Lady Vee — Grace half turned in her seat. The old Gorgon still had not put in an appearance.

Grace came back to awareness of her surroundings for Blade's big scene when "the airy form of his fair conductress was brought in as a corpse."

Here there was a bit of comedic relief while Allegra and one of the stagehands tried to figure out a graceful way to lug

Catriona across the stage. Derrick guffawed and offered several facetious suggestions. At last, the journey from stage left to right was accomplished.

"A vampyre, a vampyre," Allegra intoned in her role of superstitious peasant.

"Do try to get more inflection in that, my dear," Lord Ruthven muttered, making another note on his ever-present clipboard. A scowl marked Allegra's patrician features.

"Ianthe," Blade whispered brokenly, kneeling beside Catriona. Leave it to Catriona to look poised even as a corpse.

Grace had to admit Roy Blade was much better in the leading role of the tragic Aubrey than she had expected. True, he didn't fit her mental picture of Aubrey — at least not before Aubrey went stark raving mad. She pictured Aubrey as slim and slight and fair — more like Derek Derrick. But Derrick, as the only professional actor, had been given his pick of roles and had oddly enough chosen the much smaller (though title) role of the vampyre. Which confirmed Grace's belief that Derrick wasn't overly weighed down in the smarts department.

"We must flee, my lord," Allegra said stoically, reading from her script. "We must leave this place of doom."

"That's the second peasant's line," Lord

Ruthven pointed out.

"We don't *have* a second peasant," Allegra said testily. "The second peasant quit after the first peasant quit, citing 'queer 'appenings,' if I remember correctly. I'm reading them *both*."

Arm comfortably propped behind her head, Catriona (wearing a T-shirt that read I AM THE BAD THING THAT HAPPENS TO GOOD PEOPLE) drawled, "And very nicely too, but try to get some Gallic fervor into it, old girl." She waved one graceful arm. "We musta leave dis place of doom, ma lord!"

Everyone laughed. Even Lord Ruthven had to purse his lips to keep from smiling.

As she watched Catriona, Grace's laugh died, and her heart seemed to turn to stone. She recognized with an illogical but utter conviction that Catriona and Peter were indeed lovers.

The next moment Catriona scrambled to her feet and pointed at the maze of catwalks above them.

"There's someone up there!"

8

Roy Blade broke off his lines and craned his neck ceilingward. “Where?” Proof of how on edge everyone had grown over the passing weeks was the speed with which the cast and crew dispersed into confused alarm. People called out, staring toward the scaffolding.

“I don’t see it! Where is he? What is it?” chorused voices.

“Up there!” Catriona pointed into a shadowy recess far above.

Lord Ruthven clapped his hands, trying to regain control. “People! People!”

“I don’t see anyone,” Derek said.

“There!” Catriona’s outstretched arm seemed to track an unseen figure’s journey. “He’s wearing a cape!”

“A cape?”

Theresa gasped and clutched at Derek, who freed himself impatiently, walking beneath the catwalk.

“Hello, you up there!” he yelled.

There was no response.

“I’ll go up and check,” one of the stagehands said.

"Wait! The catwalk isn't safe," Ruthven warned him.

Roy Blade said, "I don't see a damned thing." He added, "I don't hear anything either."

"Possibly if everyone would shut up!" Catriona snapped. Her face was set. Was she really scared? That seemed out of character to Grace.

The silence that followed Catriona's words was deafening.

"You're just nervy, Catriona," Ruthven said, when several moments had passed.

The tension that gripped them all was released. Derek chuckled.

Theresa let out a bloodcurdling scream. "A bat!"

Something swooped down from the ceiling and flew straight at Grace sitting in the front row of seats.

Grace dived to the floor and heard the dull thud as the projectile hit the chair back. She sat up as the others jumped down from the stage.

Something fluttered and flopped on the floor beside her.

"A pigeon!" Allegra exclaimed. There was uneasy laughter all around.

"I know what I saw. It was not a pigeon, it was not a bat," Catriona said flatly, still standing on the stage. "It was a man in a cape."

"This is ridiculous!" Lord Ruthven said.

Grace wondered.

"The Lord of the Dead picked a good night for it," Peter remarked, locking the gallery entrance. The door shuddered beneath a gust of wind.

All Hallows' Eve was straight out of a Tom Holland novel. A spectral moon sepulchered in darkness sailed along the sky, propelled by eldritch winds. A good night for ghoulies and ghosties, as the Scots put it.

"Do you think they'll cancel the fete?" Grace asked.

"For this little bit of weather? I shouldn't think so. Why, were you planning to go?"

"I'd thought about it." She had been hoping all day he might invite her, finally resigning herself to the idea of going alone or tagging along with Sally and the kids. In the old days she wouldn't have thought twice about asking for Peter's company.

"Candy floss and Catherine wheels? Not really your kind of thing is it?"

"Why not? It sounds like fun. Anyway, I can skip a night's rehearsal. I'm not sure why they need me there at this point anyway."

"Validation?"

"Ha. I'm beginning to wonder if they just want me where they can keep an eye on me."

" 'They'? Feeling a little paranoid, are we?" He was smiling, but she had the feeling his mind was on something else. "And how goes the Theater of the Absurd these days?"

She buttoned her coat. "I guess we're on schedule. Ruthven keeps saying we are. The sets are complete. Allegra is a really gifted artist. I had no idea."

"She attended some posh art school for a few years," Peter said. He stared out the window at the weird flickering lights in the sky.

"Is it true she and Sir Gerald used to be an item?"

"Before my time."

"She does seem more like the perfect squire's lady than poor Theresa."

"It's what she was bred for," Peter agreed. "But Gerald had a different idea." He looked at the clock. "I'll pick you up at seven, shall I?"

As Grace walked across the garden on her way from the garage she couldn't help watching the shadows for signs of Miss Coke's presence. She wasn't sure what those might be. Muddy footprints? Ectoplasm?

The cottage porch light shone welcome. There was a large parcel leaning against the corner of the steps. Grace checked the label warily, then, recognizing her mother's handwriting, picked it up and carried it inside.

It took no time at all to snip the string and unwrap the layers of brown paper. A small cheery card read, *Another surprise is on its way*. Which was unexpectedly cryptic for Grace's family.

Inside the paper was a long flat box, and inside the box was a dress. Or rather a gown. A really lovely confection of cream silk faille and bronze tulle. They didn't make dresses like this anymore. She touched it with reverent fingers. It reminded her of the kind of thing Grace Kelly would have worn in *To Catch a Thief*.

The significance of this sank in, and Grace's eyes misted because she knew this was a special present from her parents. Her mother must have known in that way mothers have that there was something Grace was not saying during her last phone call home.

Her parents couldn't cure the deep hurt, the unspoken hurt, but they could fix the schoolgirl-sized tragedy of nothing to wear to the big dance. Grace chuckled, wiped her eyes and hung the dress in the old-fashioned clothes cupboard.

Grace opened the door on the first knock.

"I thought you'd never get here. I have something to show you." She drew Peter into the cottage.

"This is the kind of greeting a man appreciates," he remarked. "And may I say your sense of timing is exquisite?"

A laugh escaped Grace although she was only momentarily distracted.

"I don't mean *that.*"

His gaze flicked over the photos of her family and friends, the vases of cut flowers, the tapestry cushions and jewel-colored rugs that made the place her own, and settled approvingly on the black leggings and long burgundy cashmere sweater that Grace wore.

She was rooting amidst the day's post scattered on the table. She picked up an object and tossed it to him. "This came in the mail. Not separately as a parcel, because I did get a parcel today."

Peter caught the plant bulb one-handed.

"For the girl who has everything," he commented.

"It's garlic."

Peter arched one brow. "Someone has

discovered your unnatural love of pasta."

"Garlic," she clarified, "which is used to ward off vampires."

"And the common cold if the medical journals are to be believed."

"I'm being serious!"

"No, you're not." Peter took her coat from the back of a club chair. "Nor is whoever sent this to you."

"You don't find this . . . strange?"

"At a guess, I'd say it's meant to be funny."

"You don't think it's threatening?"

"What are you being threatened with? Bad breath?" He helped her into her coat, his fingers lingering for a moment in the silk of her hair. Slipping the garlic bulb out of her hand, he tossed it on the table. At her expression, he smiled ruefully. "Grace, I wouldn't put it past someone on the theater committee to send these out as promotion."

"They can hardly stir themselves to put up posters and flyers. I can't believe they're organized enough to mass-mail garlic."

"Right, say this was sent in earnest. It's supposed to ward off vampires, correct? So obviously it was sent to protect you. It's not a threat, it's a —"

Grace put her hand up. "Fine. Don't believe me. Just don't humor me."

As they slipped out into the garden, Grace wondered if Miss Coke was lurking amongst the rhododendrons.

Noting the look she threw over her shoulder, Peter asked, "Since when are you afraid of the dark?"

"Everyone's afraid of the dark," Grace retorted.

"Ah, you mean the great metaphysical dark." He took her hand in his, and she treasured the warm strength of his fingers linked with hers. With Peter she was not afraid of any darkness.

It was a short walk to the fete. They could hear music and the sounds of the crowd several streets away.

The smell of damp grass and popcorn, the excited screams of children and the music of the merry-go-round greeted them as they reached the village green.

"I guess rehearsal was canceled," Peter remarked.

Following his line of vision, Grace caught sight of Lord Ruthven. He stood in the shadows of an ancient oak. He wore his cape, and although many people wore costumes, he still received curious glances.

"That's just asking for trouble," Grace commented.

"Afraid he'll incite the villagers to riot?"

"It may not be as silly as it sounds. Two cast and three crew members have quit so far. There's a weird mood in the village these days."

Peter grinned.

"Okay, I probably sound like an extra from *Nosferatu*."

"The silent film?" His eyes were laughing, but he conceded, "Oh, I don't know. Your instincts aren't bad."

Instinct? Grace prided herself on her analytical skills, but there wasn't so much to analyze here. Start with a rather bad play about a vampire. Throw in a director with the same last name as the title character, a man who liked to wander around graveyards at night wearing a cape. Then what? A series of weird incidents: anonymous messages implying that a vampire walked among the village residents, free garlic, sightings of another man in a cape who might or might not be up to no good. All of which added up to what? Publicity for the show? Halloween fun? Someone's weird sense of humor?

"There's a rumor that the security guard who died was attacked by a vampire."

Peter made a contemptuous sound.

"I'm serious. People are saying that there were weird marks on his neck and that his body was drained of blood."

"Who is saying that?"

She shrugged. "It's just a rumor."

"It's ridiculous."

They watched Lord Ruthven move off through the trees. She started, "You know, I don't think I've ever seen Lord Ruthven in the day —"

But Peter interrupted, "I don't know who that bloke is, but he's not Lord Ruthven. Unless he's taken Catriona's maiden name."

It took Grace a moment to work this out. "You think they're not married?"

She could tell that Peter already regretted that moment of candor. He said, "I couldn't say, but he's not Lord Ruthven. There is no Lord Ruthven."

So the name Ruthven was genuine? But then how could there not be a Lord Ruthven? And Catriona was not married. The good news kept coming.

"But what does that mean?" Grace persisted.

Peter studied her, his eyes colorless in the artificial lights of the fete. "It's merely an observation. Don't get carried away."

Whatever, as Grace's former students were wont to say. But it was certainly a strange observation, and one that she planned on checking out as soon as she had the opportunity.

"What exactly would you like to do?" Peter asked. He was looking about himself with a detached curiosity. Grace wondered if this was his first fete.

The crowd was a mix of revelers and spectators. Children squealed with delight, racing from amusement to amusement. The air was alive with the smell of roasting nuts, carnival music and adult voices urging caution.

"I'm open to suggestion."

"Then perhaps we should start with the fortune-teller."

"Nice one. Is there a fortune-teller?"

Peter pointed out a small striped tent. A sign on an easel outside depicted a giant hand, the various lines and pressure points illustrated with numbers and signs.

Peter laughed at her enthusiastic reaction. "Are you forgetting the last time you visited a fortune-teller?"

Grace was pleased at this reminder of their shared history and forgot, for a time, that Catriona was a shapely question mark on the horizon.

The tent flap was pulled up, indicating that Madame Mignon was open for business. "Going in?" Grace asked.

"I don't believe in Fate," Peter said.

"What do you believe in?"

"Myself."

"Well, I'm going in. Wish me luck."

"That's what it's all about."

Inside the tent, the close darkness smelled of sandalwood and candle smoke. Grace could barely make out a table in the center covered with silver gauze. A globe sat on the table. An electrical current rippled through it like strikes of lightning. The modern age of mysticism, Grace thought.

She took a chair across from Madame Mignon, who was an indistinct figure beneath the layers of spangled veils. Grace got the uncertain impression of dark hair, dark eyes and dark lipstick.

"What brings you to Madame Mignon?" inquired a deep, accented voice.

Sense of humor? Curiosity? But Grace was having fun. She threw herself into her role of seeker. "I wish to know the future."

Madame Mignon was silent. Maybe she thought Grace was making fun of her.

"Really," Grace added.

"Ten bob," Madame said. She held a red-taloned hand out.

Grace paid her. The money disappeared under the table. Madame Mignon held her hand out again.

Hesitantly Grace rested her hand atop the fortune-teller's. Madame Mignon's paw was warm and soft, with fleshy strong fingers. Her hand closed around Grace's. She covered their linked hands and began to massage Grace's.

That seemed weird, but Grace made herself relax. Actually, it felt kind of good, the strong thumbs working her pressure points.

"Ah, I see, I see," Madame crooned as though the TV reception were clearing up. "I see it all." She smoothed Grace's hand out and stared hard at her palm in the glow of the electrified crystal ball.

"You are a smart girl, a girl who knows her own mind. Ah, but a choice lies before you. I see two men, two very different men. One man holds the key to your heart, but he is dangerous to you, this man. You cannot trust him. You cannot trust anyone connected with this man. You cannot trust yourself."

That narrowed it down. "Oh dear," murmured Grace.

Madame Mignon rattled on. "I see great temptation. I see lies and deceit. I see a journey. A long and dangerous journey that will lead you into great danger . . ." She trailed off as though the routineness of this prophecy was boring even her.

After a long moment of guttering candles, she seemed to squint at Grace through the veils. She spoke more slowly, even reluctantly. "I see a room. A hidden room. A treasure lies in this room. The treasure of an ancient king. The treasures of ancient Egypt. And a . . . what do you call it? A manuscript?"

"Say what?" Grace sat bolt upright.

Madame Mignon seemed to have lost the train of thought. Through the mosquito netting her eyes appeared to be closed. Had she nodded off?

"True love stories have no ending," she said abruptly, and let go of Grace's hand.

"What's the verdict?" Peter asked when Grace joined him outside the tent.

Grace ticked off on her fingers. "There are two men in my life. I am going to take a trip soon."

"No mention of tall dark strangers or coming into sudden money?"

"Just the usual."

A familiar dwarf and ballerina ran past shrieking hello, waving red sparklers.

"Friends of yours?"

Grace found herself wondering what kind of parent Peter would make. It was difficult to imagine him in that role. Grace had always assumed she would have children, but many of her assumptions had been challenged in the past year.

Two men and a choice to make?

She shook off the crawly feeling she'd had in the fortune-teller's tent, asking briskly, "What do you suppose they have to eat?"

Peter arched one brow. "You are a brave soul."

"I didn't have time for dinner."

"All right. Don't run off with the gypsies, Esmerelda. I shall return."

Esmerelda. When was the last time he had used that pet name? Months. Did tonight's date mean they were recovering their lost footing, or was he simply treating her to some of that routine charm he served up to the customers?

Peter hadn't been gone more than a minute when a hand closed around her wrist. Even without looking Grace knew those dry stick fingers did not belong to Peter. She turned and found herself face-to-face with the woman in black.

Starting, Grace stepped back.

"Do I know you?"

The claw fingers kept their grip on her wrist, but the woman said nothing.

"What do you want?" Grace tried to pull free. "Let go of me." She didn't want to cause a scene. She had the polite person's dread of public fracas. Miss Coke was not as elderly as Grace had first thought, and she was much stronger than she looked.

"What gives you the right to threaten and harass people?" she said indignantly.

Miss Coke thrust her face in Grace's and hissed . . . something. Grace couldn't make out the actual words between the moist sibilants that flecked her face.

"Now, now, girls." To Grace's grateful relief, Peter was there, moving between her and the older woman. She didn't see what happened but all at once her wrist was free and Miss Coke was yowling like a scalded cat. People turned to stare.

"My word," Peter said. "I turn my back for three minutes, and you're brawling in the streets." He guided Grace through the crowd, which seemed to engulf the motionless Miss Coke.

"That was her. The woman in black. The one I told you about. She's crazy." Grace found that she was shaking. Peter's arm felt strong and supportive around her. "I think she cursed me."

"Darling, I imagine adolescent girls have been cursing you for years. It hasn't had much effect on you, has it?"

She laughed, but the sudden whistle and explosion of a firecracker overhead caused her to jump. Golden embers drifted in the breeze like pollen.

Peter chuckled, his breath warm against her ear. "She won't get you, my pretty."

More rockets streamed off into the sky. Giant phosphorus blooms of purple, green, and blue burst wide in the night sky, following a distant crack. Glittering cosmic rain showered down on the tents and trees.

9

Chinese lanterns lit the courtyard and threw the ivy's shadow into patterns of hearts and butterflies against the stone walls. Music drifted from inside the house.

It was the night of the Hunt Ball, and everyone who was anyone in Innisdale was in attendance. Cars lined the circular drive of Ives Manor, the nineteenth-century home of Sir Gerald and Lady Ives. Every window in the manor seemed ablaze with life and color. Squares of light lit the dark lawn.

As they started up the front stairs Peter caught her hand, and as Grace turned he kissed her lightly, as lightly as the mist from the fountain. "Beautiful Esmerelda," he whispered. His fingers brushed the delicate pearl-and-filigree antique earrings she wore. The earrings matched her necklace, a gift from Peter that very evening; a lovely variation on the traditional corsage.

"Thank you again," she said, referring to more than the compliment.

"My pleasure."

A butler (or maybe it was a footman) announced them.

Sir Gerald, dashing in a scarlet evening coat, greeted them like old friends. Grace caught a whiff of his unique scent: top note, fruity aftershave, bottom note, blended whisky.

"Lovely to see you!" Lady Theresa said. Her blond hair was coiled elegantly. She wore a startlingly low-cut gown of iridescent blue.

"It could be interesting if she drops a contact lens," Grace remarked, as she and Peter strolled away from their host and hostess.

"It could be the best party of the year."

Peter rounded up champagne glasses, and they repaired to the ballroom.

Grace felt as though she had stepped into a painting she had once seen on a visit to the Metropolitan Museum of Art. *The Hunt Ball* by Jules L. Stewart.

Men in tuxedo and white tie or scarlet evening jackets and women in formal gowns circled the room to the sweep of a full orchestra. Jewels flashed and sparkled on bare arms and throats and in elaborately dressed hair. Velvet, silk and satin shone richly in light from the chandelier. Candles and flowers were multiplied by the mirrored panels between Palladian windows.

It was like a Merchant Ivory production.

"Did you want to dance?" he asked.

Grace held up her champagne glass. "I'm working on it."

His expression grew quizzical. "This is a first. Don't tell me you're feeling shy."

"A little."

Peter seemed to know everyone, moving with smiling confidence through the crush; you would have thought he was to the manor born, Grace reflected. The truth was, she had no idea to what he was born, but she had never seen anyone better suited to white tie and tails, with his tanned skin and his fair hair shining in the illumination from the chandeliers.

She glimpsed many familiar faces — and not just from the hunt. Apparently the Hunt Ball really was the social event of the season.

She recognized Allegra in slinky scarlet dancing with Derek Derrick. Sir Gerald, his receiving line duties done, was with a crowd of gentlemen not dancing.

She spotted Lady Vee in black taffeta, her hands encrusted with jewels, sitting with several other elderly women clustered like birds of prey as they watched the dancers.

"I should say hello," Grace said.

"You are a glutton for punishment." But

he steered her over to the flock.

"Petah dahling," Lady Vee greeted him. "Have you a line on that Egyptian mummy I'm interested in?"

Peter smiled his charming smile. "Lady Vee, you know perfectly well trading in Egyptian antiquities is illegal."

The other ladies tittered.

"My *deah,* I am confident you will find a way." She nodded graciously to Grace. "I understand from my niece that that dramatic travesty opens next week."

That answered one question. If Lady Vee was no longer financing the project, the Ruthvens must be putting up the capital — eliminating one motive for the play. It was not a scam to get money from unwary financiers.

"That's what they tell me," Grace said.

Lady Vee made a sound like "Paugh!" Grace covered her champagne glass.

"They're so secretive," twittered one old dame. "They've insisted on controlling every aspect of the production themselves. No one knows for certain how many seats we've sold."

Another blue-haired dowager leaned forward, then straightened as though she'd been stung. "They're here!" she whispered hoarsely.

Naturally everyone in a three-mile radius turned to look.

Lord and Lady Ruthven had entered the ballroom. He looked more cadaverous than ever in formal wear.

"Why, he looks like — like Varney the Vampire," gasped the blue-haired lady.

"That's what he wishes you to think," Lady Vee said tartly. Grace and Peter exchanged looks.

"Who?" he murmured.

"Sir Francis Varney, the antihero of Thomas Prest's 1840s penny-dreadful *Feast of Blood*."

Peter grinned.

"*She's* quite something, isn't she?" another of Lady Vee's cronies ventured.

There was no doubt to whom she referred. Catriona was breathtaking in a gown that consisted mostly of sheer black lace. Her hair was elegantly piled on her head.

"No better than she should be," Lady Vee sniffed.

Grace had been waiting all her life to hear someone say that in exactly that tone.

"Scottish nobility," another murmured.

"Says *who?*"

The ladies began fluttering and flapping at this, but to Grace's disappointment they were interrupted. She wondered if Lady

Vee's bias was based on anything or if it was simply evidence of old age and bad temper.

She and Peter moved off to make more social small talk and sip more champagne.

"So you wish to see old John Peel's hunting horn, eh?" Sir Gerald's voice blasted in Grace's ear like the hunting horn in question.

"Oh! Er — yes." Lord and Lady Ruthven stood behind the baronet. Catriona was smirking.

"Hoick together," Sir Gerald said, leading the way.

Lord Ruthven muttered something under his breath.

They traveled down a long red hallway adorned with gold-framed landscapes, passing a room where a game of billiards seemed to be in quiet but ferocious progress, passing several other white-lacquered doors, coming at last to a closed door, which Sir Gerald unlocked.

They crowded inside and Sir Gerald turned on a glass-shaded lamp that illumined a hunting dog scaring up ducks. It was a man's room. Leather furniture, prints of horses and hounds, and a beautiful cabinet filled with hunting rifles. Over the marble fireplace was a giant panorama of a foxhunt.

In the center of the room was a glass case. They gathered round.

The bugle sat on blue velvet. It looked very old, the delicate chased work at odds with the old leather straps. Next to the bugle was a small portrait of an elderly man with long white hair, dressed in hunting livery and blowing a silver horn.

"John Peel?" Grace guessed.

"That's right. He was a Cumberland farmer and huntsman. Buried at Caldbeck Church, you know."

"Why is he so famous?" Grace inquired.

"The folksong, I suppose." Sir Gerald didn't sound like he'd ever given it much thought.

"Do ye ken John Peel with his coat so gay?" murmured Lord Ruthven.

"Gray, not gay," Sir Gerald corrected. "He wore the Hodden gray, like your own countryman, Rabbie Burns." Sir Gerald rolled his "Rs" with painful abandon.

"And in those days the Lake District hunting was all on foot?"

"Still is mostly. We're the exception that proves the rule."

"How much is it worth?" Lord Ruthven asked, his eyes on the glinting curve of silver.

"Don't know. I'll never sell it." Sir Gerald

snapped out the lamp. Before the room went dark Grace caught Peter's expression. He was watching Catriona.

Derek was dancing with Theresa as they reentered the ballroom. She was laughing — too much and too loudly. He whispered in her ear. She missed a step and nearly fell. Derek steadied her. They both laughed.

Peter said softly for Grace's ears only, "She's a fool."

Grace silently agreed.

They joined the dancers on the floor. Grace had never danced with Peter before, but they quickly matched their steps to each other.

They danced the next two dances as well. It was as though she were drifting through the evening in a champagne bubble, fragile and perfect.

She caught her reflection in the ballroom mirrors, and for a moment she thought she was looking at a stranger, her gown gracefully sweeping the floor, her cheeks flushed and her eyes like stars amidst the gleam of crystal and silver, the flicker of candles on flowers.

And then the bubble burst. The music ended, and Grace found herself facing Catriona from across the room.

Catriona stood by the French windows, a

cape draped over her arm. She was staring at Peter, a long, compelling gaze.

"Excuse me," Peter said, and crossed the room, leaving Grace, who watched him drape the black folds of the cape around Catriona's shoulders. They went through the French doors and moved out of view on the veranda.

Sir Gerald appeared in the center of the room, clapping his hands.

"Time for some quadrilles!" he announced.

This was not met with the universal joy the squire seemed to expect, but reluctantly people fell into formation. Grace escaped to the dining room and heaped a plate with food. She helped herself to another champagne.

She tried not to watch the doors through which Peter and Catriona had disappeared, but it wasn't easy. People went in and out, but there was no sign of Catriona or Peter. It seemed to her that they had been gone a long time.

A woman next to her was going on and on to an earnest-looking girl in a brave but foolhardy yellow tartan gown.

"They're vermin, my dear. Like ferocious rats. The farmers *want* us to hunt. They *need* us to hunt."

"But to turn it into a sport . . ."

"*Foxes* kill for sport, my dear. Have you ever seen what a fox will do to a henhouse?"

Grace's inadvertent eavesdropping was interrupted when a small, trim woman of uncertain age dropped into the seat across from her.

Gray streaked her dark hair, but she had the loveliest violet eyes Grace had ever seen. The woman smiled warmly. "You're Miss Hollister, aren't you. I'm amazed we've never met. I'm Constance Heron."

The chief constable joined them a moment later. The three of them chatted amiably, and when they finished their supper and returned to the ballroom, the chief constable asked Grace to dance.

The orchestra was playing an old-fashioned waltz. After a few bars she recognized the tune — "John Peel."

Chief Constable Heron knew his way around the floor, and the comfortable scent of pipe tobacco and spicy aftershave reminded Grace of dancing with her father. She wished, not for the first time, that she was not always being forced into an adversarial role with the chief constable.

She heard herself thinking aloud, "After all, Peter can't be the only suspect in the entire Lake District. There must be other people with criminal records?"

Heron answered her as naturally as though they had been discussing it all evening. "It's the nature of these crimes, Miss Hollister," he said. "These aren't smash and grabs. This thief is showing off, grandstanding. We don't have that kind of local talent."

"That you know of."

Heron's smile was tolerant. "That kind of talent is rare anywhere, Miss Hollister. It's more than resource, more than nerve. More than audaciousness. These people are pros. Security systems, guard dogs, locks and safes: they walk through them like they didn't exist."

"Maybe because for them they don't exist."

Heron's currant black eyes met hers. "Exactly."

Because the thief was one of them, an accepted member of Innisdale "society."

"The man who was killed . . . I've heard some strange rumors."

Heron's smile faded. "We'll get the villains. I can promise you that."

"Is it true that he was — that his body was drained of blood?"

Heron looked startled. "It's true that he'd lost a great deal of blood, but . . . what are you suggesting, Miss Hollister?"

"Were there bite marks on his neck?"

The chief constable actually missed a step. "Good heavens!" he exclaimed. "Where the devil did you hear such a farradiddle?"

Farradiddle. Now there was a word you didn't hear every day.

"A number of people have mentioned it. I don't know who started the rumor, but I heard it from a girl whose boyfriend works at *The Clarion*." Had someone hoped to foster the notion that a vampire was running amuck in Innisdale by starting such a rumor? "So it's not true?"

"It is most certainly not true."

"Was it an accident? The security guard, Bill Jones that is, was his death an accident?"

"When someone is killed in the commission of a crime, it's murder. Maybe not according to the courts, but it's murder all the same."

That didn't sound like Jones had been in on the burglary. "Was Bill Jones involved in the robbery? Was he an accomplice?"

Heron admonished, "You must know I can't discuss the details of this case with you, Miss Hollister."

How come it always worked in books? She

abandoned her interrogation, muttering, "You may as well call me Grace since we're dancing together."

When the music ended they rejoined Constance. She was frowning, and it wasn't hard to track the source of her disapproval. Sir Gerald was getting louder and drunker. As they watched he pounded one of his fellows on the back, and the man nearly staggered beneath the blow. The circle of gentlemen shouted with good humor and waylaid one of the footmen passing with a tray of champagne glasses.

Grace wondered where Theresa was. Even more, she wondered where Peter was. He had been gone for nearly an hour.

The Herons made their way onto the crowded dance floor. Grace was navigating toward the veranda when the double doors blew open. Leaves skittered in, blowing across the tables and floors.

There were tiny screams, and the orchestra died off with trailing notes. The dancers slowed and stopped.

Allegra stood framed in the French doors. Her black hair blew around her white face; the wind gusted her red gown. Red with a darker patch of red at the knees.

"There's been an accident," she said into the shocked silence.

* * *

The shadow spilling down the stairs to the lower garden was not a shadow. It was a woman in a black cape.

One shoe stood empty on the step above her.

The crowd that had followed Grace from the house seemed to draw back at this ominous sight. Then Sir Gerald pulled back the hood of the cape and recoiled. Lady Theresa's blue eye stared up in profile. Blood welled from two puncture marks on her neck.

Theresa? Grace felt numb. She could not seem to take it in. Theresa was dead. But Catriona was the one with all the near misses . . .

Sir Gerald sat down on the steps as though his legs had given out. "Ge—" His voice cracked. He wiped a hand across his face, and croaked, "Get Heron."

Allegra knelt beside him, hand on one broad shoulder. She said something for his ears only. He nodded and wiped his eyes again.

"Lift her up, bring her inside," Lady Vee commanded.

No, wrong, Grace thought. That would be contaminating a crime scene or tampering with evidence. "Wait," she said, as a man in a tuxedo and another man in a scarlet jacket bent over Theresa's body. "I don't think we should move her. The police —"

"Police!" exclaimed Lady Vee.

"Of course the police," Grace said. "She's been murdered."

People turned faces shocked and stupid in the flickering shadows of the Chinese lanterns. What did they think, wondered Grace? Did they believe a vampire had killed Theresa?

"Miss Hollister is perfectly correct," Heron said sternly from the top of the terrace steps. "I must ask you all to return to the house."

"We can't leave her out here," Sir Gerald protested.

"No harm will come to her out here, Gerry," Heron said gruffly. "Come inside, man."

They filed back into the brightly lit room. Peter stood in the doorway watching. Grace avoided his gaze as she moved past.

"Connie, call Sergeant Stebbins," Heron ordered, and Mrs. Heron went to locate a phone.

The rest of the evening was more like the hangover than the champagne bubble. The police came and the grim process of crime scene investigation began. The guests were cordoned off in the ballroom, and Heron questioned them one by one in the billiards room.

Grace was brought in quite early.

"Tell me about this play you're involved in," the chief constable asked. "About vampires, is it?"

Grace nodded. "It's a play based on a play based on a short story that was published in 1819. It's about a man named Aubrey who befriends a mysterious nobleman who turns out to be a vampire. Theresa played Miss Aubrey, the hero's sister. The story ends with her becoming the vampire's final victim."

"And the name of the vampire?"

Reluctantly, Grace answered, "Lord Ruthven."

"Ruthven? That's quite a coincidence."

"I suppose so."

"This is a very famous play?"

"No. Rather, yes — to people familiar with the Gothic genre or into the vampire thing. To the average theatergoer, no."

"I understand there have been a number of incidents at the Playhouse. Tell me about those."

Grace related an account of the graffiti on the theater wall and the trapdoor that had given way.

"And you know about the rumor concerning Bill Jones," she finished.

Heron changed tack again. "How did Lady Ives get on with the rest of the cast?"

"Fine."

"No arguments with anyone?"

"I don't think so."

"You don't seem quite sure."

Grace said slowly, "Theresa got on with everyone."

Heron's dark eyes were canny. "There's something on your mind, Grace. Suppose you tell me what it is."

Grace gave him a troubled look. "It's not that easy," she tried to explain.

"Suppose I make it easier. Someone has suggested to me that Lady Ives was especially close to one cast member. Would you agree with that statement?"

"I hate this."

"We don't ask these questions for our own amusement. It's difficult to know what will prove to be important in an investigation. Would you agree that Lady Ives appeared to be on close terms with one cast member?"

"Derek Derrick is extremely flirtatious," Grace said. "He spent a lot of time flirting with Theresa. That doesn't necessarily mean anything."

"Very true."

He asked her a few more questions, but they were clearly routine. It wasn't long before the chief constable told Grace he would have an officer drive her home.

Something about the offhand way he said this alerted Grace to trouble. "That's all right," she said quickly. "I'll wait for Peter."

"It could be a long wait," Heron said grimly. "We've more than a few questions for Mr. Fox."

"Chief Constable, you can't think Peter had anything to do with . . . this. What possible reason would he have?"

"Lady Ives may not have been the target. Indeed, she may simply have been in the wrong place at the wrong time."

"That doesn't make sense," Grace protested.

"Ah, but there's something you don't know, Miss — Grace," Heron said somberly. "At some point this evening the silver bugle of John Peel went missing."

Moisture beaded the glistening grass. Moths batted at the light above the cottage door. The moon drifted in a smoky haze beyond the treetops.

Grace's thoughts also drifted in a smoky haze. Too much had happened during that long evening. She felt numb. Her muscles were in knots of tension. She had to clench her jaw to keep her teeth from chattering as she found her keys in her handbag.

Out of the corner of her eye she saw something move by the cottage stoop. She sucked in an alarmed breath, but the lantern illuminated the features of the man waiting for her.

"Ch-Chaz?" Grace managed.

10

“Hello, Grace.” Chaz smiled uncertainly.

The amber light gave his lean face a bronzed cast, but it was illusory. He was tall and very thin, with curly dark hair, soulful brown eyes and a meticulously groomed mustache and beard. He looked like an artist rather than a math instructor, which, according to Grace’s friend Monica, was false advertising.

“What are you doing here?” Grace’s hand closed on the collar of her coat as though she needed fresh air.

“I came to see you, obviously.”

Her mind couldn’t seem to wrap around this. After everything that had happened that evening, the sudden materialization of her ex-boyfriend seemed surreal.

“Can it wait?”

“Wait? I’ve been waiting for nearly a year.”

She took in the suitcases at his feet, the dampness of his coat. “I’m sorry. It’s not been a good night. I was at a party and my hostess was — there was an accident.” It seemed too unreal to say the word "murder."

At a loss, she unlocked and opened the door. She turned on the lights as Chaz dropped his bags inside, looking around himself curiously.

"Let me change out of this dress."

"You look . . . amazing," Chaz said. "I almost didn't recognize you. Where've you been?"

"The Hunt Ball." Somehow it came out sounding like "Tea at Buckingham Palace."

"The Hunt Ball?" Chaz's Adam's apple was prominent. She had forgotten its tendency to swell when he was shocked. She had forgotten he was easily shocked.

Grace shut herself in the bathroom, wriggling out of the gown and pulling on jeans, a white shirt and a shaker knit cardigan in oatmeal.

She rejoined Chaz in the living room. He was studying the photos of Grace and her family.

"You do look different," he remarked, turning at her entrance.

"It's my hair."

He shook his head. "Your hair is curly, but that's not it."

"Tea? Coffee?" She headed for the tiny kitchen. When in doubt, drink caffeine.

Chaz followed her.

"When did you get in?"

"A few hours ago. I flew into Manchester . . ." He frowned at his watch. "Three o'clock? Or was that Pacific Standard Time?" He went on calculating while Grace fixed coffee and chocolate praline cookies, or "biscuits," on a tray.

Carrying the tray into the main room she set it on the carved trunk Peter had loaned her for a coffee table. To fill the silence that fell between them she poured coffee and handed Chaz a cup. She offered him the plate of biscuits, still not speaking. She was too tired to make small talk.

"There wasn't a hotel," he began.

That snapped her out of her apathy. "Wait a sec," she said. "There's only one bed, and I'm sitting on it."

"Oh," said Chaz. "Well, I guess I could sleep on the floor." He looked doubtfully at the flagstone at his feet.

"I don't think that's a good idea."

"Neither do I. It's not like we've never —"

"I meant your staying here is not a good idea."

"You can't throw me out tonight," Chaz protested.

She could of course, and Chaz was civilized enough to go, but Grace would only be postponing the inevitable. She shivered.

"Are you all right? You look peaked."

"It's been a long night."

"You said there was an accident?"

She blinked at him with heavy lids. If she started explaining, they would be up for whatever was left of the night. "Sort of."

She sipped her coffee and was comforted by its warmth, though she still felt chilled to the bone despite the sweater. It was a coldness that went beyond the physical. She was too tired to think clearly, that much she knew.

"You can stay the night, and we'll talk tomorrow," she said finally.

She didn't like the gleam of triumph that she saw in his expressive eyes, but there wasn't much she could do about it. While Chaz finished his coffee, she stoked the iron stove.

The nip in the air began to dissipate from the room. After making up a bed of extra blankets and pillows on the floor for Chaz, she pulled out the chesterfield and crawled into her own cocoon of flannel sheets and wool blankets.

"My God this floor is hard," Chaz muttered in the darkness.

"Good night," Grace said.

Before her smile faded she was asleep.

★ ★ ★

"That was fast," Peter remarked.

She came back to awareness of the cold breath of morning across her face.

Grace's eyes popped open. The front door stood wide. Clad in navy pajamas with white polka dots, Chaz blocked the doorway. She kicked off the blankets and joined him at the cottage entrance.

"Come in," she croaked.

"I don't want to intrude," Peter said courteously. He looked groomed and well rested for a man who had spent the night in police interrogation. His face was expressionless.

"You're not intruding."

Chaz looked at his watch. "It's not even seven."

"And you are?" Peter inquired urbanely.

"Charles Honeyburn." He added belatedly, "The Third."

"Ah, the famous Chip."

"Chaz."

"Quite."

"Who are you?" Chaz demanded.

"This is Peter." Grace finally got a word in.

"Oh, *you're* the guy," Chaz growled.

"I'm the man," Peter corrected.

"What man?"

"The man with the power."

"What power?" Chaz turned to Grace. "What is he talking about?"

"The power of voodoo," Grace said. "It's an old vaudeville shtick."

"You'll admit," Peter said, "that this scene has its farcical aspect."

"Come in and tell me what's happened," Grace urged.

The cold morning air reached through her peach silk pajamas and turned her skin to goose bumps. It was affecting her in other ways, too, Peter's gaze informed her.

"If I'm in the way," Chaz said, in a rather huffy tone.

"It's not that," Grace said. "It's just —"

"It is that, actually," Peter said.

"Do you want me to leave?" Chaz asked Grace.

She did, but it seemed both unkind and rude to say so.

"Why don't I get dressed, and we can go somewhere and talk," Grace suggested to Peter.

"Don't be silly," Chaz said. "I'll get dressed and go out and you two can talk here."

"You're my guest," Grace protested.

"It's your home," Chaz argued.

"Fascinating," Peter murmured. "Grace, love, what I had to say can wait. I'll talk to you later."

He turned on heel.

Grace snatched one of the quilts off the floor, stepped into the Wellingtons by the front door and ran — clumping — after Peter, ignoring Chaz's protest.

"Peter, wait!"

He paused by the hydrangeas, their heads beige and papery. In the crisp sunlight she could see that there were tiny lines of weariness around his eyes and a faint golden stubble on his jaw. He was carelessly dressed in jeans and green flannel shirt beneath a leather jacket. Maybe not as groomed and well rested as she had initially thought.

"What happened last night? Why did the police let you go?"

"Why wouldn't they let me go?" His smile mocked her. "Or do you think I killed that poor silly cow?"

"I know you didn't." She didn't have to think about it. She saw an almost imperceptible relaxing of his frame. "What did happen?"

His lashes lowered for a moment, and she knew she was about to get the *Reader's Digest* version of the night before.

"Cat provided me with an alibi."

Grace considered every syllable of that neutral statement. "That means you provide Cat with an alibi as well," she said finally.

"I suppose so."

"You suppose so? Like it never occurred to you?"

"It occurred to me. Cat didn't kill Lady Ives."

"How do you know?"

"Because we really were together."

"Oh."

His eyes were the blue of the shadows that lengthen twilight. "I thought it would be better if you heard it from me."

"Sure." She pulled the blanket more tightly about herself. "What about the Peeler? The police believe the two crimes are related."

"The police are often mistaken."

"Are they mistaken this time?"

"I don't know. I didn't take the Peeler."

"Did she?"

"Not that I'm aware of."

She stood there breathing in the cold morning air, her Wellies sinking into the mud, and she became slowly aware that she was angry and getting angrier by the moment.

"Is that all you wanted to tell me?" she queried.

"Er . . . yes." She couldn't interpret his

expression, but the fact that he was smiling very faintly irked her.

"Thanks for letting me know." She turned, but the blanket caught on a shrub.

Peter freed the blanket. "My pleasure," he murmured.

She hoped she didn't sound as brittle as she felt. "You won't mind if I take a few days off? I'd like to spend time with Chaz."

"Really?"

She cast him a baleful look. "Really."

"He's not your type, you know."

There were any number of answers to that, but they all would have come out sounding childish and spiteful. Instead, she took a leaf from his own book and smiled.

It must have been a convincing smile because Peter's eyes narrowed.

Knowing she had scored, Grace swept off, quilt trailing, boots galumphing. As she closed the cottage door behind her, she had the satisfaction of knowing Peter was still standing where she'd left him.

"So that's the guy," Chaz said. "He's not what I expected."

Chaz had changed into khakis and a white shirt with a yellow ascot. He always wore ascots, Grace remembered. And tweed golf caps. She'd used to think how dashing he looked in them. How British. She wasn't the only one. Chaz had been universally popular with students and female faculty alike at St. Anne's.

"What did you expect?"

Chaz shrugged. "I didn't know what to expect. No one does. Your parents —"

"What about my parents?" she demanded.

"They're worried about you. We all are."

"Is that why you're here?"

"Maybe. Partly. I care for you, Grace. I care about us."

It was difficult, but it had to be said. "There is no 'us.' "

"You can't just call it off. Not without giving me a chance."

Chaz believed he could reason his way back into her life. This trust in the infallibility of logic probably came from devoting one's life to mathematics.

"Why now?" Grace objected. "Why didn't you say all this a year ago?"

"I don't know. Would you have listened? I thought the best thing would be to let you try it out. It was such a crazy idea, moving here. I thought the weather alone would have you home in six months."

"Well, you were wrong. All of you." She kicked off the rubber boots. "I need a shower."

★ ★ ★

The cottage was fragrant with pancakes and sausages when Grace exited the bath.

"Goodness, when did you learn to cook?" she inquired, toweling her hair as she entered the kitchen. Chaz stood at the stove, spatula in hand.

"Cooking classes are a great way to meet women," he informed her.

Grace chuckled. "Sly dog."

Chaz smiled. He had a wonderful smile, and she remembered how much she liked him and how refreshingly normal he was. Chaz would never get himself mixed up in jewel robberies or murder.

"Eat your breakfast before it gets cold," he ordered.

He had found plates and cutlery, setting the table and even making coffee while she bathed. Inevitably it brought back memories — good memories.

They breakfasted on pancakes and sausages while avoiding discussion of anything more serious than how out of control airline security had become.

"I'm seriously thinking of writing to my congressman," Chaz concluded, spooning a dollop of Sally Smithwick's blackberry jam on his last pancake.

Grace made some absent comment. She

was trying to figure what to do with Chaz. She didn't want a heart-to-heart, but there was probably no way around it. And she probably owed Chaz that much, but the timing couldn't have been worse. All Grace could think about were the events of the evening before.

She decided she needed to see the paper and read the local perspective on the murder.

"Now that you're here," she said, "can I show you the sights?"

Chaz professed himself agreeable, and Grace changed into black leggings and a long cable-knit sweater of lavender.

The narrow streets of Innisdale were quiet on this Sunday morning. Swans glided on glassy water beneath the stone bridge. The single hand on the main street corner clock ticked soundlessly. On the village green tents and the merry-go-round were being packed up. The trees had lost more leaves, limbs shivery white and skeletal.

"It's cute," Chaz conceded, as they trekked along past sleeping houses.

It is, Grace thought, but the thatched, timbered and fieldstone cottages so beloved by American readers and filmgoers were becoming a thing of the past. Standardized windows, uniform doors and a mass production approach to architecture would in time replace the unique character of the English village.

They found a news kiosk and Chaz stopped dead in his tracks as they both took in the banner headline.

MURDER AT THE HUNT BALL! proclaimed *The Clarion*.

"This was the party you were at last night?" His expression was aghast as Grace paid for the paper and scanned the front page.

The Clarion had little to add to what Grace already knew. The Peeler, hunting bugle of the famed John Peel, valued at over a hundred thousand pounds, had been stolen during the annual Hunt Ball. Lady Theresa Ives had been murdered. *The Clarion* put less emphasis on the possible connection between the two crimes and more on the fact that Lady Ives's body had been discovered with two sharp puncture wounds over her jugular vein.

And this time it's true, Grace thought. This isn't any rumor, I saw the marks myself.

It was all news to Chaz. He kept making shocked noises as he read over Grace's shoulder.

"Vampires? They think a vampire killed that woman?"

Grace listened with half an ear.

"What kind of psycho does something like that?"

Chaz's Adam's apple was decidedly mobile, giving him the aspect of a very handsome tom turkey.

"They're just capitalizing on the more sensational aspects," she said.

"And this Peter Fox is their main suspect for the robbery?"

"It doesn't say that."

"It says" — Chaz squinted, trying to get a better look at the paper — "the police spent several hours questioning local antiques dealer Peter Fox. It doesn't say that about anyone else."

Grace wasn't about to get into Peter's history with Chaz. She paid for the paper and slowly folded and tucked it into the spacious pocket of her jacket.

In uncomfortable silence she and Chaz headed back the way they had come.

As they retraced their footsteps past the village green, Chaz muttered, "Who let Mother Hubbard out of her cupboard?"

"What?" Grace glanced around. Her short hairs rose as she recognized Miss Coke trailing them at a discreet distance.

Chaz's fair skin revealed his every emotion. Just then he looked rather pink. "Is she following you?"

"Why do you say that?" Grace was hedging, and they both knew it.

"Because she's been behind us since we left your street. Didn't you notice her?"

"No." Apparently you could adjust to anything, even being stalked.

"I thought she was a bag lady planning to hit you up for a donation."

"She's the local witch."

"The local *what?* What kind of place *is* this?"

Grace barely heard him. An idea had occurred to her. "I want to stop at the police station."

Chaz opened his mouth, then changed his mind.

There was no hotel in Innisdale, but bed-and-breakfasts were numerous.

After Chaz was safely stowed in a cozy place a street or so down from Sally Smithwick's, Grace swung by the police station.

She went inside and asked to see the chief constable but was told he was out investigating the recent tragedy. The constable in charge did not know when Heron would return.

Grace returned to the tree-lined street.

Perhaps she was being overly hasty. Perhaps she was jumping to conclusions. It was difficult to know. She didn't want to start throwing accusations around, harming some innocent person merely because she made Grace uncomfortable. How much did the strange events of the past few weeks have to do with Theresa Ives's murder? Perhaps there was no connection except in Grace's imagination.

She got back in her car and returned to Renfrew Hall, parking in the carriage house and cutting through Sally's sprawling and secluded back garden.

It took only a few minutes to tidy up all traces of Chaz's brief visit. His appearance was such colossal bad timing. And the fact that her family had not warned her of his impending arrival . . . had they all lost their minds?

Perhaps it was her own sanity being questioned.

Of course there was no point brooding over it. Do something productive, Grace ordered herself. She sat down to review her notes for her book. Though intended as a scholarly work, no matter how Grace tried to downplay the sensationalist elements of last year's academic pursuit, the manuscript read like fiction. A story seemed to have happened to another Grace Hollister. Another Peter Fox. Grace shelved her notes.

Putting the kettle on, she stood for a moment at the kitchen window. From outside came a sweet warble.

Brown birdeen singing thy bird-heart song.

Who had written that? Grace couldn't recall, indication that it had been too long since she stood in front of a classroom.

The kettle whistle blew, breaking the spell. She poured herself a cup of tea and sat down at the table with a pad of paper and a pen.

Once again she considered the change in Peter. They got along as well as ever, laughed, talked, flirted as before. Sometimes she thought she was imagining his withdrawal. Instinct told her — forget instinct, she thought.

What do you know for a fact?

That everything seemed to be fine before the robberies began in late summer. Still, that wasn't proof. Maybe their trouble didn't have anything to do with the robberies. Maybe the timing *was* coincidence.

Maybe the distance she sensed didn't even have to do with Catriona. After all, Peter had known an awful lot of women, and he had never yet made a commitment to one of them. He had said that whatever was between him and Catriona had nothing to do with his relationship with Grace, so maybe she should just take him at his word.

Okay, fine, Grace thought. Let's move on to what we do know: that Peter was an ex-thief, and that he had seemed to change when these robberies began, and that Catriona was somehow involved.

Speculation?

No, because from what Grace had seen of Catriona — and from the little Peter had admitted — Catriona was clearly an important person in Peter's past. His criminal past. And her reappearance had dovetailed with the local crime wave. So maybe it wasn't *proof*, but it was surely a hunk of coincidence to swallow whole.

In fact, even Peter's cryptic denials that Catriona had anything to do with him and Grace emphasized her mysterious role in his life.

Grace scowled at the blank sheet of paper in front of her and wrote, "Conclusion?"

He's not involved in murder.

"Brilliant deduction, Holmes," she muttered.

And she had reached this conclusion how?

Just the facts, ma'am . . .

Well, there was only about an hour during

which she could not account for Peter's whereabouts at the Hunt Ball. An hour was not a lot of time to commit robbery and murder — and still return to the ballroom without a hair out of place. But he had been up to something with Catriona. Grace did not believe they had simply been catching up on old times.

Catriona was Peter's alibi and Peter was Catriona's, which in Grace's opinion meant *neither* of them actually had an alibi.

Although she was willing to believe Catriona capable of everything from leopard underwear to homicide, she couldn't see Peter standing by while poor flighty Theresa was slaughtered.

He might be lying to her about being with Catriona, but somehow she didn't think so. They had been together and, during that time, Theresa had been killed and the Peeler had been stolen. The two things might not be related, but that was an awful lot of bad luck for Sir Gerald in one night if they weren't.

11

Grace had received all the therapeutic benefit possible from catching up on her laundry when Chief Constable Heron dropped by.

"I wouldn't say no to a cup of tea," he replied to Grace's invitation. He looked as though he hadn't slept. Lowering himself into the room's single easy chair, he took out his pipe. "May I?"

Grace nodded. It might not be healthy, but she did love the smell of a pipe. She served tea and the last of the chocolate praline biscuits in the sitting room, taking the sofa across from the chief constable. There were a million questions she wanted to ask, but she knew he would not answer them. It was quite maddening because in mystery novels when the amateur sleuth made friends with a cop, the cop was always obliging about handing over all kinds of privileged information about the case.

"How is it going?" she asked. "Or can you say?"

"Too early to tell," the chief constable replied, adding heavily, "It's a bad business."

His currant black eyes rested on Grace. "Did you have some information, Miss — Grace?"

"I don't know. There's one possibility you might not have considered."

Tamping down his pipe, Heron said indulgently, "What would that be?"

"Miss Coke."

Heron's brows drew together. "Elizabeth Coke? What could she have to do with this matter?"

"Were you aware that Miss Coke is strongly antihunting, and that she expresses her disapproval through a form of silent intimidation?"

"What's that you say?" Heron looked baffled.

Grace rose and rummaged through the heavy old secretary against the wall. When she found what she was looking for she brought it to Heron. "Do you know what this is?"

Heron picked the handmade doll up gingerly. It was not a particularly attractive item.

"It's a poppet," Grace said. "I've read up since she left this on my front door. It functions like a voodoo doll."

"Good Lord. Voodoo?"

"Theresa received one. Miss Coke was

stalking her — well, following her at least — just as she's been following me. She was following me this very morning." That didn't sound as menacing as it had felt. "She accosted me at the fete."

"Accosted?"

"She grabbed my arm."

"Why didn't you report any of this, Miss Hollister?"

"Because I thought she was a harmless old crank. That's what Allegra Clairmont-Brougham told me — although she also said something about someone Miss Coke had ill-wished breaking his neck foxhunting."

"Sam Jeffries," Heron said absently.

"Maybe she's not so harmless. She's a fanatic, and fanatics can be violent in certain circumstances."

"And you think that Miss Coke might have crept onto the grounds of the Ives estate and coshed Lady Ives over the head when she went for a stroll in the moonlight?"

"Is that what happened? She was hit over the head? I thought . . ."

"You thought a vampire bit her?"

"Well, no. But I saw the marks. We all did."

"It appears those wounds were inflicted after death. They were not made by human teeth." He added dryly, "Or even inhuman teeth."

"What were they made by?"

"That we don't know. Yet."

"Why would someone want to make it look like a vampire attacked her? Obviously you would discover the truth as soon as her body was examined."

"Perhaps to confuse the issue," Heron said. "Perhaps the wounds were made by someone with little practical knowledge of how the police work. Perhaps someone was inspired by the rumors that a vampire attacked Bill Jones."

"Someone like Miss Coke?" she suggested.

"Miss Coke certainly seems to have got on your bad side," Heron said mildly.

Grace could feel her cheeks turning red. She said tartly, "It may be that I'm as stuck in the rut of my suspicions as you are in yours."

"The rut of my suspicions, eh?" Heron studied her, unsmiling. Finally, he said grudgingly, "We'll check into Miss Coke's whereabouts Saturday night, make no mistake."

"Thank you." She picked up her teacup, but her hand shook, and the words burst out of her. "It's no harder to believe that someone like Miss Coke might have done this terrible thing than it is to believe that Peter could!"

There was an embarrassing silence; then Heron said almost formally, "Thank you for coming forward with this information, Miss Hollister. If Miss Coke approaches you again, let us know right away."

She was shocked to recognize the expression in his dark eyes as pity.

The children were playing hide-and-seek in the garden that evening when Grace left to meet Chaz at the Hungry Tiger for dinner. Grace waved to them, declined an invitation to join in the game, and on impulse went round to the front of the old house and knocked on Sally's door.

Sally welcomed her and expressed sympathy for Grace's dreadful experience the previous evening.

As she sank into one of the marshmallow chintz chairs her suspicions seemed ridiculous, but Grace made herself ask. "Sally, what do you know about Sam Jeffries?"

To her surprise, Sally flushed. "What is there to know?"

"Who was he?"

"A local farmer. He owned Mallow Farm. It's gone to a Japanese gentleman now."

Sally's voice expressed disapproval. "He has an overseer to run things."

"What was Sam like?"

Was it Grace's fancy, or did Sally hesitate. "He was a good-hearted chap. Always a joke and a word of greeting. Loved his pint and his pipe."

"And he loved hunting?"

Sally's eyes met Grace's. "Yes. He was always out with the pack, rain or shine. Why?"

"Something you said about Miss Coke. Was Sam Jeffries whom you meant when you said bad things happened to people Miss Coke ill-wished?"

Sally's lips pressed tight, then relaxed. "I suppose so. There was trouble with Miss Coke living so close to Mallow. Sam would set traps, you see, to protect his livestock. One of Miss Coke's cats was killed. She began following him around like she does."

"And he was killed in a hunting accident?"

"Broke his neck not long after." Sally shook her head. "Sam was always at the front of the field."

"There wasn't anything suspicious about his death?"

"Oh no!" Sally looked shocked. "His horse didn't clear the wall, and Sam broke his neck. It was a terrible thing, but hunting is a dangerous sport."

It sounded perfectly straightforward. Grace couldn't see anything that particularly incriminated Miss Coke.

"There was an inquest, I imagine?"

"Of course."

The thought slowly took shape. "Did Sam have any other enemies?"

"Enemies!" Sally's eyes filled with consternation. "Certainly not. He was very well liked. Very popular."

"Was he married? Did he leave a family?"

"No." Sally was curt, and Grace thought she had better let the matter rest.

She met Chaz outside the Hungry Tiger. He was frowning at his watch although Grace was not late; however, his expression brightened as he spotted her walking toward him.

They went inside and were greeted warmly by Ahmed, the proprietor, who wore a lime green turban and a superbly tailored suit. His delight changed to something like dismay as he absorbed the fact that Grace was dining out with an eligible man who was not Peter.

With an air of one performing a sorrowful duty he led them back to a table in the main dining room and took their drink order.

Still looking reproachful, Ahmed returned with their beers. Chaz took a swig, frowning at the unfamiliar flavor.

They ordered, Chaz going for the *Shahi Subze,* a spicy stir-fry, and Grace settling on chicken and mushrooms in a cream-and-herb sauce.

Grace tasted her tomato-and-dill soup. It was good, but she was wishing she had not brought Chaz to a place she and Peter frequented.

She realized her thoughts had wandered, as they had a tendency to do in Chaz's company. He was waxing earnest again.

"I know you, Grace. Better than you know yourself. This . . . this . . ." He gestured to the window and Innisdale with all it represented. "This isn't you. You're smart, you're focused, and you're ambitious. You're not going to throw away everything you've worked for, for . . . Brigadoon."

"Brigadoon was Scottish."

"You know what I mean."

She did at that.

Chaz put his beer mug down with a bang as though coming to a decision. "Andrea Weicenski has used this past year to ingratiate herself with Ms. Winters."

"Andrea from the Science Department?"

"She's taken on a lot of extracurricular projects, a lot of the things you used to do, Grace."

"Well, someone's got to do them."

"This year the students elected her Most Popular Instructor. Believe me, people are noticing. She's taken every opportunity to solidify her position as Ms. Winters's successor." Chaz made it sound like there was trouble at the Machiavellis'.

"That's natural enough," Grace said. She wasn't sure if she was really as cool about it as she sounded, but common sense told her it *was* natural.

"And I can see that Ms. Winters is losing patience. If she knew a *man* was involved."

"This isn't just about a man," Grace said, finding Chaz's gaze and holding it. "This is about me deciding what I want for my life." Of course it was partly about a man and the role he would play in that life, but why confuse the issue?

They finished their soup and started their entrees. Grace glanced up to find Chaz studying her curiously.

"You always used to be on a diet."

She considered the truth of his words. Back home nearly every woman she knew was on a diet. She said, "I don't think about food the same way." Or dieting or exercise or anything else. She appreciated food more and thought about it less. Maybe it had paid off; she had given up weighing herself, so it was hard to know.

"Whatever you're doing, it's working," Chaz said. "You look terrific." His gaze was admiring.

"Thanks." She reached for her mug.

"And you never used to drink beer," Chaz added.

Grace wondered if she was going to have to hear a never-ending litany of the ways she had changed. Her eye caught a small commotion by the door.

Lord and Lady Ruthven had entered the restaurant dining room. Catriona was wearing a leather miniskirt, and Ruthven wore his usual cape. It was a toss-up as to who was garnering more attention.

Once again Grace reflected on the fact that she had never seen Lord Ruthven in the daylight. Was it something he did purposely? Perhaps he had some kind of skin or eyesight disorder that made it necessary for him to stay out of the sun. She wondered if there was a way to politely ask about that.

Ahmed attempted to seat the Ruthvens but was stymied by Catriona who, catching sight of Grace, indicated they would join her table.

"This is cozy, isn't it?" she murmured, sitting next to Chaz. Chaz made a brave effort to avoid eyeing Catriona's rising skirt hem.

Grace made some polite noise and introduced Chaz.

Lord Ruthven countered by introducing himself as Bob, which so amazed Grace she couldn't think of anything to say for a few minutes. That wasn't a problem; the conversation flowed on without her.

"Ruthven," Chaz said slowly. "So you were at that ball last night."

"The social event of the year," Catriona quipped. She turned to give Ahmed their drink order, adding another round for Chaz and Grace to the chit.

"It must have been horrific."

"It was rather. *Where* did they find that orchestra, I wonder?" Catriona queried of her husband.

Even if he had an answer, the waiter's arrival to remove the soup plates sidetracked him.

"What about this vampire story?" Chaz asked, when the waiter had moved off.

There was a funny pause, then Catriona said, "I'll tell you what I think. Someone is trying to sabotage our play."

"You can't think someone would go to

the lengths of killing Theresa to postpone the play?" Grace objected.

"Have you invested a lot in the production?" Chaz asked.

"Enough," Bob said curtly.

"You think these attacks are directed at you?" Grace said to Catriona, who shrugged an elegant shoulder.

"Isn't it obvious? I mean all that malarkey about the Crosbys' security guard. Did you hear the stories? A vampire bit him!" She chuckled. "And who, I wonder, is the most likely suspect?"

"Catriona," her husband warned.

Catriona's feline gaze met her husband's black one. Amazingly, she changed the subject.

"Will you be riding tomorrow?" she asked Grace.

"Riding? You mean there's a meet?"

"Of course. The show must go on." She glanced at Lord Ruthven and mimicked his dour expression. "That show anyway."

"Is Sir Gerald hunting?"

"I assume so." Catriona reached for her cocktail as Ahmed arrived with the drinks tray. "It's what Theresa would have wanted, poor girl. She lived for sport."

"You're going riding tomorrow?" Chaz looked from one to the other.

"Foxhunting," Lord Ruthven (Grace just could not think of him as "Bob") clarified.

Grace didn't have to look at Chaz to know he was ready to start gobbling.

"You all foxhunt?"

"I sense a bourgeois disapproval," Catriona remarked.

"Not all of us," Lord Ruthven said. "Some of us recognize it for the barbaric custom it is." He quoted Oscar Wilde. " 'The unspeakable in pursuit of the inedible.' "

Catriona laughed. "Rabbie is afraid of horses. Or perhaps the horses are afraid of Rabbie." When she said "Rabbie," the Scots pet name for "Robert," one could hear the thistle lying beneath her carefully cultivated tones.

Grace tried the *kaju katli*. Cashew fudge made with white chocolate and ground cashew nuts. It didn't quite go with the beer. She decided she needed the beer more than the chocolate if she was going to spend an evening with Catriona.

The conversation turned to plays and theater. Chaz asked Lord Ruthven what he had done that Chaz might have seen. Lord Ruthven named a couple of productions that Chaz had to admit he'd never heard of. Catriona interjected a few comments.

Grace wondered at the Ruthvens' relationship. Beneath what was apparently a successful working partnership ran an undercurrent of antagonism.

Did Ruthven suspect his wife of having an affair? Catriona seemed to enjoy baiting her spouse. Was there some past betrayal between them?

Her thoughts returned to the murder.

Why kill Theresa? What possible motive could there be?

But of course there were motives. The most obvious motive was that Sir Gerald had slain her in a jealous rage. Grace had read enough mysteries to know spouses were always the prime suspects in murder investigations. But why choose the night of the Hunt Ball? And why mar her body with pseudovampire marks? He could hardly hope to convince anyone a vampire had attacked his wife. Besides, it was too fanciful a touch for Sir Gerald.

The next most likely reason was that Theresa had somehow stumbled onto the robbery and been killed by the perpetrators. But that was so different from the death of the security guard. Even the police believed that death had been accidental. Why had it been necessary to kill her? Couldn't they just have thrown her in a shed or knocked her out? Maybe after the death of the guard they believed they had nothing to lose, but they must have worn masks. Was the thief someone Theresa would have known with or without a mask? If they hadn't worn masks, and she had seen their faces, would it have been necessary to kill her? How much was at stake?

For that matter, why had Theresa been wandering around alone outside?

Peter seemed to believe that her death was unrelated to the robbery, and, unfortunately, it appeared that he was in a position to know.

Grace's personal favorite suspect remained Miss Coke. True, she had learned nothing this evening that confirmed her suspicions about the woman in black, but she had certainly threatened Theresa; there were witnesses to that. And Miss Coke seemed more than a little unbalanced. Nobody outside of wronged women in Victorian novels and (in the words of one of Grace's former students) "freaking lunatics" carried on like Miss Coke. She was given to skulking; so it was not impossible that she might choose to skulk the night of the Hunt Ball, when all her enemies were gathered in one place.

Plus Miss Coke was said to be a witch,

and vampires were all part of the same club, weren't they?

Could Theresa have some unknown enemy? Surely if anyone had threatened her, she would have gone to the police. Her husband would know. Someone would know.

Her death might have appeared to be the result of a violent impulse except for the detail of the vampire bite. That mutilation implied planning, but surely more lay behind her murder than the wish to make it look like a vampire was running amuck in Innisdale?

One thing for sure, it was obvious that Theresa was not the random victim of a maniac.

"If someone is trying to sabotage the play," Grace said, breaking into the others' conversation, "who do you think it is?"

Catriona and her spouse exchanged a strange look.

"The old witch herself," Catriona said.

"Miss Coke?"

Catriona laughed. "Not *that* old witch. Lady Vee." She mimicked Lady Vee's ultraposh accent. "Lady Venetia Brougham, my *deah!*"

Fog damped out the sun, sponging all

color from the landscape. The occasional tree or signpost appeared like a ghost, then vanished. The scarlet and black jackets of the field were vivid against the twilight world the Innisdale Pack rode through.

It was a smaller field than previously, subdued in spirit. Even the hounds seemed irresolute, starting, then abandoning, one trail after another.

Grace noticed that the chief constable was not present — off hunting bigger game, no doubt.

She controlled the mare's eager tugging against the bit. The hounds were still uncertain, casting near and far, whining in frustration. The mare tossed her head, snaffle bit jingling.

"Easy, girl," Grace murmured, and Allegra, riding a few feet away, glanced at her sharply. In this gray void a snapping twig was as loud as a shot.

Everyone was on edge. Even Catriona looked surprisingly solemn. Sir Gerald looked ill, Grace thought. His face was puffy, and there were bags beneath his bloodshot eyes. Well, that was why she had chosen to ride: to see how those most closely connected to Theresa were taking her death.

The hounds broke into a lope, and the

rest of the pack cantered after, crossing a broad empty pasture. Grace was dimly aware of other riders as the field spread out around her, though they did not appear to have a line yet.

The miles melted away. The mist separated into patches of autumn sunlight and blue sky. The checkerboard fields of a farm loomed into view.

Mallow, Grace realized. They were nearing the property of the late Sam Jeffries.

And then one of the hounds gave voice. The others joined in, and they were off in full cry, racing across the land followed by the tattoo of drumming hooves.

"Yoi over!"

Far ahead, Grace saw the fox slip under a fence. The hounds poured after in flashes of white and brown. A rider cantered up to the gate, unlatching it, while other riders sailed over the fence. The less daring or "hilltoppers" filed through the gate.

Grace spotted a clear stretch and guided the mare toward it. Feeling the animal's approval, she kicked her forward. The mare flew at the fence as though she had wings. They landed solidly, cantering back to rejoin the others.

Grace found herself riding with Sir Gerald and Allegra. They appeared to be in some kind of old fruit orchard. The gnarled trees looked aggressively ancient, all bare knuckles and pointing fingers.

"Bloody hell!" exclaimed Sir Gerald. He halted and held his crop up, signaling the rest of the field to hold hard. "Smell that?"

"Garlic," said Allegra.

Sir Gerald began swearing. Yards ahead, Milliken turned to face them, arms spread in a gesture of defeat.

"What's happened?" Grace asked Allegra.

"These bloody saboteurs! They've sprayed the ground and foliage with garlic to ruin the scent."

Garlic? Garlic, which was used against vampires? Was there a weird connection here, or did Grace have vampires on the brain?

"They can't have sprayed the entire valley," Sir Gerald fumed.

Milliken blew the hunting horn in staccato blasts.

"Yo hote, Yo hote," urged the Whipper-in. The hounds began to zigzag, snuffling the leaf-buried ground frantically.

Slowly they advanced through the orchard.

The fog had followed them; it billowed languidly, shape-shifting through the trees.

"We don't have permission from the Shogun," Allegra said quietly to Sir Gerald.

Sir Gerald sputtered some dismissal, finishing, "I'll be damned if an Englishman needs permission from a bloody Jap to ride on English soil."

Charming, thought Grace.

If Allegra had a response, she never made it.

A shot rang out. Someone screamed. There was another shot.

Pandemonium ensued. There were shouts and cries; horses reared, appearing briefly before plunging back into the concealing fog. The hounds went mad.

Heart hammering, Grace flattened herself to her horse's neck and tried to place the direction the shots were coming from. The mare was fighting her, and Graced decided to rely on the animal's hearing, giving her her head. The bay was off like a shot.

"Retreat, retreat!" That was Sir Gerald. He charged past Grace, heading back the way they had come.

Catriona flew past, her hair whipping back from her white face. Another rider narrowly missed colliding with Grace. The wooden fence materialized out of the fog.

A crowd of horses and riders labored over it. Grace clenched her jaw and let the mare choose her spot. They were up and over — and away. The mare thrust out her neck and lengthened her stride. The miles dissolved beneath her hooves.

"There's something about a woman with a whip," Peter remarked as the gallery door opened, and Grace, dressed in full riding kit, entered.

"Someone shot at the hunt," she said. Proof of her agitation, she took a couple of steps into the shop and sat down on the nearest chair, a valuable Chippendale. She put her face in her hands.

"You've got to be joking." She clearly wasn't. Peter gave a low whistle and came to her.

"All right?" He knelt, and Grace lifted her face out of her hands.

Not many men could pose on one knee without losing either their dignity or balance, but Peter managed. His eyes were concerned, his expression serious. It was gratifying, to say the least.

"What the hell happened?"

"Someone fired shots — actual shots — at the hunt. No one was hurt, but . . ."

"Sabs?"

"I don't know. That's what everyone is saying."

His dark brows drew together. “But you think otherwise?”

“It did disrupt the hunt,” she admitted. She shook her head. “I don’t understand what’s happening.”

Peter rose. “Come on. Upstairs. You need a drink. I’m buying.”

It occurred to Grace that it was the first time she had seen him since their encounter in Sally Smithwick’s garden. She supposed it said something that he was the one she turned to when disaster struck. Then again, since he seemed to be involved in most of the disasters striking her, maybe it wasn’t so amazing.

She let herself be coaxed upstairs and plied with alcohol.

“Who rode today?” Peter asked absently, sitting beside her on the red leather sofa. His fingers found the pins holding her hair in place and removed them. He began to massage. Shivers of sensation rippled over her scalp.

“It was a smaller turnout. Sir Gerald rode. Allegra.” She couldn’t help the caustic note that crept into her voice. “Catriona.”

No comment from Peter.

“Derek wasn’t there. That’s not surprising. I think his real interest was Theresa.

Lord Ruthven never rides. Oh, and the chief constable wasn't there."

"No," Peter said dryly. "He was here."

"Oh." His long, strong fingers were working magic with the knotted muscles in her neck and at the base of her skull. She took another sip of brandy. "What do you know about Sam Jeffries?" she asked abruptly.

"Nice chap." Peter shrugged. "Rotten luck."

"But what was he like?"

Peter swallowed brandy. "Why?"

"Why not? Why does everyone clam up when I ask about Sam Jeffries?"

"Do they?" He lifted his shoulders in dismissal. "I can't speak for others, but I know you. I know what happens when you get inquisitive."

She loosened her stock. "You're still avoiding the question."

Peter sighed, sounding bored. "Sam Jeffries? He was one of these hearty man's man types. Fishing, hunting and pubbing with Sir Gerald and his merry band. Popular with the ladies."

"He owned Mallow Farm?"

"Correct."

"So he was wealthy."

"Relatively speaking." The blue eyes appraised her. "Come on, Miss Marple, give."

"I honestly don't know," Grace admitted. "But Miss Coke apparently had it in for Sam. We were on Mallow property today when we were fired on. That means we were only a few miles from Miss Coke's."

"It would be just about impossible to arrange a foxhunting accident unless you knew which way the fox was going to run, and how could you?"

"By dragging a false scent," Grace said. "A lot of hunt clubs do it if they don't want to actually kill a fox. Sabs do it. It's another method of disrupting a hunt."

"And she got Jeffries' horse to agree to miss its jump? Who is she, Dr. Doolittle?"

"Did anyone see the accident? Were there witnesses?"

"Half the hunt, I imagine. As MFH, Sir Gerald gave witness at the inquest. He swore there was nothing unusual. It's a dangerous sport. People die foxhunting."

"It's awfully convenient that two people on Miss Coke's hit list are dead."

"Accidents do happen, as the poets say."

"Theresa's death was not an accident."

"There is that," admitted Peter.

12

When Grace got in her answering machine was blinking. The first message was from Chaz asking her to meet for dinner. That was followed by Chief Constable Heron's deep voice requesting her presence at the police station. There was one last message from an alarmed-sounding Chaz, who had just heard about the shooting incident.

Grace chose police interrogation.

The chief constable looked weary as he closed his office door behind her and sat down at his desk.

"I understand there was trouble at the hunt."

Grace gave her version of the shooting. Heron listened without comment. Grace knew he was probably comparing her story to the others he must have heard that afternoon.

"So you did not actually see anyone?"

"The fog was too thick."

"Were you able to form an opinion as to which direction the shots came from?"

"Not really." Grace was apologetic. She

was annoyed with herself for being too flustered to pay closer attention.

Impulsively, she said, "You'll probably consider this another off-the-wall theory, but it's just occurred to me that Lady Ruthven, Catriona, has had a run-in with almost every member of *The Vampyre* cast."

"You think Lady Ruthven is picking off cast members?"

I wouldn't put it past her, Grace thought. She said only, "I told you about how she nearly fell through the broken trapdoor at the theater?"

"You did."

"That's not all," Grace said. "Catriona's saddle girth broke during the season's first official hunt. If she had been jumping at the time, she could have been seriously injured. I don't know how she wasn't."

Unless she was staging these accidents for some reason of her own?

Heron said nothing. Another thought struck Grace. "I suppose Sam Jeffries' billet straps were examined after his accident?"

To her surprise Heron chuckled. "Give us a little credit, Grace."

Grace blushed, realizing how officious she must sound.

"Everyone is saying hunt saboteurs opened fire on us."

"I'm aware of local opinion."

"But you don't agree?"

"I don't disagree," Heron said. "I don't know enough about the incident to have an opinion yet."

"What if it's not sabs? What if it has to do with Catriona?"

"Both incidents you've described would be imprecise methods of murder."

Grace made a face. "I know. It's probably coincidence."

"Most likely." Heron's shrewd eyes met hers briefly. After a significant pause, he added, "It is interesting that Lady Ives was wearing a cape similar to Lady Ruthven's when she was killed."

"I don't understand this whole vampire thing," Chaz was complaining.

He had attended rehearsal with Grace, and now they sat at the pub talking quietly to escape the notice of the other cast members who had stopped by for a pint.

It had not been much of a rehearsal. Theresa's death was a blow to the production, as much for psychological as practical reasons.

"You don't find vampires sexy?"

"Of course not. Have you ever seen *Nosferatu*? What's sexy about teeth like that?"

"Oh, but the modern concept of vampire is based on the Byronic vampire. Polidori's Ruthven, which he based on Lord Byron, is sort of the grandfather of all the vampires who followed, including Dracula."

"Bela Lugosi," Chaz agreed. "Now there was a sexy guy!"

Grace chuckled. "But think of all those half-naked Hammer Studio vampire ladies. They were supposed to represent a kind of unleashing of female sexuality."

"Evil female sexuality."

"Some people find evil sexy."

Chaz said glumly, "I know all about good girls seduced by bad boys."

Grace decided to ignore that. "Long before Lestat was a twinkle in Anne Rice's eye, the beautiful man with a dangerous secret was a staple of Gothic fiction. Heathcliff is sexy — even according to my jaded tenth-graders. Mr. Rochester is sexy. And by all accounts, Byron, who was, after all, the role model for all those Byronic heroes, was pretty darned sexy."

"None of them were vampires."

"Well, I guess there are a number of erotic elements to the vampire legend. What could be more intimate than the symbiotic relationship of the vampire and his chosen? I mean the victims that they turn into other vampires."

"Uh, vampires don't actually exist, Grace."

She made a face. "It's the whole symbolism. The vampire seduces his victim, feeding on the life force until he ultimately kills the thing he loves. And think about it: orgasm is sometimes referred to as the 'little death.' "

"By whom?" Chaz was plainly disapproving.

But Grace was on a roll, resting her elbows on the table in her enthusiasm. "Lovemaking involves the exchange of vital bodily fluids, and so does vampirism." She shrugged. "For whatever reason, it's very attractive to some people. You should see the Internet sites devoted to vampires. I don't mean academic research; I mean clubs and lifestyle."

"It just doesn't seem like your kind of thing, Grace."

She was startled. "It's not."

"I don't mean vampires, I mean getting involved with this play, with these weirdos."

Peter had said almost the same thing about the fete. Did she really seem so stuck in her ways?

"I don't know if it's my kind of thing. Isn't

that what life is about, growing, changing, becoming?"

Chaz's face wrinkled as though he found it hard to hear her. "I just don't know what you're doing with all these nuts. And what's with the Honorable This and Lord That? Everybody in this one-horse town has a title. It's . . . I don't know . . ."

"Un-American?"

"Hey, you're an American," Chaz said. "Don't forget it."

"I don't forget it. That doesn't mean I can't appreciate another country's culture. Especially since my grandparents were English."

"I didn't know that."

Why didn't you? Grace wondered. Why did we never truly know each other? We went out for years, but in many ways we're still strangers. Grace had been no better than Chaz. She had been satisfied with smooth surfaces.

The irony was that, while no place on earth seemed more picture-perfect than Innisdale, it was here that Grace was learning to understand about the danger that sometimes lurked beneath the placid surface.

An ormolu-and-sphinx-decorated standing

clock dominated the marble entrance hall of Lady Vee's domicile. Grace had a brief wait before the butler returned to usher her into the royal presence. She listened to the clock ticking down the minutes. It sounded unnervingly loud in the still house.

The room, like its owner, seemed to be a relic from another age, right down to the Empire furniture and gold-starred, black portieres. There was a gigantic portrait of a beautiful woman with ebony hair cut Egyptian style. She wore a sheer green gown and held a plumy fan, sort of like a flapper Cleopatra. Lady Vee in her younger days, Grace deduced.

Lady Vee, exuding lukewarm cordiality for Grace's unexpected visit, broke out the sherry bottle. It was probably excellent sherry, if you cared for sherry, which Grace did not. She murmured, "Lovely," and got to the point. "It may seem like an odd question, but I wanted to ask you how I came to be invited to join *The Vampyre* production."

"The only oddity is why it's taken you so long to ask that particular question," the old charmer retorted, refilling her own glass.

Grace worked it out. "Meaning that my presence wasn't necessary?" Or welcome apparently.

"It was necessary to someone, it would seem."

"The Ruthvens?"

Lady Vee smiled, looking uncannily like the sphinx in the main hall. "Won't you stay for luncheon, my *deah?*" she invited.

Wednesday's meal turned out to be a Sunday roast with all the trimmings. The beef was marinated in cider. It was served with a celeriac-and-potato bake topped with Gruyère cheese.

Over watercress soup Grace again brought up the subject of the Ruthvens, asking how they had become involved in the Innisdale Playhouse production.

"I've no idea," Lady Vee said. "Allegra would know. Allegra convinced me to support this project."

"Allegra has been active in the local theater for some time now?"

"Allegra devotes her time to many worthy causes." Lady Vee's mouth primly enfolded her soupspoon.

Allegra needs a job, Grace thought. She said politely, "Did Allegra mention any credentials the Ruthvens might have? I've heard several people refer to the fact that Lord Ruthven is a big name in London theater; I just wondered what that impression might be based on?"

Lady Vee's eyes flickered. "It was common knowledge."

"As it is common knowledge that he is Lord Ruthven?"

"Bah!" Lady Vee reacted predictably. "That man is no more Lord Ruthven than I am."

She had suggested as much the night of the Hunt Ball, but her conviction was interesting. "Peter said something similar. What makes you think he's not Lord Ruthven?"

"Why not ask *deah Petah?*"

"Because he won't tell me. I think you will."

The dark eyes were lizardlike beneath the emerald-shadowed lids, then Lady Vee replied simply, "Because he's not Scottish, *she* is!"

"And Ruthven is a Scottish name? But if she inherited the title —"

Such base ignorance on the all-important topic of inheritance and titles within the British nobility seemed to disconcert Lady Vee. "It doesn't work that way," she managed finally, sounding exasperated.

"All right, but she could still be —"

"I have no idea of that creature's antecedents," Lady Venetia said sweepingly. "I know only that she is what we used to call a 'wrrrrong 'un.' " Lady Vee rolled her R's as though she, too, had spent a fair amount of time roamin' in the gloamin'.

"A 'wrong 'un'?"

Lady Vee looked impatient. "An outlaw. In animals we call it 'rogue.' She is a rogue. A wrong 'un."

"What do you base that theory on?" Grace couldn't help the skepticism that crept into her voice. Pride and prejudice seemed to be thriving in this tiny corner of the realm.

Lady Vee smiled a sly smile. "Because, my *deah,* I was rather something of a wrong 'un myself once."

Grace was still chewing that over when Allegra joined them.

"Sorry I'm late." She nodded without enthusiasm to Grace. "I didn't realize we had company."

"How is poor Gerry?" Lady Vee rang the bell at her elbow.

"Dreadful. The police are hounding him," Allegra said crisply. She cast a brief look Grace's way. She looked tired, but her cheeks were attractively flushed, her eyes bright with indignation and another emotion.

Maybe things would work out for Allegra this time, Grace reflected, then guiltily, she thought of poor Theresa, who wasn't even buried yet.

Lady Vee said, "Grace was curious as to how she came to be invited to take part in *The Vampyre* production."

Allegra expelled a long angry breath, and said, "How the devil anyone can care about that bloody play after what's happened is beyond me!"

"Don't be vulgar," Lady Vee retorted. "In any case you miss the point." She was silent while a maid came in and served Allegra. When they were alone again, she said patiently, "How is it that the Ruthvens came to be so well entrenched in the theater group? Were they invited, or did they volunteer?"

Grace decided to cut to the chase. "How did you know that they were who they said they were?"

"Why wouldn't they be? What could they possibly hope to gain by pretending to be the Ruthvens?"

Once again the Hon. Al seemed to have missed the point. Still, she had started Grace thinking. The Ruthvens didn't have to participate in local theater in order to worm their way into Innisdale "society." Nor were they likely to make any money on the project. They had not solicited financial backing other than Lady Vee's; the play was more likely to cost them money.

"Did they just show up one night, or did someone invite them?" Grace pressed.

Allegra shook her head. "I suppose they turned up one evening, but we all knew about them. The entire village knew about them."

Grace tried to examine it from another angle. The Ruthvens' servants would talk, of course, but the servants would only know what they were told. They might even be in on the scam, whatever the scam was. The majority of people would take the Ruthvens at their word — why not? Everyone would assume someone else had firsthand knowledge of their background. They would really need only one local person to vouch for them, and they'd be home free.

An innocuous memory slid into her mind as suddenly as a spinout on a rain-slick road. "Has anyone besides the Ruthvens recently moved into or out of the village?"

The other two women exchanged glances. "I don't think so," Allegra said. "Why?"

"Because the night after the Thwaite robbery I remember seeing a moving van that had gone off the road in Innisdale Wood."

"And this is leading us where?" Lady Vee queried.

"I'm not sure myself, but I'm wondering what a big moving van would be doing in this neck of the woods when nobody has moved lately. We're a bit off the beaten track."

"There could be any explanation." Allegra dismissed Grace's half-formed suspicions. "It doesn't mean they were transporting stolen loot, if that's what you're getting at."

"Well, a lot of things were taken," Grace pointed out. "Furniture, rugs, paintings. A moving van would be a conspicuously inconspicuous way of transporting stolen merchandise, if you understand my meaning. I never gave that van another thought. Most people don't. Moving vans aren't unusual — except here, where people tend to root in for generations."

"What does this have to do with the Ruthvens?" Allegra asked impatiently.

"Nothing. It just reminded me —" It was obvious that neither woman thought she was making any sense. Grace changed the subject. "Getting back to the Ruthvens, did anyone know them from before?"

"Before what? I don't see what you're getting at," Allegra said.

"Just . . . did anyone actually know them in London, or did everyone assume they were theater big shots because everyone else seemed to?"

In the tone of one hoping to settle an argument once and for all, Allegra said, "Derek knew them. Derek worked with Lord Ruthven years ago."

Derek Derrick lived in a small cottage with a peacock blue door and a weather vane in the shape of a running fox. The window boxes were barren, and the house had an unlived-in air, although Derek answered the door on the third ring of the doorbell.

"Grace!" He studied her with open surprise. "Come in. I was wishing for a bit of company." He was wearing a blue-and-gold smoking jacket over a pair of trousers and slippers. His fair hair was mussed, and he needed a shave, but he was still strikingly good-looking.

"How are you holding up?" Grace inquired, following him into the front room. The room was casually furnished. There was dust an inch thick on the tables and mantel. Newspapers and movie magazines littered the floor by the sofa. Mrs. Mac clearly did not "do" for Derek Derrick.

"How sweet of you to ask," he said, heading for the drinks cabinet. "One day at a time, you know. It's a beastly situation with the police sticking their oar in." He did look tired. Or (with recollection of how some of the young ladies at St. Anne's used to drag in on Monday mornings) possibly hungover. Grace wondered if the police were "hounding" him, too, or if everyone simply felt hounded.

"Allegra says the police are giving Sir Gerald a rough time as well."

"Not bloody likely, is it?" Derek jabbed in the ice bucket with tongs. "Although he is the main suspect in my opinion. But he's one of *them*. Makes all the difference. See if it doesn't."

"It must be terrible for you," Grace sympathized.

Derek shrugged. "No more me than everyone else. I mean, Theresa was a lovely girl, and we had our bit of fun; but it's not like I was her first and only, is it? It's not like we were planning to run off together or anything daft. Even the plods can see that it wouldn't make sense for me to touch a hair on the poor girl's head."

He seemed to be trying to convince himself as well as Grace.

"I think they merely have to investigate every possibility," Grace said. "When I talked to the chief constable he seemed convinced the murder was connected to the theft of the Peeler."

"Now *that* makes sense," he said, pouring a liberal dose of gin into his glass. "Although why anyone would bother stealing that old tin can beats me. It can't be worth that much. Mostly sentimental value, I'd say." He reached for the tonic bottle.

"The papers say it's valued at over a hundred thousand pounds."

"Chicken feed," Derek scoffed. "When you think of the sorts of things those villains have been liberating, I can't see why they'd bother with that old trinket. Drink?"

"Thanks." Derek had a point. The other robberies had been meticulously planned. The Hunt Ball had been unreasonably risky — and Theresa's death was a disaster.

Derek brought her a gin and tonic and flopped down in the chair near the stereo. "They say old Gerry is talking about having Scotland Yard brought in."

"Do the Metropolitan police help out in local matters?"

"They can do. Depends on the circumstances." He took a long swallow of his drink.

Grace remembered her own drink and sipped the gin and tonic. It was very strong. "I actually wanted to ask you about the Ruthvens," she said, finally getting up her nerve.

Derek reached over and turned on the

stereo. Frank Sinatra, sounding a long way from home, crooned into Grace's ear.

"He's a genius, she's a bitch," Derek said, his smile crooked. "What else would you like to know?"

Raising her voice to be heard over Frank, Grace said, "So you'd worked with him before?"

Derek noticed his glass was empty. He rose, sloshed more gin in. She had to strain to hear him answer, "Years ago. Before he made a name for himself. Before he married *her*."

"You don't care for Catriona?"

His smile was acrid. "Does anyone?"

Old Blue Eyes was waxing earnest about "Strangers in the Night." You have no idea, thought Grace. Out loud she said, "Can I ask you something? Who suggested that I be invited in as technical advisor?"

Derek studied her curiously. "I don't know. I don't think I paid much attention to those discussions. Why?"

Grace shrugged and put down her drink. "Just curious."

Derek smiled very whitely. "You know what they say about curiosity and cats, old thing."

As female sleuths went, Grace reflected as

she undressed for bed that evening, she was afraid she was more the Hildegard Withers and less the Kinsey Millhone type. Grace had a built-in lie detector after years of teaching guileful adolescents; but while she was pretty sure no one was telling her the complete truth, it was difficult to pin down the actual lies. She knew, again from years of teaching, that people sometimes fibbed about the silliest and most unimportant things — and for reasons that made little sense to anyone else.

As her head sank into the flannel softness of her pillow, Grace hazily tried to find the pattern in all she had heard that day. After a full day of sleuthing, did she really know anything for sure, or was everything simply another person's flawed perception?

She was still counting riddles when she fell asleep . . .

In Grace's dream someone was pounding on her door. She opened her eyes and it was still nighttime. Behind the closed draperies lances of moonlight sliced the dark.

Lying there, she listened to the apple tree scratching against the walls of the Gardener's Cottage. Listened, listened . . .

An apple dropped on the roof of the cottage, making a bumping sound. Grace's heart skipped and slowed.

She had slept deeply, but was now restless with the questions that had subtly infiltrated her dreams.

Why had someone tried to make it look like Theresa had been bitten by a vampire?

Why steal the Peeler the night of the Hunt Ball?

Was Sam Jeffries' death an accident?

What was Peter hiding from her?

The moon seemed to be exerting the same effect it had on tides. Grace rose and went to the window, pulling back the drapes.

Miss Coke stood framed in the picture window.

13

The woman in black stood motionless like some ghostly apparition, pallid-faced in the moonlight, her features shadowed but somehow malevolent.

Grace sucked in her breath to scream and at the same time yanked shut the drapes. She couldn't quite explain the instinct of shutting out the picture of Miss Coke by moonlight; but as the curtain closed, Miss Coke's spell was broken.

Grace went to the phone and dialed the police station.

"Oh my gosh!" she said out loud, as the phone rang and rang on the other end. The sound of her own exasperated voice steadied her.

At last a sleepy-sounding male answered. She explained her situation. The PC, having ascertained that Miss Coke could not get into the cottage — and did not appear to be making any attempt to get into the cottage — seemed inclined to finish investigating in the morning.

Grace yanked back the drapes again.

Moonlight gilded tree and flower, but there was no sign of the witch of Innisdale Wood. Miss Coke had vanished — or possibly retreated behind a bush.

"There, you see!" The PC was triumphant.

Grace sympathized, she really did. It was a cold night. Her bare feet shrank from the stone floor, and there had been frost on the garden grass; but she felt compelled to point out that one woman had recently been murdered, and Miss Coke was a possible suspect.

The PC did not seem to agree, but he reluctantly said he'd send someone around to her cottage. Grace sat down on the edge of her bed to wait.

She was so tired. She decided to lie down and rest for a few minutes before the constable showed up. He would surely be there in a minute or two. She would consider the situation carefully. Sometimes it was easier to think with one's eyes closed . . .

"Are you avoiding me?" Chaz demanded.

"If I were avoiding you, would I be asking you out to lunch?" Grace inquired reasonably.

Despite her interrupted night's rest she was feeling much more herself this morning. She had treated herself to a long lazy bubble bath and several cups of jasmine tea while she made detailed notes of everything she had heard and learned the day before.

She had dried and dressed leisurely in her favorite garnet red chenille sweater and most comfortable faded jeans. She had filed a complaint against Miss Coke and another against the PC who had been on duty the night before and brushed off her midnight phone call for help. She had made another appointment to see the chief constable later that afternoon. She felt productive. She felt positive. She felt like being nice to Chaz.

"Where did you want to meet?" Chaz asked suspiciously. "Not that pub again. God, I'm sick of English food. And not that Indian place. I didn't like the way that guy was staring at me."

"Who?"

"Hamid or whatever his name was. The owner."

"Ahmed."

"Whatever."

"If you don't mind a short drive, we can have lunch in Kendal," Grace said, seized by inspiration. It would be good to be away from Innisdale for a short time.

Chaz professed himself agreeable, and an

hour later they were on their way to one of Grace's favorite towns in the Lake District.

Kendal possessed (according to one survey) the highest quality of life in all England. Its historical coaching inns and quaint pubs, museums and galleries and myriad shops made the twelfth-century town a bustling tourist center, but this time of year its narrow streets and alleys were comparatively quiet.

After doing a little window shopping they lunched at the Kings Arms Hotel, Grace ordering the Lake Windermere char served with nut brown butter and Chaz playing it safe with T-bone steak.

"Have you given any more thought to coming back to work?" he asked, carving his steak with a fixity that suggested this was a grudge match.

"Of course."

"And?"

"I don't know. The book isn't finished."

"Book! I haven't seen you write one page since I got here. You never even mention the thing. You aren't staying here for that book, and you know it."

"I could finish the book at home, that's true."

"Home." Chaz pounced on this. "See, you still think of home as home. Grace, face

it, your future is there. You've got people who love you, respect you, *want* you. What do you have here but a lot of inbred snobs trying to kill each other off?"

Grace sipped her wine to give herself time.

Earnestly, Chaz said, "You've got to make your mind up soon, Grace. Ms. Winters won't be patient forever. She thinks the world of you, but other people have her ear now. Luckily the only misstep you ever made was showing that R movie to your senior lit class."

Grace swallowed the wrong way. It took a minute to get her breath back; at last she demanded hoarsely, "Are you telling me that someone brought *that* up?"

"Andrea."

The single blemish on Grace's record was a mistake early in her teaching career. She had shown the film *Haunted Summer* to her senior romantic lit class. The film detailed the summer Byron, the Shelleys, Clair Clairmont and Dr. Polidori spent at the Villa Diodati on Lake Geneva. It was a beautiful scenic film; unfortunately a lot of the beautiful scenery was of *les* literary *enfants terrible* cavorting in R-rated adventures. Grace had learned to pay greater attention to film ratings.

"That was over five years ago!"

"I know, but it could be interpreted as a warning sign, a tendency toward . . . flightiness."

"Flightiness?"

"Well, it's not so far off, is it?" Chaz looked pointedly around them.

She hated to think he might have a point.

Grace tried to conceal her preoccupation from Chaz on the drive back to Innisdale, but when she could politely escape, she did so, heading straight for the library computer to see what she could find on the amazing theatrical career of Robert Ruthven. What she discovered was indeed amazing — mostly because there was no theatrical career.

There were plenty of Ruthven web pages, many of them devoted to the occult and vampires.

There was also historical information on the murder of David Rizzio, secretary to and possible lover of Mary Queen of Scots, in which, apparently, the Ruthvens had played a starring role.

According to one account the mortally ill Lord Patrick Ruthven had held a sword to the pregnant belly of the young queen while her "Seigneur Davie" was stabbed before her eyes by her husband and his noble coconspirators.

"Lovely people," murmured Grace.

However, there was not a single reference to a producer or director by the name of Ruthven. Not one. If Bob was experiencing a career slump it was a drastic one.

Since Ruthven did not have a theatrical pedigree, did that mean Derek had lied about working with him? But it was such a stupid lie, why bother?

Even more puzzling, why bother to stage a play if you were not a theatrical producer or director?

Perhaps it was something silly and sad like Bob Ruthven wanted to be a director and had faked his background in order to . . . stage an obscure provincial production that no one of consequence would ever see?

But that would require Catriona's cooperation, and Catriona did not seem like a woman with patience for foolish dreams.

In fact, Grace was willing to bet that Catriona was the one behind it all. Behind everything, from Grace's involvement in *The Vampyre* to Theresa's murder. But how? Why?

"What are you looking for?"

Grace started out of her reverie. Roy Blade, hair pulled back in a highwayman's ponytail, good eye agleam with curiosity, stood over her.

Her fingers twitched toward the close button, but she stopped herself.

"I was trying to settle a bet with myself."

"Yeah? What's the bet?"

"I was betting that Lady Vee brought me into *The Vampyre* production."

Blade laughed. "You lose. Now you want to tell me what you're surfing the Net for?"

"Who did bring me in?"

"I did. Remember?"

She did sort of, now that he mentioned it. Maybe her paranoia was beginning to run away with her. "But why? Was it all your own idea?"

"I do have ideas of my own once in a while." He was enjoying making her work for it. "I thought it would be a laugh watching you and Lady Be Damned square off."

His revelation did not fit at all with the theory that was nebulously taking shape in Grace's mind. Seeing her disappointment, Blade laughed, and said, "And Catriona kept asking about you, kept hinting that she thought you'd be an asset."

"She can't stand me."

"I thought that was interesting myself," Blade agreed.

Her phone was ringing as Grace let herself into the cottage. She picked the receiver up, but before she could speak a voice so low she could barely make out the words whispered, "Can you meet me at the theater in ten minutes?"

"Very funny, Chaz."

"It's Bob." Lord Ruthven spoke more loudly, though not much. "I must see you. I haven't much time. They're watching me."

"I see we were raised on the same movies," Grace returned. "Bob, you must realize that nothing on earth would convince me to go to a secret assignation in a deserted theater, especially when I know you've been lying about your . . . well, pretty much everything!"

"It's broad daylight," Lord Ruthven protested. "What do you imagine could happen to you? As for the rest, well . . . that's what I want to explain."

Funny that the heroines of movies and novels never had to debate the wisdom of secluded meetings with the strangers who summoned them by phone. It made it all seem less sinister and more annoying.

"I'm not coming alone. I'll call —"

"We don't have that kind of time! Look, you've got questions, I've got answers." Lord Ruthven concluded, "Park in the back and come through the side door."

"You have *got* to be ki—"

The receiver clicked, and the line went dead before she could respond.

The wind was blowing a misty silvery rain when Grace parked behind the Innisdale Playhouse. The lot was deserted. A lone cat, scrounging in the trash bin, cast her a baleful look and went back to foraging.

Grace got out and went round to the side of the building, pushing open the heavy door and slipping inside.

Rows of empty chairs sat at attention in the gloom. The stage was lit but empty.

"Hello?" Grace called. "Lord Ruthven? Bob?"

The theater creaked in the wind like a sinking ship.

This is not only dumb, it's clichéd, Grace told herself disgustedly. She knew full well what she would say to one of her girls who walked into this kind of setup. She considered backing out — literally.

"Is anyone — ?" She broke off, hand tightening on the push bar as she heard . . . what? A groan? A muffled sound of human origin.

The curtains rippled at the far end of the stage, and a hand reached out to grab the folds of material. Lord Ruthven stood swaying, one hand on the wall jamb, one clutching the curtain.

Grace left her place of safety, starting down the aisle to go to his aid. As she drew near the stage she began to notice details, like the bright red blood on Ruthven's hands. Her eyes focused on the thing that seemed out of place, the thing protruding from Lord Ruthven's chest.

She froze, hands going to stop the scream welling up. Lord Ruthven's eyes, ghastly in his cavernous face, focused on her. His mouth worked, then languidly, almost in slow motion, he crumpled to the stage floor.

The instinct to aid another human warred with the need for self-preservation. She had been lured to this theater, there were no cars outside, Lord Ruthven had been wounded and that wound was not self-inflicted.

There was a stake through his heart.

Well, no. Not through his heart, horrified common sense asserted. He couldn't be walking, he couldn't be *alive* . . . But he definitely had something protruding out of him where nothing should protrude . . .

With a terrible reluctance she approached the stage, watching all around herself for any movement in the shadows. But as she started up the steps, Lord Ruthven's eyes opened.

"Run," he whispered.

Grace backed down the steps and ran, banging out the side door. She heard it slam shut with great finality behind her.

She ran all the way to her car. Driving down to the pub, she asked them to call the police, then drove straight back to the theater.

She debated with herself whether to go back in or not, but caution prevailed. Bright rain billowed, the gusts of wind shook her car while she waited.

The police arrived within five minutes, pulling up in a marked car, lights flashing. Two uniformed constables, a man and a woman, got out and approached Grace.

"Inside," she said, and led the way across the empty lot.

The outside theater door was locked.

"It wasn't locked," Grace protested, looking from one constable to the other. She rummaged in her purse and found the keys. The door unlocked, they crowded inside. The theater was dark and silent.

The constables were also silent. Ominously silent. Grace felt around for the light switch. Rows and rows of faded chairs sat empty. Grace found another switch and the stage was illuminated.

And empty.

One of the constables sighed. She was a middle-aged woman, Asian, with a slightly pinched look around her mouth as though her feet hurt.

"I know what you're thinking," Grace said, "but this is not a prank. Do I look like the kind of person who plays pranks on the police?"

The other constable, this one chubby and bewhiskered like Bob Cratchit in a Christmas pantomime, eyed her gravely. "Perhaps someone is playing a prank on you, miss."

It wasn't inconceivable with all the weird things that had been happening, but Grace remembered the appalling look in Ruthven's eyes. She shook her head.

"At least look around," she pleaded. "Maybe he crawled backstage." And turned off the lights and locked the doors? The officers didn't point this out, but she knew if this had occurred to her it had certainly occurred to them.

"His murderer could still —"

She broke off at their skeptical expressions.

They trooped up to the stage and looked behind the props. They looked inside the wooden coffin. The woman PC knelt to examine the scratched stage boards. She shook her head.

"I'll check backstage," Bob Cratchit said. "There must be dressing rooms." He pawed his way through the first row of curtains.

Grace grabbed the edge of curtain drifting in his wake. *"Look!"*

The dried imprint of blood on the silken material could be seen in the tired overhead light.

"There have been threats. Vague threats, but . . . threats. Perhaps someone believed that Lord Ruthven really is — was — is a vampire, and attacked him." Grace rubbed her aching temples.

The constables exchanged looks. They had been doing a lot of that for the past few minutes, ever since they determined that there was no one else in the building. They were inclined to believe the bloody handprint was fake. They were inclined to believe the whole incident was a prank. Grace had been trying to convince them, but the more she theorized, the less convinced they seemed. Clearly the crime scene team was not going to be summoned anytime soon.

"Were there any cars in the lot when you arrived, ma'am?" The Bob Cratchit constable pronounced it like "Mom," which was disconcerting, since Grace was only a bit older than he. "Any indication that someone was present besides the — er — victim."

They kept saying that: "The — er — victim."

"I think there was a car out front on the street," Grace said slowly. She remembered starting for the pub and the glimpse of a parked car in her rearview mirror. Black, medium-sized . . . nothing distinct.

"Did you recognize the car?"

"Not really. It wasn't that kind of car, and I barely registered it."

"You didn't see any part of the registration plate?"

Grace shook her head regretfully.

They asked a few more questions, routine questions, then they departed, ostensibly to call upon the Ruthvens, but Grace feared more like to break for dinner.

"You will let me know what happens?" she called after their departing backs.

"You'll be hearing from us, ma'am," the female PC said, without turning back.

The lights shone cheerily in the upstairs level of Craddock House. The tang of a wood fire seasoned the dank evening air. Staring up at the windows Grace had never felt more alone, more out in the cold. She rang the bell.

She sensed rather than saw draperies move in the windows above.

It was only a minute or two before Peter let her in, his expression wary. "You're very formal this evening."

She wasted no time on preliminaries. "Did you know she was going to kill him?"

"This is obviously a trick question."

Grace cried, "How can you joke about this? She *murdered* him. She probably murdered Theresa. How can you be okay with this?"

"Would it help if I tell you I don't know what the hell you're talking about?" He was very still, his voice quiet in contrast to hers. His eyes held hers levelly.

"Bob — Lord Ruthven called me this afternoon and asked me to meet him at the theater. He said he had something to tell me."

"And you went?" Peter stared at her in disbelief. "That's the oldest trick in the world." The Chinese opera masks formed a mute and scowling chorus on the wall behind him, pale faces frozen in expressions of terrifying disapproval.

"I thought he was going to say we had to cancel the play. I thought . . . I don't know what I thought. Anyway, it wasn't a trick. He did have something to tell me, but he never got the chance because your girlfriend murdered him."

"Ruthven is dead? Have the police made an arrest?"

"The police don't believe me because when they got there she had taken his body."

"Huh?" It was a very un-Peter-like utterance. His black brows drew together.

"He was dying when I found him. He had a stake through his —"

Peter put a hand to his forehead. "Wait," he said. "Is this some macabre joke? I know you're angry —"

"No."

He stared narrowly as though she had suddenly transformed into some dangerous and unpredictable animal.

"If it's not a joke on you, it's a joke on me," he said at last.

"It's no joke. He was dying. He had a — he had been stabbed. Sort of. I went to get help, and when the police arrived, he was gone."

"Grace." He put his arms around her. She told herself she should resist, but the familiar feel of his strong arms, the warmth of his body against her own was a comfort she could not deny herself. "Don't you see? That performance was staged for your benefit. When you brought the coppers, Ruthven rang down the curtain."

Curtains, she thought dully. Curtains for Lord Ruthven, certainly.

"It was more theatrics for your benefit. Fake blood, stage makeup. I'm guessing you didn't get close enough to examine his wound."

"He wasn't faking." She could hear his heart pounding, her head pressed against his chest. A steady, untroubled beat.

"You didn't touch him."

She lifted her head, trying to read his expression. "He couldn't have faked the look in his eyes."

His lean cheek creased in sardonic humor. "It's called acting, darling. People make a living at faking that very kind of thing, Lord Ruthven being one of them. They can create believable monsters from outer space, let alone fake some blood. Ruthven's an actor."

She pulled back from him. "A director. It's not the same thing. Besides, why would he fake his death?"

"Who the hell knows? Why would he call you in the first place?"

"Because he must have known something about Theresa's murder."

"That's a stretch. Why didn't he go to the

police? Why drag you into it? You're not involved."

"Maybe I am."

"No, you're not." He had not turned on the downstairs lamp so it was increasingly difficult to read his expression in the dying light, but he spoke with a certain finality.

"Okay, then say Ruthven did lure me there solely to scare the wits out of me. Why? What possible good could scaring me do anyone?"

He didn't have an answer, and they both knew it.

14

Chief Constable Heron waited for Grace as she made her way through the soggy garden to her cottage, his black umbrella standing out like some ominous bloom amidst the wet shrubs.

"A few words, Grace."

She could not read his expression in the dying light, but she was still "Grace" and not "Miss Hollister," so at least she wasn't in complete disgrace.

She let him into the cottage and felt for the light switch. The rain peppered against the windows. Tea, she thought. Tea was just the thing she needed. But she said dispiritedly, because she was depressed that Peter had not made any move to keep her — and because she would not have trusted herself to stay even if he had, "I suppose you're going to tell me my imagination is working overtime, too?"

"No." Heron was busy with his umbrella, but something in the way he spoke that single word alerted her.

"Why? Has something happened?" She

paused, midway to the kitchen. "Have you found Lord Ruthven?"

"No."

Again, something in the single syllable prompted Grace to press. "But something *has* happened? What did Lady Ruthven say?"

"Lady Ruthven was not available for comment," the chief constable stated. He added grimly, "They've gone."

"Gone?"

"Packed up and left. The house is closed." Heron's weathered face was chagrined.

"Did they leave a forwarding address?"

His black eyes seemed to snap with some lively emotion she couldn't read. "Apparently the plan is to stay with friends in Romania."

"Romania?"

Heron's tone was sour. "To be precise, Transylvania."

The window scraped open. Grace pulled herself up, balanced on the sill, and dropped down into the dark room.

Tensely she waited for some noise, for lights to go on, for some sign that her first try at B & E was going to end in Chief Constable Heron's office.

But nothing happened.

She stood in the silence and shadows, surrounded only by a ghostly assemblage of furniture in dust sheets.

Grace switched on her flashlight.

She wasn't sure what she hoped to find — other than reassurance that the Ruthvens really were gone.

And gone they did appear to be, departing with a blitzkrieg speed and efficiency. Grace walked through room after room, footsteps echoing down the corridors.

She knew a bit about the history of the Monkton estate, tales of tragedy and betrayal during the final days of World War II. The house was still owned by the Monkton family, though it had been more than a generation since any had lived there. In fact, the house had not been leased for years, not until the Ruthvens had briefly taken it.

As she entered a long room of bay windows, drapes drawn against any ray of sun, Grace's flashlight beam picked up two eyes and she sucked in her breath. The next moment she expelled it. The eyes were painted. She knew the painting, recognized it from both *Gothic* and *Haunted Summer*. Was this a stage prop or the original of Romantic painter Henry Fuseli's *The Nightmare*?

A floorboard creaked as she approached the fireplace and the painting hanging above it. An incubus squatted on a sleeping woman's stomach. The incubus seemed to be staring straight at Grace.

She was reminded of a line by Victor Hugo, *The malicious have a dark happiness.* It seemed strangely apt in this house that had sheltered Catriona and her companion.

Was this painting a clue? Surely it was not part of the original furnishings? So what was its significance?

Grace examined the fireplace grate. It looked like some papers had recently been burned. She sifted through the gray ashes and brown curls of paper. A newspaper? She lined the largest pieces up on the floor and studied them in the circle of her flashlight beam.

. . . ossachs. Rang. LY RECORD.

It might as well be hieroglyphs. Grace sighed heavily, and her carefully accumulated clues blew across the floor. She scrambled to retrieve them, and put the crumbs of paper in her pocket to be examined later. She left the room, starting upstairs.

How could they vanish without a trace? They must have started packing the night of Theresa's murder.

Which meant what?

Obviously, Catriona was involved in the murder. That had to be what Ruthven had wanted to tell Grace, but Catriona had stopped him.

Except . . . there was a logistical problem or two with that. Catriona was strong and agile, but was it probable that she could carry an unconscious man out of a theater and clean up all traces of blood and escape without a trace within fifteen minutes?

In fact, it would take a fair amount of upper body strength to impale someone with a piece of wood. Would a woman have that kind of strength? Assuming that Peter was wrong, and this wasn't an elaborate hoax, Catriona must have had an accomplice.

Clearly *not* Lord Ruthven.

Some unknown henchman?

Or someone else? Someone she'd known and trusted for years. The kind of man who kept his head under pressure, who lied as naturally as he breathed, whose stomach wasn't turned by violence, who didn't shrink from the idea of doing something illegal.

A man like Peter.

Downstairs the phone began to ring, shrilling through the vacant hush. Grace ran downstairs and picked it up. She did not speak.

A man's voice said something she did not understand. Because he did not speak clearly or because she didn't recognize the words?

If she spoke, she would give herself away. She compromised on a toneless grunt.

"Dé?" The sharp tone was one of interrogation. The word was foreign. Romanian? She had no idea, and she did not dare reply again.

Silence stretched on both ends of the line — then it was cut by the dial tone.

She was coming out of the library the next morning — having spent a fruitful couple of hours comparing typography and newspaper mastheads — when she spotted Peter leaving the bakery a few doors down.

How anyone could be thinking of baked goods at a time like this was beyond Grace. It was even more vexing that Peter should look so relaxed and at ease with the world.

As he opened the door to his Land Rover she considered him rather critically, from the gleam of his fair hair to the dull sheen of his leather boots. He did wear Levi's well, she had to admit. Slim hips and long legs, that was the key.

As though feeling himself watched, Peter glanced around and caught her eye.

Just for a moment he looked pleased to see her. His expression changed almost instantly to wariness.

"What's up?"

"I've just been doing a little research."

His mouth thinned, but he said lightly, "Improving your mind, or are you snooping for something in particular?"

She ignored this, nodding at the white sack he held.

"Grocery shopping?" It was a silly question, but she wanted to keep him standing there, talking to her. She missed him. She hated being on opposite sides. She would have liked to call a truce — and not just to share what she suspected he carried in that paper bag.

"No, I was robbing the bakery. I've got a bag of hot croissants."

He was joking, but there was a bite to it.

Grace couldn't seem to help herself. She said, "They're gone, you know."

"Who?" She had his full attention now.

"Mary Queen of Plots and her minions. Supposedly they've gone to visit friends in Transylvania. That's what the note they left said."

Out of the corner of her eye she saw his hand tighten on the door frame. Then he relaxed. "I've heard it's lovely this time of year."

"Lord Ruthven vanished with them. But I spoke to the chief constable this morning. The police did check on that smeared handprint on the theater curtains — and it was real blood."

He was so still she couldn't see him breathe. Then he swallowed.

"I see."

She had never seen his face look like that. He was a stranger again. It was a stranger who glanced at his watch as though recollecting himself, smiled a cool, contained smile, and said, "Fascinating. Forgive me, love, but I've got to run."

He threw the sack inside the Land Rover and slid in, slamming shut the door. Just for an instant, as he started the engine, his eyes met hers through the windshield.

Then he gave her a curt nod and put the car in reverse.

Grace watched him swing in an efficient arc and speed off down the road. And she knew that he had told her the absolute truth: he was going to run.

She made her decision there and then, and went to get her car.

Speeding south along the A65, Grace kept Peter's Land Rover just in sight with one car between them.

She feared the robin's-egg blue of the Aston Martin stood out like a hot-air balloon in the gray morning, but Peter was driving fast, and Grace was willing to bet his mind was preoccupied with whatever had sent him shooting back to Craddock House and then out once more into the drizzling morning — Gladstone bag in hand.

Even preoccupied as she was, Grace could not help but notice the dramatic beauty of the rainswept countryside. Copper and gold leaves glinted against the dramatic sky, and in the distance the mountains were a pastel haze of blue and purple and mauve. The white thunderheads ahead seemed to form nebulous grimacing faces. As she drove through the lush, verdant landscape, it was easy to see why nineteenth-century painter John Constable had described the Lakes as "the finest scenery that ever was." And eighteen million annual visitors seemed to concur with this assessment.

The Land Rover was disappearing into the rolling green distance. Grace accelerated. Woods flashed by in scarlet, yellow and brown.

The tune of "John Peel" kept running through Grace's mind.

Chase the fox from his lair in the morning . . .

As they neared Oxenholme, Peter slowed and pulled into the car park. Grace shot past and a mile up pulled a U-turn, and drove back.

Peter had parked. She spotted his tall figure heading for the gray building of the station before a bus pulled out, blocking her view. It didn't take a detective to deduce he was taking the train. But which train?

She hurried across the forecourt, skirting rain puddles, and positioned herself near a kiosk where a driver in a yellow shirt and goose bumps held high a sign in Japanese.

In a few minutes Peter strode out of the station and started for a platform where a train sat idling.

Grace didn't have time to waste on subtlety. "I want to go where the man in the khaki trench coat is going."

Perhaps this was a popular route with secret agents, for the clerk said, as though hers were a routine request, "Eleven forty-three to Euston Station."

Euston Station? Then they were going to London?

Gulping over the cost, Grace bought her ticket. Because of recent deprivatization of the railway system, extensive improvements were now under way. Modern trains were slowly replacing the old rattlers; but, compared to other countries, railway travel was shockingly expensive in the UK.

Leaving the ticket counter, she looked around for a decent hiding place where she could watch Peter without being noticed until it was time to board. The bank of phones looked promising.

A young woman with a baby carriage had engaged Peter in smiling conversation. The baby, clearly a girl, was cooing at him and offering her pacifier.

There was no cash machine at the station. She would have to hope she didn't have some kind of financial emergency before she reached London. She looked at her watch. Half past eleven. It was nearly a four-hour train ride to London. Grace's stomach was already growling.

The minutes passed; then passengers began to board. Peter assisted the woman with the baby carriage.

Ticket in hand, Grace filed toward the steps of the train. A hand clamped down on her shoulder. She turned, startled.

Chaz, looking unreasonably outraged, stood there.

"What are you doing?" Grace demanded.

"What are *you* doing?"

Belatedly she lowered her voice. "Catching a train." She turned and spotted

Peter's back disappearing inside the train. "Look, I've got to go."

"You're following him!" Chaz was not bothering to keep his voice down, and they were drawing curious glances.

"And you're following me." Despite her ire, she couldn't help seeing the irony in the situation.

Chaz was attempting to draw her away. Grace freed herself. "Not now!"

"Are you crazy? You can't go running after him. Even if he's not a crook, you can't chase him all over the country."

"You don't know what you're talking about." The train whistle blew. Desperately, Grace said, "I've got to go."

"We've got to discuss —"

Grace freed herself, darting to the platform and up the stairs. The difficulty was that Peter was in the first-class section two cars up, while she was stuck in standard; it would be impossible to keep an eye on him.

She dropped into the first empty seat and picked up the newspaper someone had left on the seat next to her, opening it wide. At least it provided temporary concealment. She tried to think what to do next.

After all, Peter might simply be going to visit friends. Honest, law-abiding friends. He might be going shopping. He might just feel like a trip to London.

If he had been outraged at the idea of her spying on him in the graveyard, what would he make of this?

Someone plumped into the seat next to her.

"Why don't you poke eyeholes in the front page," Chaz muttered. "You couldn't look sillier than you do now."

Grace brought down the paper. "What are you doing here?"

"I can't let you do this by yourself."

"I *have* to do this by myself." Especially since she had no idea what she was doing.

Chaz was shaking his head stubbornly. "I've bought my ticket. It's too late now."

The train was beginning to move.

"Chaz —"

He folded his arms and sat back in his seat, ignoring Grace's exasperated gaze.

Outside the window, clouds, buildings and trees slid by as the train picked up speed. After a time Grace stopped fuming and started thinking. "Give me your cap."

Chaz looked affronted. "Why?"

"I need a disguise."

"This is ridiculous." He seemed to be addressing the ceiling of the train.

"May I please borrow your cap?"

Chaz's lips were set in disapproving lines,

but he handed his golf cap over and smoothed his dark curls down.

Grace twisted her hair into a ponytail and tucked it under the spacious cap. She turned the collar up on her blazer, and muttered, "I'll be right back."

"You couldn't look more conspicuous," Chaz informed her departing back.

This, Grace ignored. Peter would not be looking for her, so all she needed to do was avoid catching his eye. It was a risk, but she needed to know where he was. A niggling doubt suggested that if he had spotted her, he might have left the train before it departed the station.

Tipping the golf cap low over her face, she started down the corridor. Briefly she scanned the faces of the passengers crowded into the rows of seats. He wasn't in the first section.

She began to worry she'd lost him.

He wasn't in the second section. Panic set in, but then she spotted him in a window seat, gazing out at the landscape flashing by.

Grace ducked back. A couple of passengers glanced at her curiously.

Her heart was racing as though she'd just completed an obstacle course. She had to wonder at herself. No surprise Chaz thought she shouldn't be left on her own.

And she considered herself a role model for girls? Yikes!

When she was composed again, she readjusted her collar and slipped back down the corridor, finding her place next to Chaz.

"Found him."

Chaz shook his head. "May I have my cap back?"

Grace handed over the cap, took out her sunglasses, and put them on. "How much money do you have?"

"A few pounds. A hundred dollars in travelers' checks."

"I don't know how far we're going. Maybe all the way to London, although he could have purchased a ticket to London to throw off any possible pursuit. I didn't notice if this train stops along the way or runs straight through. Even so, I suppose he'd find a way to get off if he needed to."

"You should hear yourself," Chaz commented. "It's pretty sad."

"We should move down to where we can keep an eye on him."

"The train goes straight through. He's not going anywhere for a while."

There was no point arguing. Grace got up, and, sure enough, Chaz followed.

They found new seats closer to where they could observe Peter. He had ditched the mother and child but appeared to have been appropriated by a cuddly grandmother type who was showing him pictures of her cats. He really did have lovely manners, Grace reflected dispassionately.

The miles rolled by in a lulling clackety-clack of wheels on rails. Chaz read the news in sections while Grace watched the aisle from the shelter of the rest of the paper. She comforted herself that if Peter did spot them, they could pretend to be on a day-trip to London. It was reasonable that Chaz would want to sightsee. Peter shouldn't automatically assume he was being followed. In her imagination she began to argue this point with him.

"I'm hungry," Chaz said gloomily.

Grace considered for a moment. There was an onboard buffet, but that might just be for the first- or club-class passengers. In any case, they had to make sure they didn't bump into Peter. Food would have to wait.

"I know. Me too. We can grab something in London."

Chaz sighed in a way that seemed to imply that somehow his plight was all Grace's fault.

They reached London well after three o'clock in the afternoon. In Grace's mind, Euston Station was still graced with the

Great Hall and massive Doric arch entrance of old films, but these had been destroyed in the early sixties when the station was rebuilt, and the new edifice was an uninspired slab.

"Now what?" the Voice of Doom inquired as they made their way through the crowd.

"I don't know, but we have to be ready to move fast."

They waited, watching Peter from around a corner.

"I feel like a fool," Chaz groused. "What kind of relationship do you have that you feel like you need to spy on the guy?"

Stung, Grace retorted, "You're spying on me!"

"That's different."

Grace sniffed.

They struggled through the other passengers, finding then losing the tall pale-haired figure working his way quickly through the crush of people milling around them. He left the station concourse, walking out on Eversholt Street. A few yards down he went into an Edwardian-looking building on the left. A green-and-white sign read THE HEAD OF STEAM PUB.

"What now?" wondered Grace aloud. "He must be planning to catch another train, or he would hail a cab, right?"

"Don't ask me. Maybe he just likes to eat lunch here."

"But that has to be right. He wouldn't hang around here — unless he plans to meet someone who's also arriving by train."

"I can't keep up this pace on an empty stomach," Chaz informed her.

"Okay, let me think. I'll keep an eye on the pub, and you go buy something and bring it back here," Grace said. "I'm guessing he's waiting around for another train."

Chaz looked long-suffering, but went off to do her bidding. Grace checked her watch.

Chaz returned shortly with roast beef sandwiches and bottles of lemon squash. They ate hovering in the doorway, keeping an eye on the pub.

"I don't see what the point of this is," Chaz groused.

Mouth too full to answer, Grace glanced up; Peter was headed straight their way. She swallowed in one gulp, and practically fell over Chaz in her haste to avoid being seen. She dragged him, still clutching the remains of their impromptu lunch, behind the nearest magazine rack. Swimsuited models smirked at Grace from rows of glossy covers.

Peter strode past without a glance in their direction.

"Now comes the hard part." Grace fixed Chaz with the compelling look that used to work so well on her freshman class. "We've got to find out where he's headed without being seen ourselves."

Chaz looked blank; then his eyes widened. "Look," he said, "you may have noticed that I am not James Bond."

"You're doing very well," Grace assured him. "Frankly, I'm impressed."

Chaz made a harrumphing sound but looked a little flushed as he set out on his next mission. He was back after several nerve-racking minutes.

"I saw his ticket. He's going to Scotland!" he gasped.

"Scotland?"

He nodded, and, still out of breath, added, "Edinburgh. We've got to decide now. It takes twenty minutes by tube to get to King's Cross, and the train leaves at five."

Scotland. Yes, of course. Transylvania was just so much thumbing of nose. *The Daily Record* was a Scottish paper. The man who had been driving the moving van had a Scottish accent. Catriona was Scottish.

Grace said firmly, "My mind is already made up."

Chaz's shoulders slumped. "This is crazy. We don't have any luggage!"

Men. Grace had her purse, which contained all the essentials: lipstick, credit card and book. She started walking. "You don't have to come. I don't want you to come."

"Of course I'm coming," he said.

The light was gone when they crossed the border into Scotland. It had been raining for hours.

Och hush ye then, och hush ye. The night is dark and wet.

Grace put aside her book for a moment, listening to the lullaby of the rails; the wheels seemed to roll a soothing song as the miles melted away.

She glanced at Chaz. He was sleeping. No one looks his best sleeping, despite what the romance novelists write.

She reopened Paul West's brilliant *Lord Byron's Doctor*, but found that despite the seductive prose she couldn't concentrate. Poor Polidori. Nothing had gone right for him. He had loved the wrong people and pursued the dreams that would destroy him. In the end he had taken his life. Grace reflected on this final act. Suicide could be motivated by many things, including the desire for revenge.

Polidori had believed his work would secure his place in Romantic literature, but his fiction was largely forgotten and the journals of his adventures with Byron and the Shelleys had been "edited" upon his death by his sister, who had believed them scandalous. (Probably correctly!)

So in the end Polidori did not even have his final say.

He had seemed locked in a love-hate relationship with Byron, but if his suicide had been intended as a kind of payback, it seemed to have earned little more than passing comment from his famous *fratelli*.

Grace bookmarked her place and set the novel aside. She remembered discussing with Roy Blade how the lives of the Romantic poets seemed to mirror their dramatic works.

Life seemed to be imitating art in Innisdale as well.

Chaz spoke, startling her out of her reflections, and she realized he had been silently watching her for a few minutes.

"It doesn't make sense. You're not the kind of woman to sacrifice all her plans and ambitions for a man with an unsavory past. It's like something out of a B movie."

He sounded almost as though he were thinking aloud. And although he had only now truly brought it up, she felt like they had been arguing the subject since he arrived.

She tried to answer without sounding defensive. "Peter had some trouble with the law, but that's history. He's not the same person."

"You don't believe that, or you wouldn't be on this train."

"It's just the opposite. I believe it, or I wouldn't be on this train." *Did* she really believe that? Even Grace wasn't sure. She had to know what was going on, whether it meant the end to her dreams or not.

"But you're so squeaky clean!"

"Gee, you flatter me."

"I don't mean — I mean that as a compliment." Chaz straightened up in the cramped seat, his expression earnest. "You have morals and principles and goals. I just can't picture you in love with someone like that."

In love? Was it love? She didn't know. Certainly it was not the love she had dreamed of, reading by the light of a flashlight beneath an adolescent's bedclothes. The love that dare not stay up past ten o'clock. Just as certainly it was unlike any emotion she had felt for any other man in her life.

Could you love someone without trusting him?

Trust, Grace would have lectured her young ladies, is essential in any healthy relationship. Possibly, spying on one's gentleman friend was not the best illustration of trust, and yes, there was something about Peter Fox that roused instincts honed by years of supervising devious adolescents. But, the truth was, Grace did trust him. Not just with the small things, like her pocketbook. She would trust Peter with her life. In effect she had done so by moving to Innisdale.

And yet . . . she had kicked over the traces of her hitherto conventional and admirably well organized life, but she had done it on condition.

She had not truly given her heart; she had waited for proof, for guarantees.

There were no guarantees with love.

It was nine o'clock when the train let them out at Waverley Station in Edinburgh. Rain beat down on the glass ceiling supported by a network of iron columns. Commuters, haggard in artificial lighting, pursued luggage and cabs with desperate purpose in the stale air.

Tagging behind Peter, who walked

swiftly, Gladstone bag in hand, Chaz and Grace hotly debated their next move in a hissing exchange that had others moving hastily out of their path.

Peter went into a washroom.

"Go in after him," Grace urged.

Chaz balked. "I'm not following him in there. He'll see me. He might do something."

"Like what? He's not violent."

"You want to bet money?"

"Then don't let him see you!"

"How am I supposed to do that?"

Grace considered this, then relaxed. "Never mind, here he comes." She ducked back as Peter strode out, his long-legged stride quickly putting distance between them as he moved through the throngs of people engaged in farewells and hellos, struggling with luggage or searching for information on the circular signs.

Grace left her hiding place, Chaz tagging after, still protesting.

The night air was surprisingly sharp and cold. As they watched, Peter crossed the street and hailed a big black cab.

Grace flagged down another.

The driver was out before they could stop him, moving to retrieve their nonexistent luggage.

"No luggage," Grace said. "Can you please follow that car?" She pointed at the other cab pulling away from the curb, and the driver chortled.

"Oh, I've been waiting all my life for this very request." At least, that was the way Grace translated it. It came out sounding something like, "Och, ye ken fine A wantit this a guid ween year."

"Is he speaking Gaelic?" Chaz whispered.

Grace shook her head.

The cab ahead, apparently alerted to the game, began to drive with maniacal disregard for traffic, pedestrians and road signs. Its black bulk weaved in and out of the other cars.

Their own driver sped up while pointing out places of historical or cultural interest at the top of his lungs. "And there tae the left, that's Edinburgh Castle! The castle houses the Scottish crown jewels, the Scottish National War Memorial, and the Stone of Destiny —"

The black cab ahead took a corner sharply and disappeared down another boulevard, where jets of a fountain glittered among the old-fashioned streetlamps. Even at night, streaming past at sixty miles an hour, it was a beautiful city.

Fascinating to think, Grace reflected, momentarily distracted, that some of these buildings would have been standing when Polidori was a student there.

There were more twists and turns down narrow streets. Pedestrians performed intricate balletlike maneuvers to avoid the speeding vehicles. "Are you sure you've nae time for sightseeing? We're no sae far from Holyrood Palace where the Royal Family still often stay while visiting Scotland."

Their guide added with peculiar relish, "It was there that the young Mary Queen of Scots witnessed the bloody murder of the Italian Rizzio by her husband Darnley and the earrrrls of Athol, Huntly, Bothwell, Caithness and Sutherland — with the aid of the wicked Lord Ruthven."

Grace's attention was caught by the mention of this last name. She recalled that Mary had cursed Lord Ruthven and all his House — a curse that had come true during the reign of her own son, James VI.

Her thoughts were interrupted by the cabby, who suddenly yanked on the steering wheel. "Jacky Stewart thinks he's going to escape us, the daft bastard!"

They screeched around the corner in hot pursuit.

Chaz clung white-knuckled to the side of the cab. His eyes briefly met Grace's, then he closed them as if in prayer.

Someday, Grace thought — if we live — this will be funny.

"And over there is the clock tower of the new Balmoral Hotel . . ."

More squealing tires, then the cab ahead suddenly drew to the side of the road, and Peter got out, striding toward an immense building that looked like a Georgian wedding cake.

"Where's he going?"

"Pull over!" Grace ordered. "Hurry!"

Their cab rocked to a stop in the middle of the street, and Grace and Chaz piled out. Chaz paid the cabby while Grace started down the crowded sidewalk, trying to keep Peter in sight.

"Hey!" the driver called to her. "Lass! Lassie!"

Grace whirled and ran back to the cab, still darting looks over her shoulder. Peter had vanished inside the building.

"He's taken you full circle, you know."

"What?"

"Look!"

She looked. Gradually what she saw began to register: that towering pinnacle of stone, that was surely the Scott Monument. Which meant that this formal stretch of grass and flowers must be Princes Gardens

. . . The historic-looking building Peter had gone into must be the Old Waverley Hotel. Which meant that right across the street . . .

She turned, and there was the Princes Street exit for Waverley Station. They were right back where they had started less than an hour earlier.

"I don't believe it!" Chaz exclaimed. "The guy is crazy."

The cab driver laughed. "Aye, crazy like a fox!"

15

He had vanished.

The staff at the Old Waverley Hotel were solicitous but unhelpful. They could not reveal the names of registered guests; besides no one had noticed anyone of Peter Fox's description entering the building.

Chaz and Grace returned to the street. Mist rose off the pavement; the lamplight had a grainy look. It was no use. Peter had a head start and a plan. They had no idea where they were going, let alone where Peter was going.

"That's it then," Chaz said, when Grace admitted it was no use.

She could have cried with sheer frustration.

"Why don't we get some dinner and catch the next train home?"

It was a sensible suggestion. Grace heard it and acknowledged this with one ear. With the other she was listening to the little voice that insisted there had to be a way to figure out where Peter was going. After all, the entire country of Scotland wasn't as large as

Southern California.

"I'm starving," Chaz said. He looked at his watch. "Let's get something to eat," he urged again.

"Monica!" Grace exclaimed.

Chaz glanced around. "Where?"

"No, she lives here now with her husband Calum Bell. Well, in Cramond, which I think is a suburb. She might be able to help."

"Help with what? Grace, it's over. He's gone, and frankly it's just as well that you're not involved in whatever he's up to."

She ignored this, rifling through the address book in her purse. "Here we go." She looked around for a phone booth. Chaz followed, still protesting.

"Grace, he obviously knew you were following him, and he's put it just as clearly as if he said it to your face. He wants you to go home."

"Then he should have said it to my face." The answering machine picked up. Monica's chipper voice invited her to leave a message.

Grace bit her lip. Hanging up, she said, "We'll call back in a bit. Meantime, let's rent a car."

By now she was so used to the accompaniment of Chaz's objections they barely registered as they located a car rental place and hired a mini for the next few days. However, even she had to sympathize when they found their leased vehicle.

"Pink?" Chaz protested. "You expect me to drive around this country in a pink car?"

"I can drive."

"That's not the point. I'll still have to sit next to you. We'll look like — like cosmetic consultants."

"You were there. You heard the man say this was all they had."

"Unbelievable," muttered Chaz. "They'll see us coming a mile away."

Locating another phone booth, Grace tried Monica again.

This time Monica picked up.

Grace had hardly started in when Monica interrupted. "Grace, where are you? This is grand! Is Peter with you?"

"Er . . . no. I'm with Chaz."

"Chaz? *Chaz?*"

Hearing his name, Chaz whispered, "Tell her hello." His expression, however, was disapproving. He still hadn't forgiven Monica for breaking up their comfortable foursome with Tom Anderson.

"Yes, he's been visiting," Grace answered Monica brightly.

"Crikey! Well, if you can't ditch him,

bring him along," Monica ordered irrepressibly.

Directions given, they got in the rental, which, despite its rosy hue, Chaz insisted on driving.

"Are you sure you don't —"

"I am perfectly capable!"

Grace subsided.

And capable he was. It took them no more than ten minutes to get out of the roundabout, windshield wipers slapping and hazard lights flashing.

Other motorists honked impatiently and gesticulated rudely.

"It just takes some getting used to!" Chaz muttered, foot feeling once more for a nonexistent clutch.

Before heading to Monica and Calum Bell's, they stopped to purchase a few overnight things and a change of clothing at what was quaintly termed "an American-style department store," Chaz parking half on the sidewalk, which seemed to be the natives' custom.

A few minutes later, and many pounds poorer, they returned to the street and their pink chariot — now adorned with a parking ticket.

Cramond turned out to be a lovely village

on the south shore of the River Forth. Calum and Monica greeted them at the door of a whitewashed house trimmed in dark blue. Red flowers bloomed in window boxes, and a shiny brass bell hung by the front door.

"It's so good to see you!" Monica hugged Grace tight. "I've missed you!"

"Wee Gracie!" Calum said, enfolding Grace in a bone-crushing hug.

The interior of the house was ultra-modern, done in striking white and black. Posters of vintage pulp detective covers added a vibrant note of color. Walls of bookshelves were packed with books and photos of Monica and Calum looking enviably happy.

Grace took note of what seemed to be an awful lot of suitcases stacked in the front room.

"Are you going somewhere?"

Monica rolled her eyes. "There's a conference for PI novelists in Canada, and Calum is the guest of honor. We're flying out day after next."

Monica and Chaz's reunion was more restrained. Chaz's manner was a bit distant with Monica, who raised her brows and met Grace's eyes.

"He thinks you're a bad influence,"

Grace explained later, when she and Monica were alone for a few minutes in the guest room.

"The feeling's mutual. What in the world are you doing with him? Where's Peter?"

"It's a long story."

"I love long stories . . . provided there's a happy ending."

"I don't know how this ends." She tried to fill Monica in on some of the highlights.

"Wow. This sounds more like a miniseries," Monica interrupted.

"It feels more like a miniseries. Maybe something by Stephen King."

Monica chuckled. "So am I making up one bed or two?"

"Two. Definitely."

Monica nodded wisely and opened a cedar chest full of blankets.

A quantity of red wine with the pasta Monica cooked for dinner relaxed Chaz, and he stopped making scornful noises while Grace finished her explanation of what they were doing in Bonny Scotland.

When they retreated to Calum's office after the meal and Chaz saw the framed blowups of Calum's book covers, he exclaimed, "Mikey Tong? You write the

Mikey Tong series?"

"Don't tell me you've heard of it!" Then, perhaps realizing this didn't exude great confidence in his own work, Calum corrected, "That is, I do indeed. D'you mean you've read my work?"

"I'm a huge fan!"

Calum preened, if such a big, ruggedly handsome man could be said to preen. "I like this fellow," he informed Grace.

"I didn't know you read detective novels," Grace said. She accepted the snifter of Drambuie liqueur that Monica passed her.

And Chaz, or perhaps it was the wine talking, retorted, "There's a lot about me you don't know. A lot you never bothered to find out."

"Hoo boy," Monica murmured.

"Anyway," Grace said, getting hastily back to business, "we're looking for some people named Ruthven."

"Ruthven?" Calum repeated. "That's not a name you hear often."

"But it is a Scottish name? The name of a clan?"

"Aye. An old Highland family with a black-and-bloody history. I think the true line died out centuries ago with the execution of the earl of Gowrie."

"Ah," said Grace, as though she knew what the heck Calum was talking about.

Calum rose and pulled a copy of *Scottish Surnames* down from the shelf. He flipped the pages, then read, *"The peerage ended with the Gowrie Conspiracy of 1600 — an unsuccessful attempt on the life of James VI which resulted in the royal fiat that the 'names, memory and dignity of the Ruthven family' were to be extinguished and their lands shared out."* His eyes met Grace's. "Friends of yours, you say?"

"We're not that close," Grace said. "Where is the family whatchamacallit? Seat?"

Calum shrugged. "Perthshire was the original family holding."

"I would say this is probably an outlaw branch of the family."

"The entire family is an outlaw branch," Calum retorted. "You won't find them listed in half the Scottish clan books."

Grace thought this over. "Peter said that there was no Lord Ruthven."

"Technically speaking, he's correct. In Scotland the family name does survive, but the title is the earldom of Gowrie."

Grace didn't follow all the complexities of titles and endowments.

"So this particular title could be made up.

A stage name?" She was thinking out loud.

"The very name Ruthven could be made up. Even if the surname of these people is Ruthven, there may be no connection with Perthshire at all," Monica said, following Grace's line of reasoning. "It's not like Scottish families only live in their hereditary territories."

"True," Calum said, "but in rural areas you will find higher concentrations of families who have historically lived there."

. . . *ossachs* read one of the scraps of burned paper Grace had found at the Monkton estate. Not too many possible words ending in 'ossachs.' Trossachs? That was a place in Perthshire.

"I think the name Ruthven is genuine," Grace said at last. "Peter said something about it being her maiden name."

"That still doesn't mean they're in Perthshire. Or even Scotland."

This was true. Grace was not deducing, she was guessing based on some scraps of burned newspaper and a chance encounter on a rainy night. She was speculating that Peter was going to meet with Catriona, but she had no reason to think so — except that she knew of no other reason for him to travel to Scotland.

Her only clue was the name Ruthven, and

she had to investigate it as thoroughly as she knew how. She knew the name Ruthven was genuine because Peter had said so, and the fact that he knew there was technically no Lord Ruthven indicated he had some familiarity with the family lineage.

"I guess we'll start with Perthshire," she said.

Calum said dryly, "Keep in mind they don't call it the 'big country' for nothing."

"This is hopeless," Grace said, as she and Chaz walked back to their car following their tour of Huntingtower Castle.

"I'm glad you said it first," Chaz returned. "The ceiling paintings were nice anyway."

"Yes, the bright spot is you're getting to see quite a bit of the country."

Grace knew they needed a better plan. They could not simply go from castle to castle and ask if anyone knew Catriona Ruthven, although this was what they had done so far.

Huntingtower, originally called Ruthven Castle, had been held by the Ruthvens since the twelfth century. It was there that the clan had made a fatal mistake when the earl of Gowrie kidnapped James VI. In the resulting fallout, the earl and his brother had lost their heads, and the clan had lost everything else.

In a way it made sense to start their quest there, although it was highly unlikely that Catriona would be lurking around that particular tourist trap.

Grace thumbed through the guidebook they had purchased in the wee hours of the morning when they first set out upon their journey.

"According to this the Gowrie Conspiracy was nothing more than James VI trying to get out of paying back the young earl the eighty thousand pounds he owed him. This says the family honor was restored in the twentieth century and the earldom of Gowrie reinstated."

Chaz exhaled long and loudly.

Grace hastily turned the page. "The next castle would probably be Dirleton. Except . . ." She skimmed the entry. "Oh."

"Oh, what?"

"Well, Dirleton changed hands a lot of times. The Ruthvens haven't been active in the area since the sixteen hundreds. The Nisbets held it last, but it was allowed to fall into ruin. The gardens are supposed to be nice, though." She read, *"Today the Arts and Crafts North Garden is listed in the* Guinness Book of Records *as the longest herbaceous border in the world. It is 215 meters long and contains over three hundred different types of plants."*

She showed Chaz a color photo of a pile of ruins on a hillside. "This is what's left of the castle. It's used mostly as a quarry to supply stone for local cottages."

"Sounds like a good hiding place to me. Where is it?"

"East Lothian."

"Where's that?"

"Back the way we came."

They reached Dirleton Castle before lunch.

After wandering the gardens, they came upon the castle, looking very much like an incredible garden ornament, one of those "follies" the Victorians were so fond of.

Grace consulted the guidebook. "There are the Ruthven Barracks, and I suppose they could be hiding out at a national monument, but it seems unlikely."

"This entire trip seems unlikely," Chaz groused.

"The Ruthven clan motto is *'Died schaw.'* Deeds show. Someone was being ironic." She read further, and said, "Scratch Ruthven Barracks. They were captured and burned by Prince Charles Edward Stuart's army in 1746."

"That's Bonnie Prince Charlie?"

"The same."

She stared out the window at the shaggy red Highland cattle grazing. "What am I missing? It's right under my nose and I can't see it."

"What?"

"The thing I can't see." She sighed. "I give up. Let's find a place to have lunch."

They stopped for lunch at the Castle Inn, a nineteenth-century coaching inn overlooking the village green of Dirleton. The public and lounge bars had been painstakingly restored to their original glory.

Chaz was in good spirits upon learning that they were only minutes away from Cramond. Their quest was successfully concluded in his opinion.

Grace was less buoyant, eating her steak-and-mushroom pie, lost in thought.

After a time her mood affected Chaz. He studied her gravely. "What happened to us, Grace?"

Peter, thought Grace. But was that the whole truth? Peter was part of the change, but the change in herself was what made having Peter in her life possible.

"I've changed," she said at last.

Chaz's brown eyes looked more soulful than ever. "We all change. Change is part of life. Why did you have to change toward me?"

She covered his hand with hers, hating to hurt him.

"I don't know how to explain it. I feel like my life, my real life, began when I came to Innisdale." It would sound too silly to say, "I went on an adventure and learned that it was possible to live your dreams if you were brave and determined enough."

Chaz was shaking his head, refuting both what she said and what she didn't say. Chaz was an empiricist, and Grace was . . . probably out of her mind.

As they were leaving she asked the whereabouts of the nearest used-book store, and was directed down the street to a small shop where the towering bookshelves formed a twisty maze that one could barely squeeze through. Layers of dust blanketed the very top shelves, and gossamer spiderwebs floated lazily from the ceiling like leftover Halloween decorations.

Grace found the clan history book wedged in between a book on learning to speak Gaelic and a *Touring Scotland* from the 1930s.

"That's going to be completely out-of-date," Chaz objected, when she checked the copyright date.

"That's the idea. According to what Calum read us, there is no direct male descendant of the Ruthvens, which implies there are still female descendants. My clan book says that they were a prolific race. Families of ten and twelve children were common; so isn't it reasonable that all those offspring must have gone somewhere?"

"America," Chaz said. "That's where everybody goes."

Grace shook her head. "No, according to the Huntingtower guidebook there were still Ruthvens in Scotland because they were rewarded for service in World War II."

"So?"

"So traditionally in Scotland when people were outlawed they fled to the Highlands. Didn't you ever read *Kidnapped*? The Highlands and Islands were like our own Wild West. In fact, parts are still fairly remote — and they still speak Gaelic in some places."

"What does Gaelic have to do with it?"

Grace did not answer for a moment, thumbing through the yellowed pages of the clan book.

So many of the old place names mentioned in the proscription against the Ruthvens were no longer in use . . .

Chaz's words registered, and she glanced

up. "Supposedly one of the Ruthven servants spoke in a foreign language. Local opinion was German, but Gaelic is a guttural language, too, and Catriona being Scottish, it seems likely he was speaking Gaelic. I think Catriona may speak it as well." She told him about the phone call she had picked up at the Monkton estate.

"I'm not sure where this is heading."

It wasn't fair, but Grace couldn't help comparing how different this quest was with Chaz as her companion, versus last time with Peter. Peter might disagree with her conclusions, but he always knew where she was headed.

"It's a long shot, but I'm looking for a place . . ." She ran her finger along the page, then turned to the back to look at the maps.

"My gosh the light is dim in here." She held the book up, squinting at the tiny print, then handed the book to Chaz. "What does that say?"

"It's in Gaelic. I mean, what maniac came up with a language that puts 'B' and 'H' next to each other in one word? How the heck are you supposed to pronounce that?"

"We don't need to pronounce it. Just spell it out for me."

Chaz obliged, peering at the type. "A' . . . M . . . h . . . e . . . i . . . r. . ."

Grace thumbed through the browned pages of the Gaelic dictionary until she could string the words together.

A' Mheirlich Saobhaidh. Den of the Thieves. It sounded like the right place to Grace.

The village was called Eacharnach, which Grace could not find in her Gaelic-English dictionary. It was nestled in between golden hills and purple shadows.

The castle ruins stood on a small island in the loch, black pine trees concealing it from curious eyes.

"That's it. I know that's it," Grace said quietly, as she and Chaz stood by the pink car, staring out across the water at the island fortress. Smoke rose in wisps from the distant tower.

It was late afternoon by the time they located someone willing to row them across.

Donald MacLeod was as old and decrepit as his boat, though hopefully less leaky. Nevertheless, he skimmed them across the loch with powerful strokes. The water slapped against the hull of the boat. The drops from the oars sparkled in the late afternoon.

A whirring sound overhead caused Grace to instinctively duck as something winged past. She had a glimpse of a fierce-looking copper brown bird with a yellow warlike eye, and what appeared to be an eight-foot wingspan.

"Was that an eagle?" exclaimed Chaz.

"*Iolair-bhuib.* Golden eagle. She's wondering what it is you are up to."

The loch reached like the shadow of a hand down the length of the glen, shimmering like smoky glass in the burnished light. They watched the eagle skim across the water and disappear into the golden woods.

"How deep is the water here?" Chaz asked.

"Two hundred and fifty meters." The old man smiled a black-toothed smile. "They say an *each uisage* used to live in these waters."

"A what?"

"Aye."

"What's an agh iski?"

"A water spirit. Sometimes he would appear as a bonny horse, but if anyone tried to mount him, the *each uisage* would race into the loch and devour his victim beneath the water. Only the liver, heart and organs would be left uneaten to float to the shore."

"Good God," Chaz said, revolted. "What is it with you people and internal organs. I mean, what is that haggis thing about?"

The old man laughed soundlessly. "Sometimes the *each uisage* would appear as a handsome lad and suck the life from the bonny lasses he bedded." The old man nodded at Grace as though she looked like a prime candidate for snuggling up with an *each uisage*.

Vampires, Grace thought. More vamps. Even in Scotland.

The old man rambled on. "But he hasnae been seen in these parts for a century or so." MacLeod sounded like it was in recent memory, and perhaps for him it was. He bent over his oars again.

The closer they drew, the more the castle looked like one of those old Hammer Film Productions sets. Grace wouldn't have been surprised to find Frankenstein's monster waving from the battlements. Or what remained of the battlements. The place truly was a ruin.

Someone was moving around on the taller of the two towers. The skirl of bagpipes floated over the loch, a mournful, lonely sound.

" 'Flowers of the Forest,' " the boatman commented.

"It's pretty," Grace said.

"It's a lament."

They moored the boat in a stone slip that looked new compared to the rest of the island. Centuries of storms and wars had reduced most of the original structures to rubble.

The main building seemed to be a fourteenth-century keep or tower house scarred by ancient sieges. There were other smaller outlying buildings, but the smoke drifting from the foremost tower seemed the most promising indication of life.

"So what's the plan?" Chaz queried doubtfully.

"If I'm not back in half an hour, come get me."

Donald MacLeod, hands cupped around his pipe, cackled with laughter.

Grace walked up from the wharf, following a path that led between a pair of stone gateposts, winding around at last to a vine-covered and surprisingly unassuming front entrance. The door was constructed of thick weathered timber marked with scrapes and gouges that looked like the result of anything from arrows to werewolf claws. She pulled what appeared to be a bell rope.

She could hear a kind of gonging sound rolling through the belly of the castle, echoing within the stone walls. At last the door opened.

Peter stood in the wedge of light cast from the torchère on the wall behind him.

"Be careful your face doesn't freeze like that," he said.

16

The room appeared to have been decorated by a Great White Hunter on a drinking binge. Animal hides covered stone floors. African shields and spears covered stone walls. Assorted animal heads stared blankly down from strategic positions. Tribal masks glowered from corners. The place seemed to be made up of corners. There was an odd smoky smell. Brimstone?

As Grace crossed the threshold something white and enormous rose from the floor. She blinked, thinking for a split second that it was one of the stuffed animals come back to life in all its dermatitis-ridden glory, but as the creature attempted to sniff her impolitely, Grace realized it was a Scottish deerhound.

Catriona was curled on a red velvet sofa in front of the enormous fireplace.

"This is a surprise," she said lazily. "To what do we owe this honor?"

Grace sat down in a large chair and sank about two feet farther into a quicksand of bad springs and plush. She glanced at the low table beside the chair, where a stuffed mongoose and cobra were frozen in eternal combat. They reminded her vaguely of Roy Blade and Lady Vee.

Controlling her expression, Grace responded, "I happened to be visiting friends in the area, and I learned you were staying locally." It sounded as though she had been practicing it, and of course she had.

Peter restlessly circled the room. The dog wagged its tail, watching him.

She had been so intent on finding Peter that she hadn't given enough thought to what she would do when she found him. Was it just Peter and Catriona hiding out? But no, Grace had seen the piper and knew that there must be others. Perhaps an entire gang.

She made herself look away from Peter and found Catriona studying her with those strange gold eyes. "That's quite a coincidence."

"You're visiting Calum and Monica?" Peter inquired.

It was almost physically painful to look at him in these circumstances, but she made herself hold his gaze. She realized with a shock that this was the first time she had actually ever seen him and Catriona together.

They were both tall, lithe, with smooth

hard muscles. There was no wasted movement, no wandering attention, although they seemed to watch each other out of the corners of their eyes. It was like observing two panthers at home.

"Right."

"The trip's been planned for over a month," he remarked to the room at large.

Catriona considered this, then smiled.

A bald man with a cauliflower ear, who looked like Mr. Clean's evil twin, entered the room. Seeing Grace, he checked.

"Ah, tea," Catriona announced.

The man looked down at his nonexistent tea tray and backed out of the room.

Now Grace was certain she was on the right track. She was almost positive the man was the same man she had nearly skidded into that rainy night in Innisdale Wood not so long ago — although it felt like a lifetime.

"This is such an interesting room," she commented politely to fill the strange lull. "Your family is devoted to hunting?"

"My family, or rather my great-grandfather, was devoted to wholesale slaughter. His particular playing field was the African continent. This was his lair."

"Lair" seemed like the right word. Grace did feel as though she had wandered into some beast of prey's lair — or perhaps the spider's web. There was a dangerous tension in the air.

The bald man returned, and this time he did bear a heavy tray with a silver tea service complete with spooner, spoons, strainer and heavy teapot. Grace wondered if the tea service was inherited or stolen.

The man lowered the trembling tray to the nearest table. "Peter, you be mother," Catriona invited.

He came and joined her on the sofa, pouring without comment.

"Thank you, I've lunched," Grace declined, as he passed cup and saucer her way.

Clearly reading her mind, he grinned and sipped the tea, then offered the cup again to Grace.

She ignored it.

Catriona fed part of a buttered scone to the dog, who snapped up the food in one gulp.

"Is Lord Ruthven here?"

"He is," Catriona said. "Unfortunately, he's indisposed. He'll be heartbroken to have missed you." Her gaze held Grace's in open challenge.

Grace had traveled too far to back down. "We had plans to meet in Innisdale, you know. Perhaps I could see him for a moment?"

Catriona's eyes met Peter's, and she said, "No, I don't suppose it would be wise. What he has might be catching." Grace did not care for her smile. "Perhaps another time."

She could hardly insist. In fact, her safety rested primarily on this polite charade they played. "Perhaps I could come back tomorrow?"

"Perhaps."

"You must have other plans for your holiday," Peter objected. "You and Chip."

"Yes, that's true." Grace rose.

Catriona rose also in one swift movement. The dog looked from one to the other, alert, watchful. "Must you leave so soon? We've hardly had a moment to catch up on the gay old times at Innisdale."

"The boatman is waiting for me."

Catriona didn't move for a moment, then said gently, "Ah. Of course. You wouldn't have rowed yourself over."

"No, I wouldn't have."

Catriona stretched, an unselfconsciously graceful movement. "Safe home."

"I'll see you out," Peter said.

Catriona started to say something, caught his eye and subsided with a shrug.

They walked in silence down the grim serpentine hall past suits of armor and assorted weaponry. Here and there the subject of a murky portrait inspected them from across the centuries. Those Ruthvens who were not powdered and wigged ran to red hair, lynx eyes and unpleasant sneers.

"Satisfied?" Peter queried, as they walked back toward the dock.

The island was bathed in a fiery glow. Even the loch seemed to burn. The sun was setting, the tiger's eye closing in sleep.

Grace glanced his way. "Yes, of course. Why wouldn't I be? One woman is dead, murdered. A priceless artifact has been stolen, and you're the number one suspect. Lord Ruthven is missing and probably dead. You're on the lam with the Bride of Dracula . . ."

"Lam? You really did visit Calum and Monica."

"I'm on my way back there now."

"Good. Stay there."

They passed between two stone pillars topped with finials fashioned like knights in a game of chess.

"Peter, what is going *on?*"

"You've summed it up pretty well."

"You must know that by running away you've made yourself look guilty of . . . everything."

He ignored this, eyes on the boat where

Chaz and Donald MacLeod waited.

"I see you brought the faithful Honeybun."

"Why can't you tell me? Why can't I help you?" Until the moment he had opened the castle door she had believed that somehow she would find him on the side of the angels. Although all the evidence pointed against it, she had so wanted to believe that he had come to Scotland in pursuit of Catriona, not to join her. And even now . . .

Peter glanced back at the tower. "Get," he said flatly, "while the getting is good."

The storm at the Bells' had been upgraded to gale category as their departure date for the Canadian conference drew nearer.

"Are you going to the police?" Calum queried, when Grace finished recounting her visit to *A' Mheirlich Saobhaidh*.

"No." It startled all of them that she didn't have to think about it.

"Why, for God's sake!" Chaz exclaimed. "At the very least these people are suspects in a murder investigation."

He would never in a million years understand why. She wasn't sure she really understood. Loyalty? Curiosity? Love?

"I need to know more before I do anything." She selected a second piece of the rich date-and-ginger shortbread that Monica had served with tea.

"What does that mean?"

She already regretted her words. "Just that . . . we don't really have any proof."

"Proof?" Chaz was practically goggling at her. "What kind of proof do you believe you need? Do you think the cops wouldn't want to know where these felons are?"

Grace said, "I realize that, but Peter might, um, have a plan. I don't want to jeopardize whatever it is he's doing."

"You mean like stealing things and killing people?"

"That wasn't him!"

Monica said reluctantly, "We don't know that, Grace."

She didn't know it, and yet she seemed to have reached the point of impasse. The point where she either accepted on blind faith that Peter was who she believed or . . . she . . . let go.

She wasn't ready to let go. Maybe there was a third alternative.

"I can't believe this is you talking," Chaz said. "I can't believe you know what you're saying."

Monica and Calum exchanged a look.

"Whisht," Calum said, suddenly very

Scottish. "Let's leave it, shall we? A meal and a dram, that's the thing. And then we'll talk."

Calum hauled the still-protesting Chaz out into a pine-scented night that already smelled like Christmas, and Monica turned to Grace.

"Okay," she said grimly. "What's the real scoop?"

Grace shook her head.

"I can't turn him over to the police without knowing . . ."

"You're not thinking of going back there?"

"Sort of."

"On your own?"

"Unless you want to come with me." Grace was half-joking, but Monica's eyes suddenly gleamed.

"If only we could! What a lark!" Then reason seemed to cloud her mind. "We can't, and even if we could, we'd be crazy to try."

"I have to try," Grace said.

"No, but I'm serious. These people are career criminals. They've killed."

"We don't know that."

"You believe it."

Grace had no answer.

"Peter went with them of his own free

will, right? Nobody held a gun on him."

"Appearances can be deceptive."

"What does that mean? You think they're putting the squeeze on him?"

This was the short-term effect of living with a man who wrote detective novels.

"I don't know. I know that Peter couldn't have killed Lady Ives, and I don't believe he had anything to do with Lord Ruthven's disappearance because of the way he reacted when I told him about it."

"How did he react?"

"He was startled. Even alarmed. Whatever he had expected to happen, that wasn't it. I can tell when he's lying. Usually. This was the real thing."

Monica considered her argument.

"You're pinning a lot on a single reaction."

"I know. Believe me, I know."

"Okay, suppose Peter is innocent. Maybe he has a plan. Your turning up unexpectedly might throw a wrench in the whole setup."

"Or I might be able to help him."

Monica raked a hand through her short blond hair. "Then how do we help you?"

Grace told her.

Before falling asleep she thumbed through her copy of *Burke's Peerage*. Calum had not exaggerated the amazing and adventurous history of the Ruthvens. Besides an aptitude for plotting and scheming the Ruthvens were a remarkable lot, bold and courageous men and beautiful, equally lion-hearted women.

There was a legend concerning one Ruthven daughter who, fearing she would be discovered in bed with a suitor her parents disapproved of, made a nine-foot leap over a sixty-foot drop separating her lover's tower bedchamber from the rest of the castle.

Years of teaching adolescents had familiarized Grace with the lengths girls would go to, but nine feet was still pretty spectacular.

A soft tap on her door had Grace calling, "Come in!"

She expected Monica, but it was Chaz who cautiously opened the door.

"I wanted to talk to you."

She sat up against the pillows as Chaz shut the door and came to sit on the edge of the bed. The springs squeaked beneath his weight.

"It's not any use, is it?" His long-lashed soulful eyes held hers steadily.

Grace shook her head. "I'm sorry."

"Me too. I think you're making a terrible mistake."

"I hope not," said Grace. "It means a lot that you cared enough to" — she tried to make a little joke — "save me from myself."

Chaz said grimly, "It's not yourself I want to save you from, but I guess he's got you under his spell." Like those old Dracula movies, Grace was the victim sitting there in the dusk, scarf wrapped around her bitten neck, claiming she'd never felt better in her life.

"We had a good life together," he said.

"We had a comfortable routine," Grace said, "but I don't think either of us would ever have pushed for more."

"When the time was right I would have." He looked at her ringless left hand.

"I am sorry," she said again because there wasn't much else she could say. She knew, if Chaz did not, that the time would never have been right.

He sighed heavily. "Then I guess I'll head back to London tomorrow. My plane leaves Saturday."

"I'll miss you," Grace said. And it was true in a way.

Chaz leaned forward and kissed her on the forehead.

"Sweet dreams," he said. She couldn't blame him for emphasizing the word "dreams."

* * *

While waiting for the taxi to take him and Monica to the airport, Calum spent the morning instructing Grace in the fine art of lock picking.

"Of course it's theory, not practical application," he admitted, studying the array of shiny picks and jimmies spread out on the table before them.

"Hopefully I won't have to use them," Grace said, and Calum looked crestfallen.

"Calum, what else do you think she may need to break in?" Monica, sounding like a mother sending her only child to summer camp, was occupied putting together a "nice little workbox" with what she considered — probably from reading Calum's books — to be the burglary essentials: screwdriver, Instamatic camera, rope, etc.

"This is an awful lot of rope," Grace objected, joining her in the kitchen. "I don't actually plan on scaling any walls."

"You have no idea what you may end up having to do," Monica said rather direly.

"Well, I probably won't be having dinner with them," Grace pointed out, pulling a black silk stocking out of the toolbox.

"Ha. Funny. Anyway, you look good in black." Monica tossed the stocking back in the metal box.

* * *

When she reached the village of Eacharnach, the fitful Scottish sun was shining, glittering on the loch's blue water. There was a tang in the air that reminded her of the sea. Gulls whirled overhead.

The tiny village made Innisdale look like a bustling metropolis by comparison. Grace was the only visitor, and the fact that they could keep track of visitors said something about how isolated Eacharnach was.

The village boasted three pubs and one inn. Grace booked a room at the little inn, which looked out across the sun-dazzled loch. The room had sloping ceilings, and four-poster twin beds with paisley quilts. A sampler on the wall read: "Ae fine thing needs twa to set it off."

She lunched downstairs in the taproom.

"Is there a history to the castle on the island?" she asked Donnie MacInnes, the publican, doing her best to sound like an innocent American tourist.

"Aye, there's a verra fine legend about the castle if it's legend you're wanting."

"It's called the Thieves' Den, is that correct?"

"The Den of the Thieves, that is true. Och, but the castle was not always belonging to the Ruthvens! There is a story about how it came to be known as *A' Mheirlich Saobhaidh*. It was back in the days when the castle was a stronghold of the Menteiths. After the trouble between the clans —" Grace opened her mouth to ask which trouble, then closed it again, realizing the foolishness of the question.

"There was a kinsman of the Ruthvens who came to stay with the chief of the Menteiths. He dined and drank with his host as an honored guest, he slept beneath the Menteith roof, protected and sheltered by the sacred tradition of Highland hospitality."

Grace had read up on some of the sacred traditions of the warlike Highlanders, but she didn't interrupt.

"The next morning the gentlemen of the house rose to go hunting, and this son of the Ruthvens went with them. When the gentlemen reached the mainland, Ruthven's own men were waiting. The Menteiths were slaughtered to the last man. Their heads were mounted on pikes and displayed on the galleys that sailed to the island."

"Oh my gosh," Grace said, truly horrified.

"When the chief of the Ruthvens reached the island, he gave his ultimatum to Lady Menteith. If she would agree to marry him, he would spare her life and those left on the island. But she would not, and so he locked her and all her ladies in the tower. Lady Menteith's Tower they call it, for it was the mistress of the house and her ain guid ladies and the wee girrrrls that they left to starve there."

He slapped Grace's plate down on the table. "Eat up!"

Grace realized her mouth was open. She began to eat her fish and chips.

"Did none of the women escape?" she asked after a time, when there was nothing left on her plate but the inevitable molehill of green peas.

"Not one. They would have had to swim, you see. And the loch is a mile across. And there was the *each uisage* to consider." He winked at her.

A mile across and probably cold as outer space. "I've heard about the *each uisage.* And how long have the Ruthvens held the castle?"

"Ever since," Donnie MacInnes said cheerfully. "And right good lairds they've been."

Grace finished her drink in thoughtful silence and went out to rent the boat from Donald MacLeod for the next day.

This took a bit of bargaining, for the old

man was clearly skeptical when Grace told him she planned to row the boat herself.

"And why would you be wanting to paddle about the loch?"

"For exercise," Grace answered promptly. "I have to work off all the wonderful food I'm eating on my vacation."

"Vacation? A wee lassie by herself?" The old man's suspicion deepened.

The only solution seemed to be for the wee lassie to pay a rental fee that was more than the boat was worth. As she left the man of the boats mumbling darkly to himself, Grace knew word of her odd behavior would be all over the village — and probably to the castle before long. She would have to move quickly.

She spent the remainder of the afternoon walking around Eacharnach, learning what she could about the castle on the island and its history.

It appeared that while there were many stories of the old days and Ruthvens long dead, no one had — or was willing to admit to — any information on the current residents.

"Auld sins breed new sairs," sniffed the woman in the butcher shop. "Not much worrrk to be had there, not like the auld days. In those days they needed a full staff. These days it's only that rascal Hood to tend the place when she's away."

"She?"

A Highland sheep couldn't have stared more stolidly at Grace.

"Is Lady Ruthven here much?"

"This is her home."

No contradiction about Catriona's title. Interesting though not conclusive.

"Hood is the piper we heard on our trip to the castle?"

The woman snorted. "That would be Donnie MacDhomnuil. He must be back."

Grace finished paying for her soup bone.

Besides Catriona and Peter there was the bald man who was probably Donnie MacDhomnuil, and a redheaded hood. Four and possibly more.

Her next stop was the chemist shop.

The proprietor was a small, jolly man by the name of Donnie MacLean.

"Is everyone here named Donnie?" Grace inquired, puzzled.

The man burst out laughing. "Not the lassies!"

"Are you all related?"

The little man laughed all the harder. Was this an example of the subtle wit of the Gael?

The sun was sinking when Grace trudged up the road back to the inn, passing houses on the hillside where lit windows and smoke from chimneys indicated the citizens of Eacharnach were settling in for the night.

The sudden clatter of hooves sent her to the side of the road. Shaggy Highland cattle trotted down the street accompanied by a small boy and a black-and-white Border collie. The boy called a greeting to her in Gaelic.

Back at the inn Grace enjoyed a hearty supper, eating alone before the roaring fire. She skimmed a book on Scottish castles, paying close attention to a chapter devoted to mediaeval architecture, while sampling Cullen Skink, which the menu assured was classic Scottish soup. Despite the name, the hearty soup of smoked haddock, potato and leeks was delicious.

"What does the word *'Eacharnach'* mean?" she asked Donnie MacInnes.

"It's an old word in the Gaelic meaning a thing that is like a park for horses."

The soup was followed by an unimaginative but unquestionably delicious prime fillet garnished with mushrooms, potatoes and french fries. Grace drank several cups of the strong, peaty-flavored tea.

"We'll have snow before the fortnight,"

the innkeeper told her, drawing the curtains against the night.

Stars were flung across the night sky like grains of silver sand; their reflection sparkled on the water as Grace dipped the oars in the inky loch.

Sweat beaded her forehead. It might not be poetry in motion, but Grace was beginning to get the hang of rowing. Granted, it was taking about twice as long to travel across as it should have, the oars scooping and splashing in choppy rhythm.

She paused, resting on her oars. The lights of the village looked very far away. The water lapping against the hull of the rocking boat stretched black and bottomless as far as she could see.

She remembered the story of the *each uisage*. Perhaps even now he galloped miles beneath the surface, hooves pounding the floor of the loch as he searched for fresh human fodder.

Grace wiped her forehead on her sleeve and returned to rowing. Her hands were sweating inside the gloves that Monica had supplied. From her angle of approach she could not see any lights on the island. There was no sign of life except the occasional drift of woodsmoke on the breeze.

At last the boat scraped bottom in a tiny cove on the far side of the island. Grace hopped out, with more alacrity than grace, splashing through icy water onto the rocky beach. Though her eyes had had plenty of time to adjust, the deep shade of the towering pines made the night even blacker.

Dragging the boat into the trees, she stopped a moment to catch her breath. It had been harder than she expected to row across the water. She dreaded the thought of rowing back, but perhaps by then she would be running for her life, and that might supply the necessary adrenaline.

She abandoned the rock she rested on. The night was pungent with the spicy scent of the pine trees; her breath hung in the smoky moonlight.

Leaving the skiff safely hidden, she scouted around until she found what appeared to be a rocky path leading from the beach to the castle. Noiselessly, she followed the trail up the hillside and through another cluster of trees.

After a time the path disappeared into what seemed to be a rocky hillside. Grace spent a few minutes exploring the rough face of lichen-encrusted granite, until with a feeling of triumph she found a fissure wide enough to pass through.

She guessed, based on her recent reading, that it must lead to an underground passage, which would have served as a hidden or secret entrance in past centuries. She switched on her flashlight and continued walking.

Sure enough, a few feet farther the natural formation of the hillside gave way to what was obviously man-made architecture, and Grace found herself in what appeared to be a long underground tunnel. She could see smoke marks on the glistening walls where torches had burned for centuries. She could just make out marks in the stone that suggested primitive drawings of horses.

The tunnel smelled dank and slimy, if slimy had a smell. It smelled like a fish tank. Something scurried out from under her foot.

To the bats and to the moles . . .

Her flashlight beam picked out pools of oily water and the debris left by animals. At the far end pallid moonlight illuminated a narrow flight of steps leading up and out.

Picking her way through the rocks and water, she at last reached the far end of the tunnel. She switched the flashlight off and started up the steps. In the distance she heard barking, and froze.

The dog. She retreated back into the

tunnel, and fumbled into her backpack for the soup bone. Her heart thudded hard against her ribs. This kind of thing worked in fiction but probably didn't stand a chance against a well-trained guard dog. Not that Catriona's dog was a well-trained guard dog so much as a four-footed thug.

The dog went on barking but didn't seem to be coming any closer. After a moment or two, Grace expelled a long breath and abandoned the shelter of the passageway.

A few yards away stood a small tower. The tower stood separate from the main castle. It looked about two stories high, with slits for archers and an impenetrable-seeming door. Grace snooped around for a second more accessible entrance without luck. One door and no windows. A cheery place. This then would have been the prison of Lady Menteith.

She circled back to the door and jiggled the rusted padlock. Whatever was in there was worth locking up; so maybe it was worth investigating.

She pulled out Calum's lock picks but found it difficult to keep the flashlight beam propped high enough to see the lock. It had looked pretty simple when Calum demonstrated how to burgle a practice lock, but the real thing proved to be more challenging. She picked and wiggled and prodded and jiggled.

Nothing doing.

Professional pride gave way to desperation. She found a rock and banged the padlock with all her might. After two blows its hasp gave, and it fell to the ground.

Grace pushed the door wide. Hinges screeched hideously, not a bad makeshift alarm. She waited, expecting noise of discovery or pursuit.

Only night sounds met her ears. Crickets chirped and frogs croaked in unperturbed chorus. Somewhere an owl hooted.

Gathering her courage, she stepped into the tower and pulled the heavy door shut.

She switched the flashlight on, then nearly dropped it. The beam illumed a veritable treasure trove of furniture and paintings. The chamber was stacked floor to ceiling with artwork and valuables.

So this was where the loot from the Innisdale robberies had vanished. When they had filled their larcenous quota, they simply loaded up the moving van and drove straight to Scotland. Then what? A private boat ride across the loch? That would explain the modern and businesslike dock in the cove.

Keep it simple, stupid, thought Grace.

And this was so simple it was almost fool-proof.

She stepped around a fragile Louis XVI painted vanity chair and snapped a few photos with her Instamatic, hoping the flash would provide enough illumination in the pitchy darkness. She did not expect to find the jewels there. They might have already pawned those, although it would be pretty fast work. More likely Cat would keep that stuff inside under lock and key. She didn't seem like the trusting type.

In any case Grace wasn't interested in the jewels.

She began to look for the Peeler.

Finding the bugle did not necessarily prove the Ruthvens had murdered Theresa Ives, but it would link the Ives theft with the other robberies. And that would be a starting point.

Since Peter had an alibi for the Thwaite robbery, he would be off the hook for the Ives job. That was a reasonable conclusion, surely?

At least, it would be perfectly reasonable if Peter weren't hanging out with the villains at *A' Mheirlich Saobhaidh*.

Grace refused to consider the significance of that, making as thorough a search as haste permitted. She looked inside vases, opened an assortment of trunks and caskets, shifted furniture.

The Peeler did not appear to be there.

But maybe that was to be expected. The Peeler would incriminate its possessor in murder. It would be wise to hide it — even to dispose of it.

Grace straightened up, playing the flashlight beam over the walls. At the far end of the circular room was a staircase. One set of stairs ran up. The second disappeared through a square opening in the floor.

Grace shined her flashlight down the stairwell, steps glimmering palely and vanishing into the inky void. She swung the flashlight beam up. Stairs disappeared into nothingness.

Grace started down the narrow steps.

She counted fifty steps before she reached the floor of the underground chamber. There was not a flicker of light there, and she could hear what sounded like water.

The room would have been where the Menteith women were held. Grace shuddered. It was like a tomb, cold and lightless. Briefly she wondered whether Lady Menteith had regretted her defiance in the end; she could not imagine watching your friends and family slowly starve to death.

Her flashlight beam picked out a large

square tarp in the center of the floor.

Something appeared to lie under it.

Grace picked up the bottom edge of the tarp and tugged. It slid down to reveal dark hair, a high white forehead, and the staring dead eyes of Lord Ruthven.

She dropped the tarp.

It wasn't the first time she had seen violent death, but familiarity did not improve the experience.

He couldn't be three days dead, that much was obvious from the fact that he hadn't begun to, well . . . decompose. He must have died recently.

She steeled herself, picked up the tarp and gave it another yank.

Death, the sable smoke where vanishes the flame.

All that intensity, all that prickly cleverness . . . turned to cold wax. Hadn't she known all along that Ruthven must be dead? Why was she so . . . shocked to find him so?

The corpse wore no shirt. His waist was heavily bandaged in white. White splotched with red.

"But how?" she whispered. Which was foolish: *why* was the real question. Grace felt sick. The injury had been to Ruthven's stomach, not his chest, and he'd died of that wound. They — his confederates — had apparently tried to save him. But in that case, why hadn't they taken him to a doctor? It didn't make sense. Why conceal the fact that Ruthven had been injured?

Grace dropped wearily down on the bottom step and reconsidered.

Who had attacked Ruthven?

The villagers?

I'm getting punchy, she thought, rubbing her forehead. Ruthven's injury couldn't really be the result of someone attempting to drive a stake through his heart.

From far above she heard the screech of hinges as the door to the tower opened — then banged shut.

17

Grace switched off the flashlight.

Would the beam have been visible from upstairs? There was no place to hide; the cell was empty except for the thing beneath the tarp — and nothing would convince her to crawl in with it.

If she could reach the upper chamber, there were plenty of hiding spaces provided by the crowd of furniture and art.

Staying motionless, Grace listened tensely but was unable to hear anything from above.

Had the intruder simply looked in and left? Maybe they thought they had left it unlocked? *They?* That's right; it could be more than one person. But two people would surely converse — even if in whispers.

She listened so hard she thought her eardrums would pop.

Nothing.

Sweat trickled down her back. It was hard to hear over the rush of blood throbbing in her temples. What was he waiting for? Why didn't he come down here?

The darkness was thick and smothering against her face. It was like being deprived of all sight or sound or senses. Suddenly she understood Peter's aversion to small, enclosed spaces. She had to get out of the cell.

Feeling her way blindly, she moved up to the next step. She took the stairs one at a time, moving in a kind of crawl, balancing on fingertips and toes.

Step.

Pause.

Step.

Pause.

She reached up into air and knew she was at the top of the stairs. The darkness seemed thinner, the air cooler.

She crawled into the upper chamber, the whisper of her knees on stone vibrating like a shriek in her consciousness.

Was she alone? Had he gone?

Scooting quietly onto the floor, she reached unseeing and felt for the wall. Carefully she stood, using the clammy stone to orient herself. She hoped she didn't step back into the stairwell.

Grace took another step forward. All at once she knew for certain with a kind of atavistic sense that he was still there.

She was not alone.

Motionless, she tried to control her

breathing. She willed herself to be invisible, but she knew the other must be as aware of her as she was of him.

A voice spoke, dulcet tones as loud as a shot in the fraught silence. "Thou art unseen — but yet I hear thy shrill delight," quoted Peter.

Which explained why he had not followed her into the lower chamber. Peter was claustrophobic.

Grace stepped back, her foot gritting the surface of the stones. She took another step, then nearly shrieked as a hand closed on her arm. The sound, smothered by the other hand that clamped over her mouth, came out as a squawk.

Peter shushed her softly, his breath warm against her ear.

Grace stopped struggling. She stood quietly, feeling his body down the length of her own. Then, to her surprise — and possibly his own — his lips found the curve of her throat. He kissed her, his mouth like hot velvet on her sensitive skin.

Grace shivered. She tried to think of something to say. Nothing very intelligent came to mind — and his hand was still over her mouth in any case.

She was sorry when he raised his head.

"What are you doing here?" His voice was

so soft she wondered if she imagined it.

"I had to know . . ."

"And now you know."

She shook her head, stubbornly refuting the obvious.

The door to the chamber swung open. A flashlight beam struck Grace in the face. She flinched. Peter's hold had changed, grown impersonal and imprisoning.

"And what is it you are doing in here?" The figure bristling in the moonlight was short and burly, his bald bullet head giving the impression of a bad-tempered genie. His tone changed almost instantly. "What the — ?"

"Look what I found," Peter said smoothly, giving Grace a little push forward.

Donnie Hood swore.

"Is she alone? She canna be. How the hell did she get in here?"

"I hate to say I told you so," Peter said, "but —"

"Shut up, you!" Donnie grabbed Grace by the arm and hauled her out of the tower.

With Peter bringing up the rear, he half dragged, half marched Grace through a maze of broken buildings and overgrown gardens toward the main keep.

Grace did her best to map their journey in

her mind. To the west was the dim outline of what had to be the old gun battery, which meant that this long uneven stretch of lawn must be the bowling green.

A single light burned in the tower window. It looked like the cover of those Gothic romances she had read as a girl. I should have worn my negligee, Grace reflected.

They cut through the ruins of another long building and went up some stairs, bypassing what appeared to be a sunken garden. Grace was totally lost. She glanced skyward to try and figure out where she was in relation to the stars.

"The lion's den," Peter informed her. "Like so many of their contemporaries, the Ruthven lairds kept exotic wild animals."

At Grace's quick look, he added, "The last lion died back in the twenties."

Grace's captor growled something about bloody *sassunachs* and bloody tours.

Out of the corner of her eye Grace saw something. She turned her head in time to watch a shooting star slide down the sky.

"A lucky omen," Peter murmured.

The other man grunted.

"The chapel," Peter said, as they reached what appeared to be one of the L-branches of the main keep.

Grace's companion swung around like a bull ready to charge, his massive fist still clamped around Grace's arm.

"You shut your face! I know what you're about!"

Grace wished she did.

"Whatever you say, old boy." Peter sounded unruffled.

They made the rest of the trip in silence broken only by the scrape of their feet on rock.

Catriona was in the safari room. She was not alone. In fact there appeared to be a council of war in progress. Or perhaps just a war — albeit a small one.

"I don't give a damn what you think, Donnie Mac," Catriona's voice carried down the hallway, "nor Little Donnie either. I still call the shots here."

"I don't trust him!" This was a shaggy red-haired giant who reminded Grace of one of those Highland cattle — minus the horns.

They had been arguing at the top of their voices. The deerhound lay by the fireplace growling softly, but they all broke off when Grace and her companions appeared in the doorway.

Catriona went very still at the sight of

Grace. Her eyes seemed to turn yellow. She pronounced a word in Gaelic that sounded extremely unladylike.

"She knows. She was in the tower." Donnie Hood, the one who looked like one of Mr. Clean's ne'er-do-well relations, grabbed Grace's bag from Peter and threw it to Catriona. "He was in there, too."

Catriona cocked her head Peter's way.

"Don't exaggerate," Peter told Little Donnie, who began to splutter.

Catriona ignored their exchange, dumping the contents of Grace's bag on the sofa. She examined the camera, raised an eyebrow, and tossed it to the table. She unpeeled the paper around the dog bone.

"How thoughtful."

The deerhound investigated. Catriona moved the bone away from his nose. She made short shrift of the remaining items. Studying the picklocks, she laughed.

"You're a bad influence," she informed Peter.

He shrugged.

Her gaze returned to Grace. She seemed to consider her for a long moment. Grace felt the hair at the nape of her neck rise.

But all Catriona said was, "Lock her up."

The kitchen was on the basement level of

the keep. It was a long primitive hall amidst a rabbit warren of supply rooms, vaults and chambers. There was a giant central hearth with a black cauldron big enough to take a bath in, which looked as though it had not been used for some time, either for cooking or bathing. There was also a modern-looking stove and refrigerator.

Donnie Hood opened a door and thrust Grace into a small room. He locked the door behind her.

She listened to his footsteps walking away. Now what? For a moment or two Grace stood there, then common sense asserted itself, and she felt around till she found a light switch.

She was in a pantry. The deep storage shelves were stocked with linens, china, assorted household goods. She opened a drawer and there were piles of silverware. Not stainless, not silver plate: solid silver.

The door banged open just as Grace was palming a butter knife.

"Where is it?" This was the red-haired Donnie, the piper; and he had the lungs for it, given the way he bellowed at her.

"Where's what?" Grace was guiltily conscious of the knife up her sleeve.

"The bloody bugle. The Peeler."

"I don't know."

That appeared to be the wrong answer. He pulled her out of the pantry. In the main kitchen stood Little Donnie. They escorted her back upstairs.

Catriona was pacing back and forth before the fireplace. Peter leaned against the wall watching her.

Another man sat on the sofa.

Even before he turned her way she recognized the back of his blond head and the set of his broad shoulders. He faced her, and she stared at his handsome, chiseled features.

Derek Derrick?

Her first and foremost thought was that he was a better actor than she had given him credit for. Or she was a worse sleuth.

Now he smiled, but there was no warmth in his eyes.

"Hallo, Grace."

"Looks like the gang's all here," Peter remarked.

Was he trying to tell her something? Grace's brain felt sluggish. Two and two seemed unreasonably complex.

A slide show seemed to play across the blank screen of her memory: Derek diving to Catriona's rescue when the trapdoor gave way; Derek staying behind when Catriona's saddle broke; Derek everywhere Catriona was, despite his professed antipathy.

Derek who had provided the equivalent of a letter of introduction for the Ruthvens.

He rose, coming toward her, and Grace instinctively stepped back.

"Where is it, Grace?"

"I don't know."

"We need that horn. We're going to get it from you, whatever it takes."

Donnie MacDhomnuil shoved her forward. She stumbled, and Catriona caught her by the arm, saying flatly, "I'm going to count to three, and if you don't tell me where it is, I'll break your little finger."

Instinctively, Grace made her hands into fists, trying to protect her fingers. "I don't have it! You searched my bag."

Like a playground bully, Catriona pushed her back toward Derek. "Search her."

"I think it would be rather difficult to conceal on one's person," Peter pointed out lazily. "Those unsightly bulges. Or bugles."

"Search her," Catriona repeated.

Grace struggled. It was instinctive. She knew she wasn't going anywhere.

When she risked a peek his way, Peter's face was impassive. His own position seemed to be precarious, unless she misunderstood some of the crooks' comments to each other; even so it was hard not to look to him for help.

Derek's hands slid over her breasts, her hips. It was humiliating, which was no doubt the point. He patted her down roughly and the butter knife fell out of Grace's sleeve, clattering on the flagstones. Peter laughed.

"Brilliant!" Catriona exclaimed. She glared at her henchman, who stared at his feet.

"Where the hell did you hide it?" Derek demanded.

"I couldn't find it!"

She wrested her arm away as Derek tried to grab her. "So help me God, I'll do more than break your finger," he threatened.

Peter moved between them. "No fair. Two against one."

Derek halted. "What about him?" He jabbed his thumb at Peter. "He could have taken it."

There was an interesting silence.

"He's in this as deep as we are," Catriona said with a glance at Grace.

"Not quite," Derek said. "There's a crucial difference, and let's not forget it." There was a note in his voice . . . Anger? Desperation? Grace struggled to classify the emotion underlying his words and was startled by her own conclusion.

"You killed Lord Ruthven!"

It was a guess, but Derek recoiled.

"Of course." She gained conviction. "It had to be someone familiar with the theater, and someone strong enough to carry a body out. Someone strong enough to impale —"

"It was an accident," Derek exclaimed. "It was self-defense."

Peter sounded interested. "Which was it, an accident or self-defense?"

Derek cast him a baleful look. "Both."

"You do seem to have your share of accidents." Peter sighed. "Not like the good old days, is it?"

"Shut up, Derry," Catriona warned the other man as his face darkened. "Let's stick to finding the Peeler."

Grace had already figured out that her best chance lay in exploiting the emotional tension she sensed. She began, "Lord Ruthven —"

"Christ, stop calling him that!" Catriona exclaimed, suddenly losing her temper.

The fire popped loudly, and a shower of sparks flew up.

"That's right, there is no Lord Ruthven," Grace said. "So who was he?"

"A liability," Peter remarked.

For some reason this annoyed Catriona into reply. "An associate." Her eyes held

Peter's. "A former friend. A former lover."

"Not much of a retirement plan in that line of work," Grace said to Peter. She couldn't help it; she wanted to snap the invisible link that seemed to tie the other two's gazes.

"Not much, no."

Derek laughed. "Lover! He was trying to kill you."

"Some girls have all the fun," Grace said without thinking. Peter made a sound that wasn't quite a laugh.

Catriona wheeled on Grace. "Enjoying yourself?"

"I've had better nights."

Peter said, "Tell her. She's come this far."

Catriona sneered, "You tell her. You're so good at sussing out what makes people tick."

"Not always." They broke eye contact, and Peter said, "I'm guessing that Bob didn't appreciate being blackmailed into taking part in another of Catriona's schemes. Especially after the guard was killed. He decided to pull the plug."

Catriona stared at him. "You think so?"

Derek said, "That goes to prove you don't have a clue, mate. Ruthven tried to pull the plug all right. On Cat."

The accidents plaguing Catriona . . . who

had better opportunity than the man she lived with? But there was something in the way Ruthven had watched Catriona, something that, despite the current of hostility between them, would have led Grace to believe he still cared for her.

"Why?" she questioned.

Peter suggested, as though it was only of academic interest, "I suppose if it wasn't that he objected to being blackmailed, he resented being phased out?"

A falling-out of thieves? It sounded as melodramatic as anything Polidori might have devised.

Grace worked it out. "So it was Lord Ruthven — Bob — who killed Lady Ives? Thinking she was you?"

There was another one of those moody silences.

"And, in character as Lord Ruthven, he left the vampire marks?"

Again it was Peter who responded. "It sounds rather like a bad movie doesn't it? *Curse of the Vampyre.* Deranged thespian runs amuck acting out his stage persona."

She supposed it made sense, except Ruthven, like Catriona, was a schemer, a plotter. His previous attempts on his "wife" had all been staged to look like accidents. Why had he suddenly lost patience, bashing her head with a garden ornament? It was such a brutal, clumsy crime. Not really Ruthven's style at all. And why the night of the Hunt Ball, with so many people wandering around the garden?

How convenient, Grace thought, to blame the murder on a dead man.

Surprised at her own cynicism, she barely heard Peter's insolent, "Except jolly old Ruthven wasn't the actor in the house, was he?"

Derek swung at him. Peter sidestepped neatly. The dog jumped to its feet, barking as Derek knocked into a table.

"Derry, don't be an ass! He's baiting you." Catriona raked a hand through her mane. "Donnie, take her back downstairs — and I don't mean leave her in the pantry this time."

Donnie Hood escorted Grace down through a labyrinth of poorly lit halls and stairways to what appeared to be an actual dungeon. He gestured for her to step inside a long, rectangular room and locked the heavy door with an air of finality.

Grace slowly took in the collection of antiquated devices, possibly intended for torture but looking as much like farm equipment as anything. There were brackets on the wall for torches and casks for wine. It was damp. She could hear something dripping, the small plop of sound magnified in the moldering darkness.

Time for some quick thinking, Grace instructed herself; but all she could focus on was that the situation upstairs was deteriorating fast, and the more desperate and panicky the crooks became, the greater her danger.

And Peter's.

Chapter 18

Grace had plenty of time to reflect on the error of her ways: hours if her watch was correct. She kept holding it up to her ear, and it did seem to be ticking. She was relieved Chaz was not with her. Not only would she be responsible for imperiling him, she would have had to listen to a never-ending I Told You So.

She wondered, with Chaz returning to England and the Bells on their way to Canada, how long it would be before anyone reported her missing? Of course, they would notice at the inn when she didn't turn up for breakfast, and Donald MacLeod would know his boat had been used during the night. Hopefully they would come straight to the island. But if the lady of the loch swore that she hadn't seen Grace — ?

How long would they hold her? That was probably a dumb question since she was in a dungeon, and they could probably leave her there forever and not be even slightly inconvenienced. Grace refused to consider the alternative, that they might do away with her — although there was something in

Catriona's eyes that made her uneasy.

A key grated in the lock. The door swung open.

"Come on," Peter said softly. "Chop-chop."

Grace, seated on a large barrel, looked at him warily. "What's going on?"

"Jailbreak."

"I thought you were on their side now."

"I'm on my side. Are you coming or not?"

"I may as well."

In the uncertain light his shadow loomed ten feet tall as he started for the stairs. He was moving fast but very quietly, and Grace instinctively switched to tiptoe as she sprinted after him up the serpentine coil of steps.

It was not easy to converse and climb, but Grace managed a whispered, "Where is everybody?"

"Derek and Cat have retired. Hood is on watch. Donnie Mac is drowning his sorrows. That's the story anyway."

"You mean this could be a trap?"

"Of course it's a trap." He sounded surprised that she could doubt it.

"Then what are we doing?"

They started another winding flight. "What are you doing with these lunatics? Why did you leave Innisdale?" Grace questioned, not waiting for his last answer. She knew the answer, in any case. Trap or not, this was the best opportunity they'd have.

"Sshhh." He pressed his head against a dome-shaped wooden door, listening. He nodded at her and opened it.

They seemed to be back in the kitchen. Peter headed for what appeared to be a back door. There was no doubt he knew his way around the castle like the back of his hand.

They stepped out into what must have originally been the castle garden. A tangle of vines covered one wall. The herb beds were overgrown with weeds, and the fishpond, which once would have been stocked with trout and pike, was dry and filled with debris.

Grace, following her own line of thought, said, "So Derek was in on it from the start? He was just pretending to dislike Catriona, and she was pretending to dislike him." She reflected. "She does truly seem to dislike me, though."

"Hard to believe, I know."

"Derek and Catriona are lovers?"

No comment. Maybe he didn't like the idea.

Grace chose not to pursue that line of thought. "Was he pretending to have an affair with Theresa Ives? Or did he have an affair in order to get close to her for the robbery?"

"Will you be quiet?"

"I am being quiet," she hissed back. "Did Derek kill Theresa? Did she find out about the robbery; is that what happened?"

"I thought you had deduced that Ruthven killed her in mistake for Cat?"

"Is that what they said?"

"It hasn't come up in conversation." He raised a hand, and she paused, her heart beating fast. Someone was walking along one of the overhanging ledges. Peter knelt in a single fluid movement and seemed to melt into the shadow. Grace squatted, and her knees popped. It sounded as loud as a firecracker to her, but the person on the ledge kept walking. For a moment Donnie Hood was silhouetted by the moon.

When his footsteps died away, Peter stood, placed his hands on the wall and swung himself up. He reached down, helping Grace scramble up. Sticking to the deep shade of the castle, they edged their way around the expanse of green.

When they stopped to rest, Grace said softly, "But it doesn't make sense. Ruthven loved Catriona. I know he did. Well, maybe love's not the word, but there was passion there." She remembered his face when

Catriona had nearly fallen through the trapdoor. "Or obsession."

"It's a fine line sometimes." She didn't like the way he said that.

"So the truth is Ruthven became jealous? He and Derek fought, and Derek killed him?" She reconsidered. "Or did Derek try to kill him for trying to kill Catriona? Or did he kill him to try and take Catriona away from him?"

Peter threw a look over his shoulder that suggested he was having second thoughts about the rescue attempt.

"But no," Grace continued, "that can't be right because they did try to save him. Sort of. And why would they do that if they were trying to kill him? And they wouldn't need to kill him since they weren't really married — the Ruthvens, I mean. But how could it be self-defense? They would have had to follow him to the theater — unless that whole scene was a setup?"

Peter stopped dead and stared at her. "What are you talking about?"

"Don't you see? It's more than the fact that Theresa's death doesn't make sense. None of this makes sense! What was the point? What was the big scheme?" Grace pressed. "It can't be a coincidence that they chose Innisdale for their home base. And surely there's more to all this than a bunch of robberies? Why the charade of the play? Why did Lord Ruthven pretend to be a vampire?"

Peter quoted huskily, "Sweet is revenge — especially to women."

Grace was still mulling this over when they entered the ruins of a long hallway.

Something took flight from the broken rafters overhead.

"Was that a bat?" Grace gulped.

Peter started left, stopped, then went the opposite direction.

"Are you sure you know where you're going?"

He cast her a withering look.

"Is there a phone? Maybe we could call for help?"

"Why, I never thought of that!" He looked exasperated. "There's no bloody phone."

"What about my stuff? My camera. It's proof —"

"Proof of what?" Peter interrupted, and his voice raised briefly for a moment. "You've just admitted you still have no idea what's going on, and it's painfully clear you've missed a vital point."

"Which is what?"

"Which is that they can't decide whether to kill you or simply leave you locked in the dungeon for the next decade."

"All I can figure is — *kill* me? But why? If Lord Ruthven killed Lady Ives, and his death was an accident?"

Peter didn't respond and Grace stopped in her tracks. "I knew it. So Lord Ruthven *didn't* kill Lady Ives?"

"No."

"But —" She broke off as they spotted Donnie Hood at the far end of the hallway.

Hood held up his lantern and recognized them. They turned and saw MacDhomnuil at the other end of the hallway. Hood pointed, shouting, and MacDhomnuil bellowed back.

"Children of the night, what music they make," Peter murmured, grabbing Grace by the shoulders and sending her climbing out through the shattered wall of the passageway.

They ran across the green, and Peter, like the fox he was, suddenly jinked left and cut back toward the pile of stone. Grace risked a look over her shoulder and saw their pursuers huffing and puffing many yards behind them. She sympathized; she was getting a stitch in her side.

They raced on, weaving around obstacles that Grace belatedly realized were gravestones. She made out a rudely carved skull and crossbones twinkling with the frost now glazing the grass. Beneath this grim obstacle course of markers and stones Menteiths and Ruthvens boarded together in "that dark inn, the grave."

Full circle, she thought crazily, her feet squelching through the wet grass. Peter sprinted a few feet ahead, clearly checking his speed to match hers.

After what seemed miles but could have only been a few yards, Peter stopped running. Grace took advantage of the break, leaning against the stone wall and trying to catch her breath. Her calf muscles were burning.

How many calories do you burn running for your life? she wondered.

When Peter touched her shoulder, Grace straightened. He gestured, unspeaking, showing the way into what must have been the original chapel.

Keeping to the shadows, they crept across the floor of the old chapel, overgrown with wildflowers and weeds. High above, stars scintillated through the open roof.

Behind them came the circles of flashlight beams probing through the ruins.

She could hear the Donnies calling back and forth to each other.

Crawling out through a stone shelf that had once been a window frame, Peter led her up some broken stairs and across another flagstone patio. Grace stared up at the grim stone facade. This part of the castle looked vaguely familiar.

"This way."

They seemed to be balancing on a wall looking down into an enclosure or private garden.

Peter put his finger to his lips. Grace nodded but nearly squeaked her surprise when he leapt down off the wall.

He stood up, waist high in grasses and brambles, and gestured for her to jump.

Grace hesitated, but there did not appear to be stairs. She took a deep breath and jumped.

Peter caught her, helping to break her fall, but even so her shins hurt.

"Down this way. Quietly."

Taking her hand, Peter led her through the yard of the lion's den. He moved soundlessly; but to Grace, the soft scrape of her shoes on rock, the shifting of earth sounded as loud as explosions.

Peter squeezed around the iron gate nearly barring the entrance, and Grace wriggled in after him. It smelled weird and animal in the cell.

Afraid she could be seen in the startlingly bright moonlight, Grace backed up. Something sharp stuck her in the shoulder. She turned. A polar bear towered over her, paws outstretched, jaws gaping. Grace sucked in breath for a scream.

Peter's hand clamped over her mouth. His lips at her ear whispered, "It's stuffed."

She slumped against him. His heart was beating fast beneath the damp wool of his sweater. His arms held her tightly, with reassuring strength. Something brushed the top of her head, and she wondered if he had rested his cheek there for a moment. But the touch had been too fleeting.

They waited with the dead bear, watching the shifting light of moon and clouds.

It seemed like hours but it could only have been minutes before Peter said, his voice low, "Right. Where's the boat?"

"I hid it in the pine trees by the tunnel."

"The — ? The postern, you mean?"

She nodded.

"We'll have to assume they've found it by now or are looking for it. Our best chance is to take the launch. Can you steer a motorboat?"

"Me? But you're coming, too. You've got to. You can't stay now. They know you've helped me —"

He was shaking his head, drawing her out of the cave.

They picked their way across the yard of the den, and Grace tripped. She looked down. It was a skull, definitely animal in shape. Too small to be a cow. A deer?

They cut back across the green, keeping to the shadows, and slipped between the stone pillars with the horsehead finials.

Clambering onto the stone dock, they ran for the boathouse. Peter paused outside the wide door.

"Don't wait," he warned her. "Start for home tonight."

"Start for home? I'm going straight to the police!"

He was shaking his head. "There is no policeman in Eacharnach. And if you call the police, you're turning me in as well."

"But you can explain . . ." She faltered, not sure herself what his explanation was. She tried again, knowing it was useless. "You can't stay here. You've got to come with me. They'll kill you, too."

He was shaking his head. "If I leave now, I'll spend the rest of my life looking over my shoulder."

Because of the police or because of Catriona and her gang? Or both?

She controlled herself with an effort and managed to ask fairly calmly, "What are you going to do?"

"Not sure. I'm making it up as I go." He grinned with unexpected cheerfulness.

"Do you know who has the Peeler?"

"It's not enough."

What was he hoping for? A signed confession?

"Why isn't it? I can . . . back you up."

He was silent for a moment, then said lightly, "All the more reason to keep you alive."

"Gosh, I didn't think you cared." She got it out, but she swallowed it so that it sounded uncomfortably like she was close to tears. Even if his former associates didn't do him in for this treachery, he would be starting life on the run. When would she see him again? This felt too much like goodbye.

Peter said quietly, "Then you haven't been paying attention." He touched her hair lightly. "You may not hear from me for a bit."

"Please be careful. That woman is insane."

"I can handle Cat." He bent forward to kiss her.

Catriona stepped around the corner of the boathouse.

"Do tell," she said.

The gun she aimed at them was the size of a blunderbuss.

19

"Scratch a lover, find a foe," quoted Grace.

"Eenie meenie, miney mo." Peter's voice was muffled as he worked to pry the grate off the floor of their cell.

Grace studied the lightly muscled line of his back. "I think I've figured it out."

"Marvelous. Explain it to me one of these days." He wiped his arm across his face.

"It's Grand Guignol," she told him. "Someone staged a big dramatic production full of violent, frightening themes for our benefit. Or maybe for your benefit."

Peter did not respond, shifting position on the stone floor for better leverage.

"All the mysterious events of the past few weeks have been so many stage trappings. Vampires, sinister occurrences, jealous lovers and a stolen treasure — they were just red herrings, MacGuffins."

Grace believed, though she did not say so aloud, that the true purpose behind all the melodramatic machinations was a dark one and possibly as Gothic as anything Polidori or Byron could have conceived: revenge.

Revenge against Peter.

But surely something had gone wrong. Surely Lord Ruthven's death had not been part of the original plan. Unless it was a really bad plan.

Peter made an impatient sound and straightened, flexing his back. "Your logic is impeccable, Professor. You seem to have missed only one detail. A minor one, but you'll find it of interest."

But the rest of what he would have said was cut off by the grate of the key in the lock of their cell door.

"Let's go." Both Donnies were present and armed with a mediaeval but quite effective-looking assortment of weapons. They narrowly eyed Peter as he stepped out of the cell followed by Grace.

"Move your arse," Red Donnie snarled at Grace. With his bristling red beard and hair he reminded her of those Hagar the Horrible cartoons. She bit back a hysterical giggle.

They marched up the stairs in uneasy formation.

As they passed through the doorway Grace caught Derek's words, and her heart forgot how to beat for a moment.

"We're going to have to kill them," he was saying. "We've gone too far to turn back."

"Let me think." Catriona massaged her temples. She sat in a yellow brocade Queen Anne chair that looked like a small throne; the old pistol lay on the table beside her. Derek paced up and down before the fireplace.

"There's nothing to think about. He's been playing you. And she knows too much."

"Actually, I don't know that much," said Grace.

This was a smaller room and empty of the grotesque hunting trophies of the lair of Catriona's great-grandfather. There was a gorgeous brown-and-navy Persian carpet on the floor. Isfahan by any chance?

Grace tried to imagine growing up in a mausoleum like this castle, and decided it was no wonder Catriona was more than a tad odd.

"Do sit down," Catriona invited.

Grace took the chair opposite Catriona, who studied her sardonically.

"What a transparent face you have. Would you like to hear the story of my life? Or no, I imagine it's the story of Peter's life you'd most enjoy."

Her golden eyes shifted to Peter's. Grace was reminded of a quote from Byron. *"These two hated with a hate found only on the stage.*" But in truth that better applied to Derek and Catriona — their dislike had been feigned. Whatever lay between Catriona and Peter was not feigned, and it was somehow the crux of this "case."

"She's heard it all before," Peter said.

"I doubt that, lover."

Grace said to Derek, "If you're going to knock me off anyway, you may as well fill in the blanks. What did happen at the theater?"

"Not much," drawled Catriona.

"I mean to Lord Ruthven. If you didn't kill Lady Ives, and Lord Ruthven's death was an accident, and the security guard's death was —" She couldn't help but swallow on that. "An accident — I guess — I don't see why you're so set on killing us."

"Possibly because I would enjoy it," Catriona said.

Until then Grace had been thinking Catriona held a grudge against her because Grace had stumbled into the middle of her revenge on Peter. It was sinking in that the "minor detail" Peter had referred to was Cat's jealousy of Grace. Jealousy and possibly hatred.

"Oh."

Catriona's eyes glinted. "Anyway, we've already explained it for you once. Rabbie wanted out. After the fiasco at the Hunt Ball, he hit on the idea of confiding in you. Derek went to the theater to dissuade him. They fought. Rabbie got the worst of it."

"It was an accident," Derek insisted. "He tried to hit me with a chair, and I jabbed him with the broken handle of a broom."

You impaled him, Grace thought, but she said only, "If that's true, why can't you go to the police? It's clear that you did try to save him." Sort of.

Catriona shrugged an elegant shoulder. "We don't enjoy the camaraderie you do with the coppers. And I don't imagine our innocent intent will go far with the authorities; not given our other activities."

Probably not, Grace silently agreed, thinking of the dead security guard.

"Who was driving the van that hit the security guard?"

"Donnie Hood," Derek was quick to say. Grace understood what people meant by "looking daggers." Catriona looked daggers at Derek.

But with one possible murder charge hanging over him, Grace could see why Derek wasn't covering for anyone else's fatal mistakes.

"And what was the scheme Lord Ruthven wanted out of?"

"The usual." Catriona gazed at Peter. He gazed back.

"Quite," he said.

"You did have a choice. One always has choice, as you used to say."

Grace said, "You wanted Peter back in the gang?"

Catriona sighed in mock sorrow. "It just wasn't the same without him."

"We made him an offer he couldn't refuse," Derek said. He laughed, and looked to Catriona for confirmation.

"Who said I wanted to refuse?" Peter said reasonably. "We simply need to negotiate the details." He nodded at Grace. "Like her."

Grace said, confirming her own theory, "And all the vampire stuff was just . . . stage trappings?"

"Very good."

"*Was* there anyone on the catwalk the night the pigeon was trapped?"

Catriona's grin widened. "Nope."

The power of suggestion, Grace thought ruefully. Catriona had manipulated them all beautifully. "Who followed me from the pub that night?" She had been guessing Derek, but now she wondered.

"Who do you imagine?"

She purred the words, and Grace had a picture of herself as the mouse Cat had been toying with, batting between her sharp little claws as she savored the thought of . . . this moment? A moment made possible by Grace's own stubbornness.

"And Lord Ruthven killed Lady Ives?"

"That's right." But Catriona hesitated just a fraction too long.

"Who killed Lady Ives?" Grace pressed.

Derek's gaze slanted toward Catriona. Catriona's eyes slid toward Derek.

They don't know, Grace realized. *Or* the one who did it was pretending to believe the other was guilty.

"Now I have a question for you," Catriona said. "Where is the Peeler?"

But she was not asking Grace, she was talking to Peter. She cocked the old pistol she held and pointed it at Grace.

"I hid it," Peter said.

"I'm going to shoot her in the kneecap."

"I'll be happy to show you where it is."

Catriona looked suddenly very weary. "I've got a better idea. Bring it here. Derek, go with him."

"I'd rather not be left alone with her," Grace remarked.

Derek laughed. Peter's eyes held Grace's for a long moment. If he was trying to signal her, Grace couldn't read the message.

They left.

Catriona turned to her two henchmen, who had been watching the proceedings with beady-eyed interest. She spoke to them in Gaelic. Their eyes went to Grace, then they exchanged a look.

Grace felt cold in the pit of her stomach.

"Put the dog on the boat," Catriona added.

The two Donnies left the room, the deer-hound trotting after.

Catriona studied Grace. "Nothing personal."

"No?"

Her smile was scornful. "No."

So much made sense now, including Grace's inclusion in the production of *The Vampyre* — perhaps even Peter's careful distancing of himself from her. She watched Catriona saunter to the fireplace, leaning one elbow on the mantel and staring into the orange flames. She seemed lost in her thoughts.

"I've known him since I was nineteen," Catriona said at last. "How long have you known him?"

Grace didn't answer.

"Everything was fine until Istanbul. It all fell apart in Istanbul. The whole goddamned world fell apart in Istanbul." Her profile looked like marble in the flickering firelight.

Birds of prey mate for life. The thought came unbidden to Grace. Not something one wanted to get in the middle of, really.

"They caught him," Catriona said. Her voice was barely audible; her mouth twisted bitterly.

"We couldn't get him out." Her head turned briefly Grace's way, and Grace saw the brilliant sheen of her eyes. Too brilliant, she realized with a jolt.

Long moments passed before Catriona spoke again, and Grace knew that the other woman had traveled miles and years in her thoughts.

"I thought he was in China," she said quietly. "He used to joke about retiring to China. But he was in England all the time."

"How did you find him?" Grace asked curiously.

Catriona laughed without humor. "By accident. Danny spotted him." Her eyes met Grace's. "Danny Delon."

Danny Delon. The little man who had quite inadvertently brought Grace and Peter together. It was a small world after all.

Inexplicably she thought of the maps in Rogue's Gallery, the pale and beautiful drawings of mysterious landscapes — and the ferocious monsters lurking at the edges of the uncertain world. She remembered

Peter quoting a Chinese proverb. *Wherever you go, speak the language of that place.*

Reaching down, she grabbed the edge of the Persian rug. She yanked with all her might.

Catriona's feet shot out from under her and she crashed to the floor, dropping the gun.

Grace lunged for the gun. Catriona scrambled for it, too.

They wrestled on the floor. Grace's fingertips brushed the gun. She pushed it farther away. Catriona rolled over and jerked a fistful of Grace's hair. She tried to bang Grace's head on the floor. Instinctively Grace's hands locked in Catriona's hair, and she used the other woman to leverage herself so that her head didn't contact the stone.

Lips drawing back in a snarl, Catriona used her free hand to try to grab Grace by the throat. Grace let go of one hank of hair and tried to punch Catriona, remembering too late that she should keep her thumb on the outside of her fist. Her blow landed ineffectively on Catriona's shoulder as Catriona whipped around.

It could only have been a few seconds, but it felt like they had been struggling for hours. The muscles in Grace's arms ached.

Her thumb felt sprained.

Footsteps down the hall indicated someone was returning — at a run.

Catriona kicked her hard, and Grace yipped. This was her first fight, and, unless she won it, probably her last. She let go of Catriona for a second, grabbed for the statue on the table, and brought it down hard on Catriona's head.

Catriona's arms slid out from under her, and she flattened on the carpet.

Peter skidded to a stop in the doorway. His eyebrows were raised in startled inquiry.

"Girl Scouts," gasped Grace.

Their dash down the hallway was stopped short by the figure advancing on them. Moonlight outlined the newcomer, gleaming off fair hair and patrician features — and the blade of the sword he carried.

"Oh, hell," Peter said.

He didn't waste further breath on speech, but went to the nearest wall and ripped a basket-hilt broadsword down. He barely had it free when Derek ran at him swinging wildly.

Peter parried, although it was more like swinging a bat. The blades met with a ferocious clang. This was not fencing like in the movies; it was violent slashing and cutting at each other.

Blood trickled from Derek's hairline down his face. Peter must have hit him — though not nearly hard enough. Grace was a little surprised at her own bloodthirsty impulse.

Derek was fearless; Grace had to give him that. He charged at Peter again and again, and was driven back — though each time with a bit less energy.

Their blades rang out once more. Peter narrowly missed being sliced. He grabbed a carved chair and threw it in Derek's path. Derek avoided falling over it, and charged forward.

Peter backed up a few steps and slid over a table, keeping it between himself and Derek. Derek swore.

His eyes were slits of concentration, his mouth a straight line; Peter used the point of his sword to shove a pewter *quaich* in Derek's path. It clattered noisily on the flagstones.

Grace, sticking to the edge of the hall, moved around the duelists, starting back toward the room where they had left Catriona. She thought that Catriona's blunderbuss might come in useful, although she shied mentally from the idea of shooting anyone. She told herself the main thing was to keep Catriona from using it — not that there weren't plenty of other weapons available, and Catriona was probably adept at wielding all of them.

Once she had the gun, perhaps she could find her knapsack and the rope and other goodies that Monica had packed . . .

The blades chattered against each other and broke free.

She watched Peter grab the end of a faded tapestry and yank it down. His attempt was clearly to tangle Derek in its folds, but the other man ducked nimbly away.

Grace threw one last glance at Peter over her shoulder and raced on.

She reached the sitting room in time to find Catriona on her hands and knees. She had the blunderbuss. Raising her head, she saw Grace and fired. Grace ducked back with a yelp. There was a chunk out of the door frame about the size of her fist.

She tore back to where Peter and Derek were still whaling away at each other.

"Peter!"

He spared her a quick glance, then had to fight hard to push back Derek. Apparently he had registered the shot and recognized the source of her panic.

"Up." He sounded breathless.

Grace ran for the main staircase. Derek tried to intercept her, and she pushed a suit of armor his way. It made a horrendous din, breaking apart as it rolled down the stairs.

Derek half fell, but clumsily regained his footing as Peter lunged for him. Peter wasn't fooling around, Grace realized. He would have skewered Derek if he'd connected.

She ran up to the landing, but had to stop and watch. Peter was fighting furiously, fighting for his life and hers. Both men were fast and agile. Peter had a slight advantage of height, but Grace realized for the first time that Derek was younger by several years, and in this game that might mean the difference. Her hands clutched the banister so tightly her knuckles ached, but she didn't feel the pain.

Both men were moving more slowly, their swings wide and less focused. Sweat shone on their faces.

And then it was over so fast she didn't see it coming.

Peter took an incredible chance, dropping down beneath Derek's two-handed sweep, and thrusting up. Derek cried out, at the last second managing to deflect the blow, so that the sword pierced him over his hip instead of sliding through his gut.

Grace felt sick, which was probably nothing to the way Derek must have felt. He swayed, crumpled, and rolled down the stairs to the bottom. Peter dropped his sword and bounded up the staircase, panting and white-faced.

"Go!"

A shot rang out behind them, and the wall splintered.

Catriona, her hair Medusa-like, appeared in the hall below. She shrieked like a Banshee in Gaelic.

Racing up another flight, they fled down an unlit hall. At the end of the hall was a door. Peter tried it. It was locked. Apparently there was no time to waste on picking locks; he delivered a swift hard kick to the door. It gave with a splintering crash. Too much of a crash. Grace looked down and in the paling darkness she saw that there was no floor behind the threshold.

There was . . . nothing. The ceiling of the great hall was beneath them — a story or so down.

She looked up. A large portion of the roof was gone, too. An icy moon shone hazily through the skeleton of broken beams and sky.

"We're trapped!"

"No." He pointed across the nonexistent

floor to a trefoil recess. "See that? Make for it."

"You've got to be joking! Am I supposed to fly?" From down the hall she could hear slow, deliberate footsteps.

"The ledge goes all the way around." Peter's voice was calm, but she could feel his urgency.

"It's only about a foot wide!"

"It's wide enough. For God's sake, *go*."

She went — even more afraid of Catriona than of falling to her death.

Glued to the rough stone, Grace inched her way along the edge toward the alcove. She tried to reassure herself that if the structure had lasted this long, it would probably hold up for one more night.

"That's it," Peter encouraged. "That's the girl, Esmerelda."

Ah, yes. The old Esmerelda routine. Wasn't Esmerelda the girl Quasimodo carried off to the bell tower of Notre Dame Cathedral? Or was that Esmeralda with an "A"? Grace tried to focus her thoughts on anything but the fact that she was about a hundred feet up in the air on a ledge about the width of a balance beam.

"Don't look down," Peter warned.

But it was impossible not to look down.

She had an amazing view of the entire

island. The sparkling black water stretched out for miles. She could see the roof of Lady Menteith's Tower powdered white with frost several feet below them; and to the south, the harbor, which seemed to be lit up. The rumble of a motorboat engine drifted on the breeze cooling her sweating face.

The Donnies were preparing for escape in the launch.

A rusted nail snagged in her sweater and for a second she was off-balance. She caught herself, pressing back against the grainy wall, her heart tripping and skipping.

"Steady," Peter said.

Great, she thought dizzily. If I don't die in the fall, I'll probably get tetanus.

Soaked in perspiration and trembling, Grace made the last few sliding steps, and crawled into the recess.

Her fingers brushed something cool and metallic. She heard the silvery whisper of metal on rock. The Peeler!

Peter's decision made more sense, but they were still trapped up in the rooftop.

Catriona appeared in the empty doorway.

She said conversationally, "I wondered if you'd forgotten this place."

"I like what you've done with it," Peter remarked, equally offhand. He was midway across the ledge. There was only room for one in the trefoil recess, and apparently he thought it better to keep Catriona focused on him.

"So glad you approve," Catriona replied, "since you'll be spending eternity here."

Grace screamed as Catrina fired.

She waited for Peter to sway and fall.

Peter jerked as a chip of stone grazed his cheek, but his footing never wavered. Catriona had missed. But there was nowhere for him to go. He was like a pop-up in a shooting gallery.

There must be something I can do, Grace thought desperately. I can't just sit here and let this happen. But what could she do? She had no weapon. There was no room to move on the ledge, and beneath her was a dizzying view of the tower and, beyond, the loch.

Catriona took aim again.

"I am thinking it would be wise, *mo leannan,* to be looking to the immediate future," Peter said, imitating the Gaelic phrasing.

Catriona didn't lower the gun, but she looked around, as did Grace.

There were too many lights in the cove, Grace realized. Too many people moving around the docks for it to be simply the Donnies.

"It's the coppers," Peter said evenly.

Catriona stared across at him for a long moment.

Grace was afraid to breathe. Then, as lightly as a cat, Catriona dropped the gun and ran out along the opposite ledge. She stared for a long moment down at the tower.

It's impossible, Grace thought. It must be nine feet across . . .

Catriona circled back again, raced at the ledge and leapt.

For a moment she seemed suspended in thin air, legs outstretched in a perfect grand jete like some supernatural element of the sky.

"She won't make it," Grace whispered, leaning dangerously out of the alcove to see.

"She will," Peter said quietly.

Catriona landed on the opposite roof and rolled.

Sounds from below caught Grace's attention. A mob of men with high-powered lights pounded at the entrance of the keep. The entrance bell rang, the chime rolling through the castle.

Farther out in the harbor, the launch had been stopped. Men were boarding from another, larger boat. She could hear the dog barking from here.

She looked back to the tower in time to

see Catriona crossing the roof, running lightly, keeping low.

"She'll take the skiff," Grace realized aloud.

"Yes."

Peter had moved along the ledge to the recess. He rested on the edge, half-in and half-out of shadow. She wondered if his legs felt as weak as hers. Not likely. Staring at him, she stated, "You want her to get away?"

His profile seemed carved of moonlight. "It's simpler that way."

Simpler for whom?

"She would have killed you," Grace said.

His mouth twisted.

When she looked back, the tower roof was bare of anything but moonlight.

"I knew Chaz would have to have the last word," Grace remarked, smothering a yawn.

The last rays of sunset filtered through the lace curtains and threw snowflake shapes against the walls. It was twilight — the gloaming — and they were back at her room in the inn after spending the remainder of the night and most of the day with the Edinburgh police, who had been tipped off about the activities at *A' Mheirlich*

Saobhaidh by Charles Honeyburn III during a last-minute phone call from Waverley Station.

Peter, lost in study of the twin beds, glanced up. "What's that?"

"Chaz. Not that I'm not forever grateful, but calling the police was so . . . so . . . like him."

Peter's cheek creased. "But not like you?"

"Oh, well, maybe a little . . . once." She swallowed the rest of it in another jaw-breaking yawn. "Perhaps you are a bad influence."

"Mmm."

There was a fine-drawn tautness to his skin and little lines of weariness around his eyes that she didn't remember seeing before. She would have liked to reach out to him, to comfort him, although the idea that Peter would need or accept anyone's comfort was probably ridiculous. She said prosaically, "Do you think the police will really let us leave tomorrow?"

"If I'm correctly interpreting the official noises, it sounds that way. They've got their hands full — literally. That haul from the tower must be worth several million dollars."

"Do you think they'll catch her?"

She couldn't read his expression.

He said unemotionally, "They know who she is now. She'll be on the run for the rest of her life."

Grace just couldn't get too broken up over it.

She mused, "I wonder why they didn't destroy the Peeler? Since it incriminated them —" She paused at the quick look he threw her from beneath his lashes. "What? *What?*"

Reluctantly, he said, "You've got that part wrong. The bugle was their alibi. That's why they were so desperate to get it back."

"That can't be right." Grace was frowning. To her surprise, Peter reached over and gently rubbed the frown line with the edge of his thumb. They were so close she could smell the smooth texture of his skin, the warmth of his breath.

His mouth was a kiss away from hers. "It doesn't matter," he said quietly.

Grace's eyes opened. "Yes, it does!"

He drew back. "Right then. Think back to that evening. How long was Theresa gone from the ballroom?"

"I don't remember. I wasn't watching her. I assumed she was with Derek."

"Derek was with Ruthven, breaking into Sir Gerald's study."

"You mean there wasn't time to steal the Peeler and kill Theresa?"

"It would be cutting it fine."

"What about Catriona?"

"I was with Catriona."

Grace preferred not to pursue this line of investigation. She wondered if Peter had been tempted even for a moment to throw aside his law-abiding existence for the lure of the old life.

"Even with the Peeler that will be pretty hard to prove. Ruthven's dead and can't corroborate. And from the way the police sounded I don't think that Derek's story about finding Theresa dead and puncturing her neck with his picklock is going to fly."

Peter's mouth twisted ruefully. "It's such a stupid story. It's probably true."

"But why try to confuse the issue with fake vampire bites?"

"I think he was inspired by the wild rumors following the security guard's death. He must have imagined it was a way to divert suspicion from himself. His affair with her wasn't much of a secret; he had to know the police would suspect him. And as half the village believed Ruthven was running around playing vampire . . ." He lifted a dismissing shoulder. "Or perhaps it was sheer malice. By then Derek and Cat suspected Ruthven was behind her 'accidents.' "

"But Ruthven couldn't have killed Theresa because he was stealing the Peeler?"

"Apparently."

"While you were busy with Catriona."

He shot her a sideways look. "While I was with Catriona."

"Talking."

"We had a lot to talk about."

"Gosh, I could sleep for a thousand years." She flopped back on the other twin. "The bed is spinning."

The room was nearly dark.

Grace's eyes flew open as Peter's weight settled on the bed beside her.

"Oh, hi."

"Hello." He traced the outline of her lips with a light finger. "Why don't I trust this sudden lack of curiosity on your part?"

"I don't know. After all, we each have our little secrets."

His fingers stilled.

Grace smiled. His head bent, but before he could kiss her, Grace sat up, narrowly missing denting his rather haughty nose. She turned on the bedside lamp.

"Speaking of secrets, if Derek didn't kill Theresa, and you didn't, and Catriona says she didn't, and Lord Ruthven didn't . . . who *did?*"

The chief constable was studying a report and sucking meditatively on his pipe when Grace was shown into his office.

"Glad to see you safe and sound after your adventures, Grace," he said once she was seated on the other side of the desk. "You took a great chance."

"Sometimes you have to," Grace said.

Heron shook his head, and to head off the dire prophecy she suspected was coming, Grace said, "I believe I know who killed Theresa Ives."

"Indeed." He knocked the bowl of the pipe against the ashtray.

"I think it might even have been an accident."

Something in Heron's shoe-button eyes told her she was on the right track.

"He had been drinking heavily that night, and I think he knew that she was having an affair. I think it wasn't the first time for her."

"Nor for him," Chief Constable Heron said grimly.

Startled, Grace met his eyes. "Then . . . it's true?"

He nodded curtly. "Oddly enough, it was

your suspicion of Miss Coke that put us on the right track."

Momentarily sidetracked, Grace asked, "What's happening with Miss Coke? Did she shoot at the hunt?"

"We believe one of the Shog— Mr. Okada's former caretaker fired in the air to scare the hunt. The man has since returned to Japan, and there's no way of verifying whether he intended real harm, but it seems unlikely."

"And Miss Coke?"

"Miss Coke has received official warning about her antihunt activities."

"That's *it?*"

Heron's eyes narrowed a little.

"I'm not suggesting we burn her at the stake," Grace said defensively. "I just don't think she's quite as harmless as you seem to."

Heron shook his head a little, as though Grace was demonstrating some uniquely American paranoia.

Through the closed door she could hear someone typing. Typing? Did people still use typewriters? She gave it up, returning to the thread of their original conversation.

"You looked into the death of Sam Jeffries?" she guessed.

"That's right. Jeffries was always one for

the ladies, and Lady Theresa, well, she was a bit younger than her husband, and had time on her hands. He blamed it the first time on Jeffries, I suppose, but when it happened again . . ."

"He decided to solve the problem once and for all." Grace was thinking aloud. She could almost see it from the murderer's standpoint: humiliated and betrayed by his younger wife, a wife unsuited to the role she had been granted — so unlike Allegra Clairmont-Brougham, who was everything a squire's lady should be . . . and still available after all these years.

Perhaps it had seemed like Fate.

Jeffries' death had most likely been an impulse, and he had gotten away with it; so when he found his wife alone in the garden fresh from making a spectacle of herself all evening with Derek, perhaps he had struck out in jealous rage. Perhaps he had simply seized another opportunity.

The door to Heron's office opened. A PC stood there with crisply typed sheets. "We've got the warrant, sir."

Heron rose slowly and wearily from behind his desk. Grace preceded him out, watching as he got in the black car and drove off to arrest Sir Gerald Ives for the murder of his wife.

Epilogue

The parcel arrived with the first official snowfall, an ordinary brown package addressed to Peter.

The postmark read Paris. Grace did not recognize the handwriting. She was sure she had never seen that precise black script before, but she recognized Peter's reaction to it.

He slit the brown mailer open and slid out the book.

Opening it, he smoothed his hand down the frontispiece. Grace watched his face, caught the tightening of his jaw, the way his lashes lowered, veiling his eyes, keeping his thoughts.

Then to her surprise he handed the book to her and went to the bow window, staring out at the white feathers pouring out of the leaden skies, blanketing the world in mysterious white.

Curiously, Grace examined the book. It was a leather-bound volume of Byron's poems. She read the inscription. It was a fragment of a poem first published in 1812.

And Thou Art Dead . . .

Yet did I love thee to the last
As fervently as thou,
Who didst not change through all the
past,
And canst not alter now.

She felt a pricking beneath her eyelids, without understanding quite why, and closed the cover, setting the book aside and joining Peter at the window.

The snow was falling more heavily, shrouding the woods in a white hush.

Peter put his arm around her shoulders, drawing her near and kissing the top of her head. They stayed so for some time.

Then Grace said, "You know, that gypsy fortune-teller was wrong."

Peter smiled wryly. "I can be trusted?"

"Not that." Grace brushed this aside. "There was no hidden room, there was no lost treasure of an ancient king, there was no lost manuscript."

His eyes were the blue of shade on new-fallen snow. His head bent, his mouth seeking hers. "But you know," he said softly, "the story's not over."

About the Author

Diana Killian is the author of *High Rhymes and Misdemeanors* (available from Pocket Books). She also wrote *The Art of Dying* and *Murder in Pastel* under the pseudonym Colin Dunne. She is coeditor of the anthology *Down These Wicked Streets*, and the founder of the Wicked Company writers' community for mystery and crime writers. She lives in Los Angeles, California.

Visit her website at www.girl-detective.net.